i

Beside the
Broken Trail

Thomas F. Sheehan

Pocol Press

Clifton, VA

POCOL PRESS
Published in the United States of America
by Pocol Press
6023 Pocol Drive
Clifton, VA 20124
www.pocolpress.com

Publisher's Cataloguing-in-Publication

Names: Sheehan, Thomas F., 1928-, author.
Title: Beside the broken trail, / Thomas F. Sheehan.
Description: Clifton, VA: Pocol Press, 2017.
Identifiers: ISBN 978-1-929763-78-8 | LCCN 2017961606
Subjects: LCSH Frontier and pioneer life--West (U.S.)--Fiction. |
Cowboys--Fiction. | Outlaws--Fiction. | West (U.S.)--Fiction. | Short
stories, American. | Western stories. | Historical fiction. | BISAC
FICTION / Westerns | FICTION / Short Stories (single author).
Classification: LCC PS3569.H39216 B47 2017 | DDC 813.6--dc23

Library of Congress Control Number: 2017961606

ACKNOWLEDGEMENTS

Tom Sheehan's stories have appeared in *Rope and Wire Western Lifestyle Magazine,* *Western Online,* and *Literally Stories.*

TABLE OF CONTENTS

A Daughter in the Mix

The pickings were slim, if there were any at all, and Thorn Lavery looked down the length of the ranch and saw one mule, three cows, and four cowpokes, all idling like scarecrows, and he made a quick decision.

He saddled his horse and rode toward town; there was payment due and he was on the short end. He carried no side arms and no rifle showed in his saddle scabbard. Some locals said he was average height, average weight, with the usual blue eyes that come with sandy hair the wind often played with. They also said he was short of bad habits, good with good friends, a decent employer at times who was not the best businessman, but he was long on determination.

Most of those people liked Lavery, but Gus Marshall did not like him. Nobody knew the reason why, except Marshall who had heard Lavery had spoken out against him several times, saying, "That man wants everything he sees, takes much of it, plays to beat everybody at whatever he's involved in, and does what it takes to stay ahead of those who have and those who don't have."

At Pecos Hill, Gus Marshall, owner of the massive Circle Ought-Bar-Ought spread, was waiting for Lavery, his arms folded across his chest as he sat outside The Pecos West Saloon in the only chair on the boardwalk, the chair generally not used by anybody else when Marshall was in town. A few of his ranch hands were hunkered near him, trying to squeeze themselves out of sight, and a few others had scattered into the morning crowd. Marshall rarely went anyplace without a likely amount of force at close call. Older folks at Pecos Hill hinted often that he was like the queen bee with all the drones scrambling for crumbs off the earth.

A few of those folks were convinced this day promised action before noon, tempo in the air for one reason or another.

The sun, meanwhile, shot its slanting rays into the heart of Pecos Hill. Even so early in the day that orb sat like a fist on top of the town, much like Marshall sat on the town; oppressive in his way, making people come to a uncanny standstill and show their worst under the pressure.

As he rode into town, Lavery entertained several thoughts, foremost being that he'd never tell Marshall all the facts in their ongoing problems lest he appear to be alibiing; he had never stolen a cow in his life, or a horse, and especially had never cut a man's fence, even though he hated fences and the people who put them up ... like Marshall did on every new piece of land he grabbed out from under someone who "owed him."

Lastly, Lavery'd die before he'd let on that daughter Penny, 12, had overheard two of Marshall's men discussing her planned kidnapping. "She's the only thing Lavery loves, and the boss knows it. That's why we got to get the edge on things for the boss, the way he likes them. He don't like no odd chances."

The other man, in a deeper voice, said, "He don't like to lose no way out of the barn, but he ain't plannin' on hurtin' her, just gettin' that edge he needs all the time, force an issue."

Other knowledge stayed in the mix of Lavery's mind as he mulled things over.

One of them was that Penny should never have been out there alone, at the edge of the foothills, her horse run off towards home, and her hiding in the higher limbs of the tree, the two Marshall hands sitting under tree taking a break from fence repair, and each one shooting off his mouth about how they ought to "cash in on that little Penny."

One of them left a permanent thought in Penny's mind when he said, "She's a troublemaker like all girls this side of The Pecos West." His laughter was shared by his partner on fence duty, who said, "Give her a year or so and see what you get then."

That brought a round of laughter she faintly understood.

Later, she said to her irritated father, "Why do they want me, Pa?" Her eyes looking as big as flapjacks. She was as pretty as the summer mountain in the distance, or the winter copy of it when snow topped it off. He'd say she warmed every room she entered.

"That squirrely one," she put forth, "that Doak Witherspoon, he's always thinking he's the best looking man on the whole side of the mountain, just 'cause he is. Don't give him the right to say what he said, about grabbing me and taking me up to Peanut Hill to their line camp up there?"

"Penny," Lavery had burst out with, "are you damned sure that's what he said? He ain't a bad guy though he thinks awful big. You said stuff before about him. What the hell were you doing up in that tree? You could have been killed."

His nerves jumped at the thought.

"I told you, Ginger run off on me when I was picking flowers. I think she got spooked by a snake in the rocks that are spread all over the hill."

His nerves jumped again, but she had artfully shifted some of the focus again, the way her mother had been able to do, manipulating in a mostly innocent manner, and his eyes now making off with most of the elusive mischief. Lavery found the images of strewn rocks filling the back of his mind along with poisonous snakes.

2

He finally allowed one hidden thought to stick in his mind as he rode and all the images it carried with it.

He saw her again with the cards in her hand on the evening before at the kitchen table, as though she was going to wave them and make you think she'd show them off, a wicked smile curving her lips, her eyes lit up by the lamps. She had even said during the half wave, "Watch the cards, Pa. Watch the cards."

Then a new idea grasped her attention. "Didn't Grandma or Grandpa or somebody say something like that, Pa ... Watch the cards?" The lamplight still sat in her eyes as though it had picked her out for special reflections.

He had shaken his head, but she hadn't let it go. "It keeps coming at me, Pa," she said. "Like just now. Like last night. Like when I think of Ma leaving so early. Think it's her saying, 'Watch the cards?' That mean anything special, Pa?"

She closed her eyes, slowly tilted her head as though one suitable image was clutching for room, and offered up a new measure: "Think that makes me a special messenger, Pa? Think I really got something to say? All I have to say is, 'Watch the cards. Watch the cards.'"

Thorn Lavery, never a card player outside of his own home, noticed her eyes change, her face striking for some message too old for her few years.

Girls were a mystery to him. Always had been. And he was continually amazed at Penny's looks, nothing like her real father, that miserable creature sitting in town waiting for him, but like her mother. She was the prettiest thing in the whole valley, her mom gone just as she gave birth, her mom's hand out to her best friend, Thorn Lavery, her last words saying, "Don't ever let Marshall know I had a baby, Thorn. He stole me off one night and took me up to a line camp and got me this way." She looked away from Thorn Lavery for a moment.

"Him and my pa would have had a war and my pa would have died. I couldn't stand that. Told him it was an Indian and he near went crazy. That's when he tossed me out and you found me, took me in here. I'm sorry to lay this all on you, Thorn. It was no Indian, but Gus Marshall. Please don't tell him I had a baby by him. I'd die."

She had looked off again, adding, "I hope pa is there waiting for me. I miss him." She did die. She was dead in seconds after the birth of her daughter, the baby swept into another room by the Mexican lady that worked Lavery's kitchen ... from then on working for the infant, from then on working for the whole house. Her name was Lily-do, the name coming from Lavery saying so often, "Lily do this, Lily do that."

They laughed at it as the baby grew, but the name stuck. "Lily-do."

And "Penny," the name they gave the infant, stuck too.

Thorn Lavery was alone with the infant girl and the Mexican woman, him the apparent father to the whole town of Pecos Hill, as well as to the girl as she grew. He gave his all in raising her, his hate for Marshall falling away more and more each year as Penny came to be a beautiful young girl. Marshall's name never came up in rumor or silly talk from Saturday night drunks.

It was apparent that nobody knew.

Including Gus Marshall.

In town, seeing Marshall in repose in the chair on the boardwalk, like he was holding court, Lavery slowed his horse, dismounted at the rail and tied his horse to the rail. He looked at Marshall sort of apologetically, still wondering what he was going to do to pay his debt off to Marshall, sitting on his IOU from the general store. To pay now would hold off on his purchase of one good build to start a new herd.

Marshall looked up, saw he was unarmed, and said, "Hell, Thorn, you didn't have to come all the way into town to pay off that debt. I would have ridden out there to collect in a week or so. No trouble at all."

He smiled, looking around, seeing that his boys were spread around town like always, and Lavery coming alone, not that there was going to be a fight, but Marshall always liked odds in his favor.

"I'm not sure that I'll pay it off today. I got more than a week to go before you tally the new stuff I'm going to pick up today."

"Uh uh," Marshal said. "I'm not giving you any more credit until this one's paid off." He looked around, saw all eyes on him, like the lord on high had made a pronouncement. He figured, with the opportunity right in his hands, he'd make it go as far as possible.

"You never come into town except to buy at the store. You rarely have a drink with the other boys at the saloon, you don't go to the barbershop, and you've never stayed at the hotel. Hell, Lavery, I never saw you in a card game in my whole life. You afraid of the cards, Lavery?"

His smile ran right through the crowd that had filtered from sundry sources at the sight of the two men talking, two gents at odds.

"Cards were never for me, or haircuts, or a hotel bed when I have my own bed back at the ranch. And why would I go to the saloon if I don't drink? That thinking throws me off. Is there something else there that I'm missing?"

As soon as he said that he heard Penny say, a dozen times if once, "Watch the cards. Watch the cards." A strange feeling came over him, as if he was in the grip of a surge of energy or a light was trying to shine in him.

4

Marshall, feeling he was in absolute control of the whole scene, said, "We could play poker, Lavery. You could bet what you owe me, if you don't happen to have any cash in your pockets right now."

It was one of his standard ploys.

The snickers ran through the crowd, much of it spawned by Marshall's men.

Not believing what came out of his mouth, Lavery said, "Why not? Let's play poker. I'll ante up some of the debt I owe you, if that's okay with you."

"That's fine by me," Marshall said. He yelled to one of his men, a sly looking cowpoke, thin as a split rail, a mustache just as thin, like a black wire sitting on his upper lip holding a sneer tightly in place.

"Jake," he said, "go pick a table for us and set up the cards and the chips like usual. We're going to have a big game of poker. Thorn Lavery's going to play poker!" He yelled out his words, which worked slick as a veil.

"Can you imagine that? Me and him, me and Lavery, like it's a Duel at Pecos Hill. Ain't that the top of the day for you? The Duel at Pecos Hill, and right here at the card table in The Pecos West Saloon. Don't that beat all hell."

He shook his head in false disbelief and uttered a laugh rife with derision.

The gathering in The Pecos West Saloon caught it on the first toss.

The two men went at it, virtual as sworn enemies. They played and played and the game went back and forth, Lavery winning some, losing some, and the edge slowly sliding away on the hands with bigger pots. At the far end of the room, silence hanging in the air like a prairie mist, a few men heard the whisper of cards being dealt, chips falling in place, breath abated at raises, cards tossed onto the table top. Some of the watchers wished they were right in the game, but others knew their place; this was trenchant, extraordinary, the salient game in the history of The Pecos West Saloon.

At length, thirst working, Lavery accepted a drink from Marshall, then another. He appeared to be getting dizzy, and after winning one good pot, turned to one of Marshall's men and said, surprisingly, "If you caught me cheating, what would you do, Doak?"

It was the good looking gent that Penny had mentioned a few times. He would agree with Penny that he was a good looking fellow.

"Hell, mister," Doak said, "if you was caught cheating at cards we'd do a couple of things I've seen done before … either hang you right outside the door or run you out of town all slickered up with tar and feathers on your own horse." He slapped his thigh and yelled a loud, "Yippee! Ain't that a sight to bust your britches!"

Lavery turned to another one of Marshall's men sitting at the next table. It was Jake Preble, the one who had set up the table, the cards, the chips. Jake Preble had huge grin on his face.

Lavery looked at him righty in the eye and asked, "You wouldn't be so quick as your pal there, would you, Jake? Would you run a cheat out of town, or worse, hang him out front?"

Preble laughed loud enough to be heard outside and down the boardwalk. "I sure would, mister. I'd hang you on the spot. I wouldn't waste my time slickin' you up on a horse. I'd do it good, quick, right and proper, and right out front. It'd be a good end to the Duel at Pecos Hill." He let loose another loud laugh that bounced off the walls of the saloon.

"Would you really do that to a cheater, Jake?" Lavery looked all around the room, finding few eyes in the room that had ascertained fully what he was saying. Most faces were thick with other thoughts, other leanings.

It was only the bartender, smarter than some folks, who had a slight grin beginning its place on his lips, thinking about pouring himself a beer before the situation developed into an interesting episode.

"What the hell did I just say, mister?" Preble said. "Can't you hear me any good at all. What did I just say?" He was standing beside his chair, his hand too near his revolver to be incidental. On his face an old scar threatened its perceivable redness, liquor dotted his eyes, and anger was having its way with him.

The bartender put one hand on the butt of a rifle under the bar, and with his other hand he slid a beer mug under the tap. The taste was on his lips, in his throat ... and a bit of suspense, like seeing a cougar preparing to leap.

Lavery wanted to be as quick as Preble's gun hand appeared to be. "Well, Jake, what you just said was that you'd hang a cheater quick and good and right out front. Am I right on that?"

The bartender poured himself a beer and waited for the suds to settle on the top before he wiped them off. One hand was still on the butt of the rifle.

Lavery, thinking all the time about Penny, what would happen to her if he messed things up, knowing full well what had developed in front of him, alerted from the first word to be watching the cards, as she had advised, as she had foresworn, as she had prophesized from the beginning, was not worried about Marshall.

Lavery took stock: Marshall was now the pawn in the whole mess, in this place, in the seat he would never have chosen. His guns sat hanging at his hips.

Doak, the good looking kid, didn't bother Lavery.

But Jake Preble did. Jake had set up the table. Jake Preble had set down the deck of cards. Jake was Marshall's man from the very first minute, Jake Preble with the thin mustache, like it was clipped from a strand of barbed wire, like it could twist a smile into a snarl.

It was Jake Preble he was worried about. But Jake Preble, at the same time, seemed to be the key to it all and Marshall the mere pawn.

Nothing told him he was wrong.

Lavery knew it had to be quick. It had to be firm. It had to be so open there could be no complaint. No false moves. No alibis or excuses or mixed words tossed into the mess to twist it further, to hide reality.

Lavery, turning slowly, noted that Preble and Witherspoon, as well as Marshall, were all of a like mind. His eyes, in a sweep of the room, caught only they eyes of the bartender, with minute admiration … and hope.

Lavery knew some men were smarter than he was … and he hoped the bartender was one of them.

But he made his move, depending on Preble's attitude, Witherspoon's youth and basic honesty, and the bartender's alertness. He did not know the man's name, but he hoped he was accountable.

He looked at Preble, his eyes narrowing in intentness, and said, his words coming alive across the whole room, "If I told you the deck of cards we're using had 5 aces in it, would you say that was cheating? Would you hang the guy that put it there? Would you hang that gent who would stoop as low as a common barn rat?"

The room was deadly silent.

The bartender gripped the rifle under the bar and slowly lifted it onto the bar top. Many customers in the saloon saw the move.

Preble, frozen in place, coming up as bare as a sudden decoy, did not move, except for the grimace that traversed his face, a grimace that carried all he knew.

Doak Witherspoon, the handsome kid, stuck in a spot, was stunned; he knew who always set up Marshall's card table.

Marshall, caught in the midst of his usual way of odds-leaning, seeking the edge, seeing Jake Preble about to break a long trust and the handsome kid Doak Witherspoon now caught without a paddle, his own status brought into the open, slyly reached one hand for his pistol.

"Don't," said the bartender, pointing the rifle directly at him, his single word resounding in the room.

Marshall reached anyway, measuring all the consequences, coming up the loser no matter what happened, and the bartender fired the rifle at him as he pulled his revolver free of the holster.

Marshall never knew he had a daughter, about the prettiest girl in the whole valley, and Penny Lavery, 13 and going on 30, never knew that Gus Marshall was her real father.

Downwind of Murder

As Shasta Corbin, sheriff of Polatta, rode into the canyon in the heat of the day, he saw a pair of vultures high overhead floating on a thermal, which most likely had risen from the heart of the canyon. With that sight, also came a putrid odor. In one drawn breath he caught the ripe smell of death. It was a stench he'd never get used to, and recognized instantly.

He hoped it wasn't Coyle Magnan baking away in the stove of the canyon. Hell, it wasn't murder that Magnan was running from, or stealing someone's horse, but was accused only of stealing a few hundred dollars from Doc Filmore, a thief in his own right, but the cardsharp had sworn out a warrant on Magnan in public display. "You get him, Sheriff, that's what you get paid for. I don't care if it's horse stealing, rustling, murder or outright theft, it's the law. He broke the law and you got to enforce the law."

Of course, it was like Filmore in his usual way, saying it in front of a couple of dozen men in the saloon, all of them nodding in agreement, though not many of them really liking the card man. Witnesses meant strength and order to Filmore, like cards in his hand; neat, of one purpose, to be properly handled. Corbin had to hand it to him, the way he handled the group of men, making each one feel as though it was his money that had been stolen.

And, of course, he said to himself again, Filmore got his nickname from the belief that he could doctor a sick hand of cards back to good health with his quick fingers and a degree in swift shuffling of the odds. Corbin could not remember who said that about Doc, but it was one of the town fathers who had probably been caught too often with an ailing hand and a big pot on the table. The faces of the lawyer Juspin and Overby, the owner of the bank, lurked in a narrow part of his mind. There were times he thought the pair of them could be as devious as any common criminal. He quickly admitted it was only a suspicion kicking around in his mind, but he had survived believing in suspicions that came upon him from nowhere in particular, except that he also believed his experiences built upon themselves a kind of caution not to be ignored.

The vultures, meanwhile, continued their graceful but deadly looking maneuver as the sheriff moved deeper into the canyon. There were a few ways of leaving the canyon, in amongst a huge mass of fallen rock walls, but he did not believe he'd have to seek out those escape routes, not with the smell getting stronger and the big birds staying put overhead. With thermals working for them, they'd outlast him in the long run.

He saw the horse first. It was a big gray that had fallen onto a cluster of rocks, dead forever, and the saddle gone. When he checked the animal, the wound was quickly evident; the gray had been shot at close range, part of its head shattered, but no legs showed broken. Sudden hate for any man that shot a horse ran through Corbin as if he had been shot himself. He'd shoot a man for doing that to a healthy and useful horse. We'd still be walking west if it wasn't for horses, the lot of us, he said in quick judgment.

A swirl of dust lifted off the canyon floor, picked up by a breath of air. A bit of debris fluttered in the dusty air, and then Corbin saw a gray Stetson start to roll near a slab of rock, for a bare moment as if on its brim, but it sat down on its crown in a sudden dip. And the stench had gotten viler, heavy with death. He hoped again it was not Magnan smelling up the canyon, dead as his horse. No clear tracks of another horse appeared on the rocky surface. The thought of a bushwhacker came to him, and he dipped in the saddle and looked all around the canyon, watching for any movement, for the sun glinting on a rifle sight, or for a hat barely moving behind a rock. A chill ascended his whole frame, running up the back of his neck. He hoped he had not missed a slight movement, a quick flash of sunny reflection, a bushwhacker in the act. A man who'd shoot a horse like he'd found would have no hesitation to shoot a sheriff on the move.

"Hellfire," he said. "Keep low in the saddle." He ducked, pulling his head down from the firing line. It would be true irony to feel the shot before he died. There came an immediate flash when he equated a bushwhacker with the vultures still soaring overhead, waiting for the moment of truth, the moment of opportunity.

Even as he ducked he saw the body of Magnan, the face a mess, bloody and torn up, feasted on by some carrion eaters. His revolver lay on the ground beside him. He was 40 or so feet from his dead horse, and Corbin tried to picture his ending at the hands of somebody who'd shoot a horse. It didn't come easy.

Bang! A shot came from nowhere it seemed, a sharp but echoing blast that the canyon made louder, more threatening even in missing him as the bullet splattered against a rock face directly in front of him.

Corbin leaped from his saddle, whacking his horse on the rump, hoping he'd rush off and not be shot like the other horse. His own big gray, at a gallop, was gone from sight in a matter of a seconds, behind a rock, onto a hidden curve, the hoof beats echoing off the walls even as the boom of the shot leaped off other surfaces. The shot had corrupted the very air in the canyon, the sound waves bouncing off the high vertical walls like ricochets from a repeating rifle.

His rifle was in one hand as he rolled behind a rock looking immediately at the higher levels to see if some bushwhacker was about to shoot a fish in a barrel.

Perhaps the vultures would lose their grip on a thermal, he thought, and fall a hundred feet before they'd correct their fall. He looked overhead again for a brief second, and the second shot came, from far off to the left he figured, from among another cluttered mound of fall-downs, break-offs, debris of a thousand years in the pull of time, and the steep rise of the canyon wall. In the wall of the canyon he spotted the blackness of a crevice looking like a black stroke of lightning, a jagged, broken darkness running up the wall. There was a heavy sense of darkness, of depression, in one section; that's what he'd best immediately concentrate on.

But it was not from high above him. So he would have some space to move though he might be pinned down to a low level.

"Draw fire," he said in self-direction. "Make him give himself away. Make him use his ammo. Get a shot off in return."

With deliberate ease he pushed a smaller rock off to the side of the boulder he was hiding behind.

There was no answering shot. But there was a voice he did not recognize, as the words came to him: "I'm not a dumb cowboy, Sheriff. I got you where I want you and I have all day and your horse has gone off with your canteen and it's getting hotter than Hell in here. I have water, and you have none."

Corbin nudged the small rock further, and then tossed another one beyond it.

A shot rang out again, a sharp boom of a shot, and the bullet hit right beside the tossed rock.

"He's got a good eye," Corbin said, "but don't answer him. Don't speak. Let him do the talking." And even as he talked to himself other facets of his own intelligence were at work. "Draw him out. Draw him down. Get him exposed."

He felt his imagination making headway, demanding to have space. "Tossed stones won't do it long," he added. "It's got to be glitter, shine, reflection. Something different, eye-catching." The word "glitter" came back again and he leaned back against the protective rock and let loose his imagination. "Don't use the rifle to do it, because you'll need that before this day is over."

Where it came from he had no idea, except that it was some part of him waking up another part, drawing on experience, known circumstances. He looked down the length of himself and it was his badge that caught his eye. And the connection was immediate. "I always keep it shined, and polished. I'm damned proud to wear it."

He'd use the badge other than a symbol of his office, of his trust. "Make a tool of it," he said, almost aloud.

He'd have to use what was on him, as there was nothing in sight that he could adapt to the idea that suddenly ran clean through him.

With the most deliberate move he removed the badge from his shirt and the belt from his pants after his gun belt was laid aside. The pants belt, when folded upon itself three times, was about a foot long, and almost as stiff as he needed it to be. Tearing his bandana into strips, he tied each strip around the folded belt, slipped the pin of his badge onto the end of the belt and felt the belt remain stiff in his hand.

"Now," he said, as he looked at the bright sun riding down into the canyon, the heat coming off the face of rocks and the walls, and the vultures still glued to their endless arc above the canyon and the remains of the dead man and the dead horse. He held the folded belt in one hand, checked the sun's rays, saw the slim angle of them, and twisted the belt as a wand and held it beyond the protective rock.

The reflections leaped off the face of the badge in several directions, and an answering shot came from the darkness of the crevice. He reassessed his use of the tool, arranged a few rocks in place at the right end of the rock, stuck the belt into the small pile of rocks so that the badge was fully exposed, and he rolled quickly to the other end where he had placed his rifle.

There were two quick shots from the crevice, the bushwhacker, Corbin assumed, thinking the reflections were coming from his rifle.

With quick and sure aim, the sheriff poured four rounds from his Springfield into the crevice, heard the surprised cry of a wounded man … and ensuing silence.

He waited almost an hour, hearing a few cries at first, and then nothing.

The vultures continued their wait in the hot sky, the sun baked the canyon, and thirst built up in the sheriff. He flashed the badge a half dozen times and saw no reaction. He fired another round into the same fissure, and there was no response.

He realized he could sit all day if he didn't move, but the thirst would eventually force him to do something he might as well get done as soon as possible. The bushwhacker did have water.

He slipped out from behind the rock, firing three more rounds as he moved.

The echoes died out.

He found the bushwhacker, a complete stranger, at death's door, a bullet in his chest, lots of blood spilled on his clothing. The man was an older man, rough in the face as he continued to breathe, his lips twisted in desperation.

Corbin gave the man a drink from his canteen and then had some himself. The man came conscious and Corbin said, "Why'd you kill Magnan? Were you hired? Who hired you? What's your name?"

"I'm dyin'," the wounded man said. "I'm Johnny Quick from Lima. I got nobody. But don't let them vultures get me. The Doc hired me. Told me right where Magnan'd be, right here."

"Why? For a few dollars?"

"No. He got to Doc's sister, over in Alberville. Messed her up some. Doc was waitin' for an excuse, I guess. But then he found out Magnan had money in the Polatta Bank, 'cause Overby the banker told him, and they was goin' to split it soon as Magnan was dead, but Overby don't want no part of the killin' end, just the bankin' end. Some of the money's from a bank robbery in Alberville. And Doc's sister knew Magnan robbed the bank. He even told her, but didn't know she was Doc's sister."

Two burials were on him now, Corbin conceded, and he'd do them as best he could, under rocks, away from the vultures and what carrion eaters were not rock movers. He'd promised Johnny Quick that much, so he'd do the same for Magnan.

Both of them were messy, but done, and in a few hours he found his horse in the shade of an overhang. With water from his hat from Quick's canteen, his horse was his horse again.

He rode back to Polatta with the news of Magnan and Quick and further duties on his plate as sheriff of the town, featuring Overby the banker and Filmore the card shark.

There'd be a trial. He had one live witness he could lean on; that was Filmore the card man and he'd bring Filmore's sister into it if necessary. He knew who Overby would have as his defense attorney and wondered what approach the defense would take.

His imagination didn't reach all the way to what that approach would be. So he let it rest. That imagination had already completed a neat job for him and the badge he wore.

Hobie's Sugar Still

Hobart Bridgewater, Hobie to most folks, was a freighter who promised delivery of whiskey to several saloons along the Snake River. "I go get it for you and bring it back, and then you pay me. If you don't pay me, you don't get the load and I don't bring you no more. That's all easy for you gents and tough for me. Some days out there on the trail I have to keep my rifle leveled and ready, that's why I have the best shot in all the territory riding up there with me. Burke Molton ain't never missed a target he took aim at, and that includes those three scallywags who tried us on for size on the river road just last week and he knocked two of them right off their mounts with two shots and them riding hard at us all the while and trying to get the best whiskey in the west from us at the point of their guns."

All those in the Broke Bronc Saloon agreed with Hobie, some of them having heard his spiel before, some knowing what his intention was, some finding a bit of admiration for an older man who'd brave the elements and the dangers of the trail to keep all their throats up-happy and wet.

He raised his glass and said, "To a natural killer, gents, who don't miss, Burkey Molton." It was nothing short of him saying, "That's a promise of death next man tries us on."

Red in the face, sticking out now like a target, Molton realized that Hobie had used him the way he'd promised right from the beginning; "You're going to be kind of famous, Burkey boy, right famous, if I do it up the right way, and that's getting all the edge we can on those we do business with and those who try to do their business on us, if you know what I mean."

Off in a corner of the saloon, sorely missing two riding pards now gone, one man felt the anger crawling in him like a desert spider. In the past, prior to his last sentence in a Wyoming court and two years in prison before he broke loose of his cell one night and escaped with the warden's own horse, Nightrider Berwick vouched his own promise, though keeping it in his thoughts: "I'll drink right from your wagon one of these days, Hobie, and leave you like you and your pard left my pards."

It took all he had in him to walk out of the saloon and into the deep night, memories and old images cutting their way into his mind. "Damned fool lucky shot," he said into the dark night.

It was assumed right from the beginning by Hobie Bridgewater that all saloon owners cut the delivery of "decent whiskey" he brought to them with a wide assortment of ingredients, all of which came cheap to hand. Such cutting stuff included chewing tobacco with a decent taste to it, plain old alcohol otherwise known as the man killer, and sundry other mixes where the basic supply was easy to find.

With all that said, cowpokes would oftentimes blame the freighters for delivering plain old rot gut, where the next day their stomachs were damnation's curses coming alive. But the saloon gents didn't know that Hobie had a private stop on the way where he did his own cutting, "making the slice of the profits go into some different pockets."

When he stopped on the road, at Sarah Henderson's place on the long run of grass running up to the Snake, the small shed beside the barn was his own "private still of sorts." Even Sarah had no firm idea of what he was up to on the night when she saw the candlelight flickering late in the night, and still going as dawn neared. In her heart she had a soft spot for the old freighter who had befriended her father so long in the past. Cantankerous old men, she would argue, had a right to their own bit of privacy.

But on each visit at Sarah's place, Hobie would off-load some part of his wagon's contents and take it inside the shed. She never asked questions, because of the past favors, and he paid up at each stop at her place. It was good money needed to keep her place going, and Hobie stopped in every time he passed by.

Hobie and Burkey Molton, once inside the shed where they took turns sleeping, treated a portion of their load with extra ingredients that included sugar and corn squeezing they got by dickering with farmers and settlers on the routes they traveled, and any liquid supply that added volume to their load.

Sometimes Hobie added turpentine, gun powder ("That'd give the Devil himself a kick, Burkey," he'd say), ammonia or any native liquid he got his hands on from Indians ("This one'll be called Bend in the Road or Paw Paw Juice or plain old Stumpleg by the boys on the next day.") From this activity he'd maintain a keg or barrel of his "own stuff" eventually peddling it to saloon owners on top of their own orders. The special cut might come up with names the cowboys gave it when they celebrated the end of their cattle drives with a turn in a saloon, names that came easy on them, like Brokefoot, Spider in the Glass, MexTex Lightning or Fools' Lightning and Bugberry from the Bughouse.

But all that stuff was put aside for the time being, except for Nightrider Berwick's intentions of getting even with the old freighter and his hired gun. He was positive that Bridgewater had not recognized him during the attempted robbery because he had kept back from his two fellow bandits, him having the only prison record and wanting to keep it from adding to it.

It came to him that he should follow Bridgewater on his whole route and see what might become a special advantage.

So it was he saw the stop at Sarah Henderson's place, some part of the load being moved into the small shed, the lamp light burning in the window for most of the night. It was, he figured correctly, a stop to water down a portion of the whiskey.

But it was Sarah Henderson who spotted a man watching her place that same night as she and her foreman came back from a visit to a nearby ranch, saw the glimmer of a fire in a small copse, and snuck in to check it out. They saw a man step away from the fire with a small telescope, climb to the top of a rise and study her ranch through the glass. His silhouette was easily seen by them. They watched him for more than an hour before they slipped away in the night and went home.

But Sarah, for the first time ever, knocked on the door of the shed where the lamplight still showed in the one window.

Hobie Bridgewater, somewhat surprised, stepped out and Sarah said, "My foreman and I saw a man off in those woods yonder watching what we think was you here in the shed tonight with a spyglass. You have any idea who he might be?"

Hobie said, "I do, Sarah, and I want to thank you for warning me. Me and Burkey will set up something special for him, that's for plumb sure."

Sarah, not asking any more questions, left the pair of freighters to their own means, and went off to bed.

Before dawn came, the plan was devised and set into operation.

In the mix of shadow and faint light, the freighter's wagon left Sarah Henderson's ranch, with two figures sitting up on the front seat of the wagon, the load still sitting low on the wagon behind them. One of the figures was Hobie Bridgewater, talking his fool head off, giving continuous orders and condemnations to the other figure, a still figure made of some planking and dressed with Burkey Molton's hat and coat, and Bridgewater's old shotgun propped at a 45 degree angle. As if ready to fire.

Fifteen minutes after the wagon went down the road, and after a figure on horseback slipped out of the woods and followed the wagon at a good distance, Molton gently led his horse out to the main trail and mounted his horse after the furtive rider had gone out of sight ahead of him, a half mile down the trail.

In a matter of an hour down trail, and out of Henderson ranch hearing distance, Bridgewater stopped the wagon, climbed down, and yelled loudly at the figure still seated up on the wagon, the shotgun still in hand, "You stay up there, Burkey, and keep your eye out for any bandits while I fix this damned broken piece here."

He waved his hands around and yelled out in the early morning air, his voice rising with morning clarity, his anger as evident as the clear air, "Why'n'cha fix that damned thing last night like I told ya. Damned disgrace is what you are. Gotta do this myself while you sit on your useless rear end."

He stomped around, yelled loudly, "Keep your eyes open and don't fall asleep again." His voice was strident, acidic, an old war horse at his sourest bit.

There was some banging and more cursing and a general mix of commotion in different degrees of delivery. But it wasn't musical.

Nightrider Berwick, out of the saddle, smug with the upper hand on a sworn foe, placed his rifle down on a stump, listened to the commotion, and twisted his face into a relishing grin at the sight and the sounds.

His right eye settled down on the rifle barrel to where the sight was squarely on the figure sitting up on the wagon with the weapon of undetermined type in his hands, the gray Stetson and the short gray coat assuring identification of the killer of his pards.

Berwick heard more noise, felt a wild sense of joy surge through his frame, but was still able to lock tightly on the still figure. With added glee accompanying his mind set, he squeezed off a dead-on shot right where excruciating pain would set in like a grenade exploding.

He harrumphed his triumph.

The gray Stetson jumped off the figure sitting up on the wagon. Hobie Bridgewater, down on the ground, dove down under the wagon. The team of horses, securely hobbled, only made noise on top of the other noises: the echo of the rifle shot, the sound of the plank being ripped by the bullet, Bridgewater's curses rising in the air, a second shot slamming into the main plank that had held the Stetson and still supporting the gray coat, now horribly rent by lead.

Berwick, leaning on the stump, was dumbfounded; the figure of Burkey Molton had not moved. He was positive he had hit him dead-on. The man's hat had jumped off with the hit. It had fluttered to the ground where Bridgewater still yelled out his anger.

He fired again, his eye dead-on again, on the headless figure! Had he decapitated him? Was it now all even? All squared away? His pals paid off in spades?

Nothing was happening ... except the pain now in his leg, in his back, riding up his whole body from an unknown cause, an unknown source. When he managed to spin around, the rifle gone from his hands, fallen useless now to the ground, and his sudden inability to reach for a side arm, Burkey Molton, true dead shot of dead shots, was advancing

17

on him still in the saddle, his rifle aimed at the heart of the failed bushwhacker, smoke coming from the barrel of his rifle.

Under the wagon, his voice still rising in the morning air, an image of Sarah Henderson accepting a gallon of 100 per cent uncut whiskey showing in the back of his head, the old freighter knew the true glee that never came to the bushwhacker on his last breath ... and he was still in the still business, him and his pard, Burkey Molton, sure shot for sure.

Hourly Bastion, Bastard Hero

He was "that boy" in town, born in a room above the Bull's Head Saloon, living there most of his early life, subjected to scornful castigation, taunts, and frequent beatings at the hands of bullies. He spent limitless hours of young exploration in the alleys of Westcott, Arizona, sometimes hounded by peers who maligned him with the harshest nicknames, all speaking directly to his birthright, "that bastard boy born upstairs at the saloon."

His name, given because of the barrage of questions from the upstairs ladies about when the expected birth was due, came from the house madam's usual reply, "Hourly," and so his mother, Sally Bastion, one of the loveliest of the ladies, called him "Hourly" from that hour on. Without realizing it, the name came back upon the boy, and his mother, as a brand, a stigma from the start. A few saloon wags even made up songs about the mother and her son, their tawdry refrains phrased with the cruelest indignities.

But, in truth, the vocal stigma toughened up both of them, her for her frightful role in life, the boy for the life that was trying to pin him down to a singular role in the long run.

Hourly Bastion, it could be seen early on, wasn't going to stand for it.

As a result of the many indignities tossed at him, he found solace in odd places about the small community on the river. In those hours he "lost" himself and "aged" himself in the strange games of human interplay caught up in his mind. Hourly saw people, all kinds of people, at their best and at their worst. It made him sit up and look closely at some of those he saw in both normal and extraordinary actions around town, knowing it was just like being in an outdoor schoolhouse. He found escape in the created adventures, and from them gained experience he'd not otherwise achieve. Hourly, it was evident to any keen observer, was maturing without realizing it.

The horses got him first, the parade of them into and out of town, him hiding behind some small barricade so he could see them all, their spirit, their muscled frames. He loved them with a ferocity that seemed born with him, dreaming of them, seeing their eyes wild and bright, manes flying in the wind, their huge chests like prairie barges, miracles on the run, and when they ran in bunches, fast, then faster, like longhorns in a stampede, he loved them more, the grays and pintos and sun-gifted palominos and quarter horses as talented as athletes. Incessantly he dreamed of a huge remuda under his care, a huge herd of cattle out on the vast prairie, and him on his favorite horse singing a soft song to the herd and the remuda, a song that he had not yet heard, and never knew the words coming out of his mouth.

It was a significant joy for him, a trade-off with pleasure for the daily pains that otherwise came at him.

Horses, of all things western towns featured, came with their assorted colors and patterns, especially the ones called paints and pintos; he loved their variety and color schemes, the lively camouflage of them at a distance. From an early age, barely out and about by himself, he watched the parade of riders coming into and leaving the livery run by an old man with a crooked leg and a deep voice. The crooked leg frightened him and the scary deep voice as if coming from a dark cave, but the feeling were altered by the way the man treated horses; he knew that was special, and thus so stood the man with the bent leg and the scary voice. It was, he learned in piece parts, a lesson taking place, and to which he must pay attention … at all times. These lessons lead to warm fuzzy feelings, which meant lunch, a late sandwich when he was ravished by hunger, or a hug from his mother or one of the ladies who smelled like the prairie flowers that ran right up to the fence beside the Westcott cemetery on the edge of town.

Those who did not know his background would say he was a handsome boy, his hair keenly gold as corn tassel, eyes as deep blue as one of those prairie flowers, and bore an intensity for a youngster that made people take a second look at him, oftentimes setting him apart from others his age. They'd exclaim mightily and with an exultant joy, those who did not know of his background, when he said his name was Hourly. The name drew "hallos" and "howdy-dos" and "whatta ya knows" from them and now and then a "Whoop-dee-doo." A few new-comers to town tried quick attempts at jokes about "What's your second hand up to?" or "How many minutes you got to spare, Kid?" After a few of them, gaily delivered, he understood them to be curious kindnesses, and made room for them.

His mother, and the ladies upstairs who doted on him, had helped him to read at an early age, and that let him spend time at books and small tasks he found on his own. One of the tasks was making a list of all the horse breeds he saw in the town with all the information on each one that he could get by studying horses, by asking questions, and he was eventually able to tell one from another in an instant. He insisted that his mother and the ladies help him make his list, and the list grew; quarter horses and mustangs and appaloosas and paints and pintos and Arabians and Morgans. He'd ask anyone a question about horses to fill his book. Certain touches of the wind became readable and colors and scents of animals began to form a litany in his mind. The scent of animals developed name tags for him, as did their colors or paired colors with a basic white, as with the paint horses, where white mixed with a variety of bay, black, brown, roan, buckskin, champagne, chestnut, cremello, dun, gray, grullo, palomino, perlino, red dun, roan, smoky cream, or sorrel. He stockpiled all he learned, and his collection of note pads, grocer's wrappings, throw-away paper were tucked away on a roof beam in the saloon's upper structure.

When the horse book was full, he started on guns, hand guns and rifles, small bore to blunderbuss, and made up a list that also became a book. Hourly became so adept at certain tasks, and with grasping all kinds of know-how, that some of the cowpokes became irritated and muttered, loud enough to be heard by ladies on the balcony, "That little bastard gets more favors than we do and we keep the damned place running, don't we?"

Stories circulated that a few of the ladies, angered by cowpokes' attitudes, imposed their own demands on the noisiest of them.

While on his livery lookout the boy saw how riders mounted a horse, and dismounted, took care of their horse and gear, made way to the saloon where his mother spent all her days and nights. A few of the repeat riders became favorite sights and he could spot them at the far edge of town as they rode in from wherever, his eyes quickly finding known elements of identification: color schemes of clothes, a wide hat with a special band on it or a brim flipped at a cocky angle, how the sun bounced off a steel spur or a magnificent belt buckle or now and then off a lawman's badge, a proud adornment he began to dream about.

He noticed how men rode in the saddle, how they sat, what kind of saddle they favored, how they found rhythm from the hooves of their huge gray or black or red horse or a pinto, as he moved each horse into its appropriate breed and class of horses that came or rode off.

All the garnered knowledge of familiar figures found its way into his memory structure, and he sought additional characteristics that separated each man from the next man he saw. Soon, he could spot the differences at first glance.

At noon when he came back to the saloon from hunger's stir, climbing by a side entrance to his own room, little more than a closet space, either his mother or one of the ladies would provide lunch for him, each one of them having somewhat adopted him as her own in her own way. "Hourly's one of ours and we'll do whatever to take care of him."

Some of that, unknown to Hourly or his mother, was carried to another level where customers were advised how special Hourly was to each lady on the second floor and it would be best for all customers to have the same considerations for "that little boy you see around here, Hourly, our boy Hourly."

His mother kept saying she didn't know who his father was, but each of them had a serious suspicion of who he was because of the boy's looks and the looks of one likely looking customer. The name was always a whisper among the ladies, and never once mentioned in Hourly's presence.

But Hourly, as dictated by his genes, had some backbone in him, and some smarts, and thusly from the age of 14 was a willing volunteer to go on posse hunts with the sheriff, Will Tonger, the first man in Westcott to really look upon him with something other than distaste. This favor was not one asked or suggested to him by one of the ladies, but from something he ascertained in the boy as a scraping child, an exerted will, and Hourly making his way around town and on into adolescence, a survivor all the way in spite of his beginning.

The pair of them went through several dangerous situations on a few posse hunts, and the bond grew stronger with each incident. The boy's natural instincts and wisdom were consistently exposed to the sheriff, and he felt comfortable with him as a riding pard. Someday, he was positive, there'd be a turn-around for Hourly Bastion, the way things happen with people he found notable, worthy, beyond their start in life. He'd seen ordinary mountain men assume greatness on the land, coming off as near-godheads in the crudest but survivable way, knowing the land as only the native tribesmen did, living off it, succoring it, giving back to it. They were heroes.

The sheriff addressed it openly one day when he said, "Hourly, some day when you go out on one of these challenging rides, you'll come back different than when you left. And things back here will be different for you too. Don't ever let it get away from you, that chance at change. Like they say, It's in the books, the books about heroes. I've got my hands on a few of them hero books from drummers and hustlers and you can read them any time you want. My door's never locked."

On his 18th birthday Hourly Bastion was hired as a full-time deputy by Sheriff Tonger. "Do it up the way you think about it, Hourly, and I know you do that with your own special tools. Do it good and honest and as quick as you can. You bring a lot to the job, so you should be able to walk away with something from it."

Two days later, as fate might have set its spring, the bank was robbed by two masked men who moved as smooth as a good clock at each of the small details in the big heist.

No volunteers would go with the sheriff on the posse because three people had been killed already as the robbers made their way out of town in a running gunfight mounted by alarmed citizens. The three dead townsmen changed the town, but Hourly Bastion was ready to ride in minutes.

They left, the two of them, tracking the robbers of the bank, the leader having said to the bank manager, "We're not taking it all. Only what we need right now. You'll have enough left to run the bank. Perhaps someone will come along to put a big deposit in the bank and really make it grow."

A few days later, while Sheriff Tonger and Hourly Bastion were still on the chase, a cattleman, at the end of a profitable drive, put up a ten thousand dollar reward for the capture of the two robbers, and made a hefty deposit in the bank. His name was Mort Gloster, and he owned a sizable ranch a dozen miles up the river from Westcott.

At about that time, in a canyon up river, Tonger and Bastion cornered the two robbers, and forced them to drop their guns in a deadly crossfire. The two, both known by their captors as ranch hands at the Gloster Ranch, proclaimed their innocence in a flurry of talk. But Hourly Bastion had seen one of the men in operation before and remembered some things about him.

He asked Tonger if he could question him. "'Course you can, Hourly. Take your time. We'll get them back to town and then have a quick trial."

Bastion said to the robber, "All of a sudden, Clarker, you left a difficult trail to follow to one like a kid trying to hide from his mom. Too simple and easy, wasn't it? Ain't it? What else you guys got going?"

He knew the card table expression on Clarker's face, a giveaway to some other ruse or ploy already well into play.

"Nothing, I swear it," he said, but his looks did not agree to what he was saying.

It had been warning enough and just as Bastion saw a reflection from above and yelled out a warning, two gunshots went off, one atop the other, like they were fired from rungs in a ladder. They echoed down from above and Sheriff Tonger and one of the robbers fell dead from their saddles. Bastion scrambled for cover, still holding the reins of the other robber's horse, the robber's hands trussed to the pommel, him going nowhere.

Both men had been shot in the back.

Deputy Hourly Bastion brought two dead men and the prisoner back to town, two bodies across the saddles of their horses, the prisoner trussed up for jailing. He was hailed as a hero in the town that had castigated him and taunted him for years, and at times still did the same to his mother ... but no longer where Hourly Bastion could hear it.

Bastion heard the sheriff's words about coming back to town different than when he went out ... but it couldn't have been about the sheriff's death ... he wouldn't have meant that. It still eluded Bastion.

There was hell to pay around Westcott for the whole day, and the judge in the next town was sent for. The judge had one trial going and would in Westcott in a few days.

It looked to be a quick trial on the bank robbery and a new posse, under Hourly Bastion, would go back out to find the bushwhacker who killed the sheriff and the prisoner.

The next morning, however, a quick meeting of the town council was called by the mayor, where Mort Gloster made some devastating accusations against Hourly Bastion. "I got a couple of my line riders who saw the deputy, who probably wants the sheriff's job and figures this is the only way to get it, shoot both men in the back as they sat their horses in Big Horn Canyon. Shot them right out of the saddle he did without so much as a howdy-do. That's your sheriff, gents, going today to the cemetery. Now I don't know how long you gents are going to take that kind of stuff from the likes of him, and you know what I mean by that, but I'll say right here and now me and my boys won't stand for no tricks from him any longer."

The mayor said to Bastion, "Hourly, you don't need to give me your gun and your badge, not now. We can wait till things develop once Judge Carlton Shavers gets here. We'll see then. Just consider taking a rest from the job unless something happens before the court sits on this serious matter."

"So you'll let me keep my badge and guns in case something happens, huh? Well, Mayor, I don't think that will work out in my favor, so you take them now or I carry on like always."

"Oh, all right, Hourly. I was just trying to be fair about this."

"There ain't nothing fair about any of it except the sheriff gets a decent burial, and I'm going to see that it happens."

In the morning they rang the bell in the church and the trial soon got underway, the saloon stuffed with the curious, the faithful, the thirsty. The mayor said, "Please rise now for Judge Carlton Shavers who will sit here in judgment of the case against Deputy Hourly Bastion."

Shavers, an ordinary looking man, with a beard, a Stetson sitting squarely on his head, a pair of Colts displayed on his belt, sat at a table in the saloon. He cast a stern eye about him and said, "That's the end of all drinking while court is in session. No more beer. No whiskey, not so much as a glass of water or a glass of sarsaparilla gets passed to a customer." He added, "The law of the land," as he looked at the long row of men standing at the bar, the driest looking lot in the saloon.

He harrumphed a few times, took a drink of water that had a faded orange color to it, and banged the table with his fist. "I have read the charges against the deputy you call Hourly. Who is the defendant's lawyer?" He looked around the room for someone to stand up, be announced.

It was Hourly Bastion who stood up and said, "I am the defendant's lawyer."

The judge said, "You ain't no real lawyer."

Hourly Bastion, in his best imitative voice, said, "And you ain't no real judge." There followed a slow laughter, most men aware of what Bastion meant.

"When they were going to try Cody Twitchell for murder back in Pega Verdi, Judge," Bastion continued, "you were the barkeep and the only one who had no interest in the trail and that's how you were chosen to be judge and you've plain kept at it ever since. I ain't saying you haven't done some good at it, but these accusations could make me real uncomfortable if I don't take some real precautions that a real lawyer would try. So I suspect that we agree on all that, don't we, Your Honor?"

"Oh, alright, Hourly, you can carry on by the minute if you will," and he squeezed out a smile that went to the farthest corner of the room, and took another sip of the off-color water. "Who do you want up here to get sworn in as a witness?"

On the landing above the temporary court, from her room down the hall, Sally Bastion watched her son Hourly, and admired the way he was going about this whole mess. More than once she looked down upon the man who most looked like her son and whom she knew to be his father, neither one of them ever guessing about the relationship. At the same time she saw another son, one she had given up, sitting at a table with his adoptive farther while his real father, also with no knowledge of their kinship, sat at the very next table watching all that was going on, and none of them knowing what was most important to them.

The ironies could have crushed her, except for the gifts she got when she decided to keep Hourly in spite of all the talk that surrounded them, and much of it because of the son she had given up.

Hourly Bastion looked at his two accusers, Jonas Salt and George Spanger, and noticed the grimace moving on the face of Jonas Salt.

"Jonas Salt, come up here, please," he said, his hand out to one of the two witnesses, a cowpoke on the Gloster ranch, a weekend drinker with few equals, a cowpoke who more than once Bastion had seen beat his horse with a whip. He picked Salt, having seen him for a few years at his best and at his worst.

Salt sat in a chair beside the judge, and Hourly Bastion said, "You were out on line work and that's when you saw me shoot Sheriff Tonger right in the back from close up and didn't do anything about it. Is that your story?"

"That's just what I said when the mayor asked me."

"And you didn't do anything at all but run and hide?"

"We was too far away to do anything."

"You just said you saw me from close up."

"I didn't say that, you did."

"But you agreed, didn't you?"

"That was part of the trick work my boss said you was goin' to use."

"You work for Mort Gloster, don't you?"

"Yup, all the way." His smile reached around the room.

Hourly Bastion, self-defending lawyer, said, "If I was to tell you that there is a witness that says you were not out there on line work the other day, but someplace else, what would you say to that?"

"I'd say he was a dad-blamed liar all the way."

"Well, his name is Epaminondas Anganistickoulus." Bastion laughed loudly, gauged the reaction in the courtroom, and said, "I swear by all that's holy that his name is Epaminondas Anganistickoulus. You know the man? He came here from one of those Greek Islands we hear about every once in a while." With a pard's move, he placed his hand on Salt's shoulder. "How's that sit with you now, Jonas?"

Judge Carlton Shavers twisted his head sideways, and tossed off the most curious look at this information.

"Well, Hourly, that's a real easy one for me," Jonas Salt said. "I never knew the man, I never saw the man, I never spoke to the man, so he can't say where I was anytime at all, or what I was doing, or where I been any of these days. And that's the honest truth." He glowed in the face as he looked around the room again, a bit of crow in his talk, a nod to the table where Gloster sat.

"So, Jonas, that's the whole truth just like everything you said so far is the whole truth and nothing but the truth, so help you in the face of the good Lord. So true without a doubt about the next witness and where you were when I was supposed to have shot my best friend in the whole world, Sheriff Tonger?"

"Sure as I'm sitting here." The look on his face came up for the third time.

"Truth is a strange thing at times, Jonas, and comes from right where it is when you need it the most. Now, I admit I didn't make that part up, Jonas, but Sheriff Tonger said it one day and I plain just remember it."

Jonas Salt smiled his understanding and Hourly Bastion whirled about near the judge's table and said, "Will Epaminondas Anganistickoulus please stand up."

The whole courtroom, from Judge Carlton Shavers and the witness Jonas Salt and the accused Hourly Bastion looked around the room and waited for the man named Epaminondas Anganistickoulus to stand up.

Behind the bar, not working since the judge's dictate about no drinking, the bartender known as Sticky raised his hand and said, "Here I am."

Jonas Salt almost fell out of the witness chair, and stared at his boss, Mort Gloster, who pushed his thumb up under his chin as if to say, "Stick with it, Jonas, or you're on your own in all of this."

Jonas Salt yelled out, "He never told me that was his name. We always called him Sticky. Sticky's his name. His one and only name."

Hourly Bastion said, "You think his mother called him Sticky 'cause he came all glued up?" Even the judge laughed at that.

Upstairs, on the landing, somewhat out of sight, Hourly's mother smiled at her son's question and Jonas Salt managed a weak smile, fearing some strange thing about to work against him. Sally Bastion also knew a nervous twinge pass through her body. Perhaps something was about to break loose.

Sticky, the usually quiet bartender of the Bull's Head Saloon, sometimes but most infrequently known as Epaminondas Anganistickoulus, walked from behind the bar and took the chair beside the judge as Salt went back to his boss's table. Mort Gloster did not acknowledge him.

"Sticky," Bastion said, "you heard everything Jonas Salt just told this court, didn't you?"

"Every word."

"Did he tell it the way it really was, Sticky?"

"No, he didn't, Hourly. He was right at the bar, him and Georgie Spanger, that other fellow he's sitting with at Mort Gloster's table. He'll be another witness for you if he tells the truth about him being there or not being there at the canyon. They couldn't be anyplace else but drinking up a storm right here in this room when they said they were up there in the canyon watching you shoot down your best friend, the sheriff."

"Is that the full and only truth, Sticky?"

"It sure is, Hourly, and they are the damnedest liars I ever heard in court." He turned to the judge and said hello in his birth language, "Υειά σου, Carly. Nice to see you again. It's been a spell, hasn't it?"

"Sure is, Sticky," obviously understanding Sticky's hello. "I ain't seen you in a hound's age. You been well, I take it." He slammed his fist down on the table and said, "Charges dismissed against Hourly Bastion."

27

And he turned back to his old pal and said, "Get back to work, Sticky. I got a real thirst goin' in place."

Mort Gloster made a move for the door, and Hourly Bastion, with a sudden change to his voice, said, "Hold on there, Mister Gloster. You got some explaining to do, you and your lying friends and who else was in your employ. I want all your ranch hands in here to stand up now and tell us where they were when Sheriff Tonger was killed by some bushwhacker or bushwhackers – and I want the truth 'cause I have more witnesses ready to swear the god-awful truth about all of this – and you all know, every last man in here, that I got no quit on this one, not when it comes to my first and best friend ever, Sheriff Will Tonger."

It was his turn to slam the table top and he did so right in front of the judge, who stood up and said, "This here court is back in session and the bar is still closed." He shrugged his shoulders at old friend Epaminondas Anganistickoulus.

Mort Gloster, wealthy rancher, prominent citizen, made another desperate move for the door, and Sheriff Hourly Bastion, quick as a slick gunman, drew his weapon and leveled it at the unveiled manipulator bearing the heaviest suspicions, being a possible murderer of the town's most recent sheriff, looking as if he was about to flee true justice at the hands of the bastard sheriff.

Fate does have its way with some of its heroes. Hourly Bastion, supposedly fatherless, born into a tragic life, despised and continually set upon by his peers, knowing the ironies swiftly piling up from one more sweeping statement, stood at last at the head of the line among his peers, his unknown father identified, his birth covered by sudden attrition as his mother, Sally Bastion, seeing him take aim at Gloster as if he was about to shoot him, leaped from a corner of the balcony, and yelled, "Don't shoot him, Hourly. He's your father."

Hourly Bastion had come home, all the way home as a hero, as foretold by his dearest friend, Will Tonger, hoped for by his mother, and definitely foreseen by the ladies upstairs at the saloon.

Kid Bullet off the Trail

Travis Henry, young sheriff of Winslow Hills, in the Wyoming Territory, was back from his honeymoon of sorts, and was on the job after a quiet period when he was away. He was 21, three times wounded in his short life, and considered lucky by most men who knew him, and gun-fast by everybody else in town.

Going back to work was easy, with a smile on his face.

It didn't last long, that quiet period, with Bog Morchant in town and his gang of sour faces, poor dispositions and hands generally too quick to their guns. The lot of them was a mix of anger, greed, boisterous energy as long as things were tilted in their favor. It was easy to say that they could spoil any evening of any week, summer or winter, as long as they were together, bunched, interdependent, a precursor to unionism. It was their way, feeling it was their due, losers all the way trying to get something free they figured was owed them, fate at work for them.

The camaraderie had come into the ranks of a bunch of losers who had been banded by the energy, and evil, of one man. Morchant knew how he came at people and used it, fond of his mean edge and how he could slip it in against most anybody, like setting a branding iron on the lot of them who might get in his way.

A testament to the gang's creation was offered up by one of its minions. Lucky Cadre was so misnamed that it never hit him. He was rotten-spoiled, a sore loser, sick mostly of what life served up for him, but knew he had found his haven within the gang, with Morchant as a leader. The man was steady in his way and little deterred him short of success, no matter what the cost amounted to.

Cadre said to a pard in their hideout cabin one night, "We was a bunch of loose lifes that Bog gathered under his wing, under his eye. I ain't ever felt so good as when we run the way we want and take what we want. I swear to you, Turkey, that I used to dream about this, getting' even, stickin' my nose in their stinkin' business and drawin' off what I want. You got to say Bog got us this way. We were nothin' alone, but now we're somethin'. Now we're our own army. Our own army, man."

That made him think some more and he said, "Think he'll ever make us corporals? We was here almost ahead of all the others."

Earlier, Morchant had earmarked Winslow Hills as a soft target after he had visited several times, always at night, always at the saloon, listening to every conversation he could, picking up all the pieces of information floating about from the loose lips, the drunks, the smart-asses in their nice clothes and fancy hats sitting at crowded tables.

He hadn't come across the sheriff in is visits, but had heard all about him and his good luck, how young he was, his new bride, his mouthy father.

"That Winslow Hills is a pot shot waitin' for us to happen to it. We can have a barrel of fun there, boys," Morchant said to his crew. "They got a kid sheriff, a babe right out of the wrapper if you want to know, and green as new corn. We ought to think about lockin' him up in his own jail."

He dwelled on that point for a long stare into possibilities. "Ain't that one hell of an idea, boys, chuckin' the sheriff in his own hoosegow? Set a stain on that town they can't shake loose no matter how long they try and we can become part of their history, part of their legend. They'll remember us forever." He licked his lips, flashed the lascivious smile they all had come to expect and enjoy.

"It'll be easy as lickin' butter off a knife." He made off he was doing just that, sliding his fingers down across his thrust-out tongue.

The whole crew of them laughed at the imagined sight; a jailer jailed, a town on its knees, the booze flowing, the women free and easy. Hiding the sheriff behind his own bars loomed as the idea of a master criminal mind at work. To a man they drooled over it, this knock-out punch for Winslow Hills; each of them admiring the boss's imagination, wishing they had thought of it.

"Get thinkin' what you boys want to get done," Morchant summed up. "Don't wait for it to happen. Get it straight now, set a target, get it done, and then you can make your way around town. Them ladies ain't goin' anyplace lest we say so. You boys remember that; they ain't goin' no place lest it's with us." He slapped the tabletop in their hideout in the hills and the whole cabin rocked with that slamming fist.

Though Travis Henry worked mostly alone on the job, having a part-time deputy, a former but tired sheriff, he did have a few allies and good friends in Winslow Hills. He had a few pals working in the saloon and a few others around town. It was part of his method of work, his way of the law.

One of those helpers was a porch percher, a boyhood pal with a bad leg, by the name of Chuck Herring, who sat most of the day looking out over the town from his porch at one end the main street. When he saw odd circumstances or strange happenings, he made sure that Henry heard about it through messengers that delivered the news like a loaded bee going back to the hive. So it was that Henry heard a strange gang had come into town, in separate entrances, and were merged somewhat later behind the livery where they probably were planning what they'd be doing based on information gathered so far about Winslow Hills.

After getting the word from Herring, the sheriff, from a vantage also behind a building near the livery, managed to view the meeting and guessed what was happening. He noted each man, what he wore, how he moved, how he carried his guns. Nothing of his observations was wasted, knowing he could spot each one of them any place in town. He departed the scene before they did.

The first thing he did was to change his shirt at the office, going in the back door, then going out the same way and heading to the saloon. He entered the saloon leisurely, wearing not his usual brown shirt but a light gray one, and his father's old Stetson, long turned to a sad white. He carried his badge in his pocket, set his mind alert, his guns loose, his hands loose, but kept up his casual entry. In one quick scan of the room he spotted two of the gang drinking at opposite ends of the bar, neither one paying any attention to the other gang member.

At a table down near the middle of the room, Henry spotted two of the gang sitting at the same table, drinks sitting in front of them. Behind them, alone at another table, was the big man who had been doing all the talking behind the livery. Henry knew, from wanted posters from outside the territory, that the man was Bog Morchant, a man with a reputation for wildness and vindictiveness, and guilty of several crimes elsewhere ... but not wanted here in Winslow Hills.

"Not as yet," Henry said as he kept his eyes averted from eyes of gang members, though he wondered if any of them had recognized him yet. That's when his eye settled on those of the bartender who had not said a word to him yet, having seen strange men in the room, and the sheriff not wearing his badge, or his regular shirt or his regular hat.

"The boy's up to something," the bartender said under his breath, setting a glass on the bar top.

Henry pursed his lips for silence, casually tipped his head at the strangers around the room, and tweaked his own ear.

The bartender, looked overhead when he heard a door close, saw Sally Keith standing on the second deck. He likewise nodded at the men in the center of the room and tweaked his ear. Sally Keith nodded back, off on a task she had done before.

In her red dress, a blazing red dress, her hair piled up in a big city fashion, shaking her bird cage in wanton glory, and her beautiful face caught up in a matching smile, she descended the stairs, moved slowly through the room and sat at the table where the two bandits sat, directly in front of Morchant's table.

"Either one of you gents going to buy me a drink? I'm real thirsty for top shelf if you do, if you care to share some time with me. This place is usually dead as a snake under the hoof. You gents might make a little excitement for a change." The two looked wide-eyed, as if a fire had sat at their table.

"Oh, we got that in mind, Ma'am," one of them muttered through his teeth. "We're gonna turn this place on its ear tonight. You betcha on that. We aim to lock the sheriff in his own jail and then raise all the kinds of hell you been lookin' for. How's that set with you, honey?"

"The name's Sally, handsome, Sally Keith, and I just can't believe you gents, just the two of you, are going to take on the law and put the law behind its own bars. That's really putting on the spurs, now isn't it?"

They both laughed, and one of them said, "Oh. We ain't that dumb, Ma'am. We got more help right here in the saloon, and some more outside."

Both Henry and the bartender saw Morchant, sitting behind them, trying to make them shut their mouths. Morchant finally coughed loud enough and gave them the shut-up sign.

One the men got up and said, "I'll get us a jug of dynamite."

Sally Keith, her hand touching on his sleeve, said, "Tell the man behind the bar I want boss whiskey, from under the bar, from his hiding place."

The talker brought back a bottle from the bar and poured Sally a drink, a beer glass supposedly half full of boss whiskey.

She said, "You boys wait right here. I want to see what the other bottles look like down there under the bar. I want to make sure we got the best stuff. I'll be right back."

She walked off swinging her hips like matched tassels, drawing every eye in the saloon.

"Hey, Josh," she said to the bartender, "Did we get boss stuff in that jug. It looks funny." And in a near whisper said, "They're going to lock up the sheriff in his own jail and raise hell all over town."

The bartender, fully upright, said, "You got the best down there I got, Sally. The damned best of the lot. It's the only stuff I drink myself." His smile was as wide as his beard.

Sally walked back to the table. "It's okay, boys. We got the best in the house, now pour me another and let's get this night going. I'm thirsty, real thirsty and craving real excitement."

She flounced herself into a strange pair of arms and began what she hoped was a short night with a nice thank you following, from somebody else.

Twenty minutes later, after Henry had slipped out of the bar, a young man in a gleaming white hat, a brown shirt and black pants, came into the saloon and stood just inside the door. He was also wearing the 5-pointed badge of a sheriff. In a casual manner, as though business was moving as usual, he sauntered slowly toward the bar, the bartender staring at him, nodding, saying, "Hi, Sheriff, what'll you have this time?"

The ruckus started as soon as the sheriff felt the gun in his back and the hard voice coming from Morchant screaming at the top of his lungs, "Don't nobody move or we kill the sheriff right here and now. There's more than me." He waved his gun and said, still as loud as ever, "Look around. There's a whole bunch of us, in here and outside spread around the town."

Several men were standing and waving their guns at those closest to them.

Morchant continued: "We aim to own this place, at least for the night. So you all go about your business, do what you always do, and don't do any gun play or a shot in here will tell the rest of us around town to start shootin' who's ever closest to them. That's a damned good promise I'm making."

He stopped, looked around again as one cohort took the guns out of the sheriff's holsters and stuck them inside his own belt.

Morchant added, "But we have a surprise for you gents while we lock the sheriff in his own jail. Don't you think that's great stuff, the sheriff locked in his own jail, and he laughed heartily and added, "one more nice surprise comin' too. The bar's open. The drinks is on me. All the way. All night." His stare was at the bartender who only nodded back.

Three men, including Morchant, walked the unarmed sheriff out of the saloon, down the street and into the sheriff's office with the jail cells in the back. Morchant grabbed the ring of keys off a wall hook, handed it to the sheriff and shoved him toward the cells.

"Open one of 'em up, Sheriff. You're gonna spend the whole damned night in there, along with anybody else who gets foolish or darin' on their own."

The cell was opened and Morchant was about to shove the sheriff into the cell, when he was knocked on the side of the head by Winslow Hills' real sheriff, Travis Henry, wearing his own badge, the different brown shirt, his father's faded Stetson, and brandishing his own weapons.

Morchant was on the floor of the jail from Henry's smack on the head, Henry having come in behind them from the side door to the office.

Henry said to the other two gang members, "Not a word out of you two or you're dead without a trial. Now pick him up and put him in the cell. You'll stay in there with him. We're going after your pals real pronto. It's going to be a jig from here on."

Around town in the next ten minutes, with surprise, four men were caught in silence and at gunpoint and jailed in a separate cell.

The crowd in the saloon was drinking its way toward oblivion, Josh the bartender pouring freely under the watchful eyes, and guns, of two gang members standing at each end of the bar. Another man was at the saloon door, just inside. He moved to see who was coming in, felt the gun slam into his gut, and folded up.

Sheriff Henry, all 21 years of him, saw one man at the end of the bar go for his gun and slapped a bullet into his wrist that at another angle might have torn the man's hand from his arm.

At the other end of the bar, his other partner measured what he had just seen and simply raised his arms in the air. He had already heard too many stories about the real sheriff of Winslow Hills, who this man must be. He was a sudden believer in all he heard.

Winslow Hills, for the next fifteen years, except for a few sporadic incidents, was generally a quiet town as the sheriff and his young family founded their ranch, saw it bloom and blossom, all heading to the day in the short future when the sheriff would retire and begin ranching in earnest.

He still felt lucky as he set out on a new career, Morchant long forgotten as he spent those years in jail, and the wounded member of the gang, his gun hand gone forever, had become a lefty and a trusted member of Henry's outfit.

Lucifer's Saddle

He was not a gunfighter, not a killer, not a bank robber or prairie brigand, but he was as mean looking as a cornered peccary. When he stepped off the weekly stage in Cross Roads, Utah, the only passenger, a dozen people were waiting around to see and size up new arrivals. It was a game they played calling on insight, first impressions, internal likes and dislikes, guesswork, and open curiosity that had been engineered by the imaginative bartender at the Close Call Saloon, Shank Bellbin. None of those folks checking on the arrivals realized it, but it was Bellbin's shot at increasing business at the saloon, drawing folks into discussions of newcomers right there in front of him as he spurred the discussions, fueled the differences, and kept pouring the drinks. A share of proceeds was his due.

From first sight, Jebediah Morgan Elmsworth was sure to increase business, the man who wore a Stetson so white it was brilliant, as if it had never collected dust, felt the ground, or knew grime. The hat, some folks offered, nearly shone.

But he had not been the only one to come into Cross Roads on this day.

There were two other known arrivals.

A stocky man, riding a paint, came to the backside of a small cabin on the outskirts of town, banged on the door, and was let in by a another man who looked like a brother would look ... stocky, thick at neck and arms, eyes wide apart as though he had been frightened right from birth. Brows on them appeared as formidable ledges, shadowing those dark eyes. Over the deep-set eyes and the formidable brow, on the visitor, sat a hat looking like a left-over from a second hand sale. When either of them talked, diaphragms operated at lower levels and made note of a frightening power buried underneath all their talk. Their names were Clocksdale, Erwin and Mortimer Clocksdale; robbers, bandits, road agents, brigands, you name it and they had done it. And not yet a day in jail for either one.

Mortimer Clocksdale was the new man in town.

The other newcomer to Cross Roads came on the distaff side.

Young, twentyish, looking like she'd been abused and left at the side of the road, she walked into the Close Call Saloon seeking work. She was dressed in near-rags, bruises on her face where the sun sat too long, knots in her brunette hair thick as barn rope. The bartender gave her short thrift, threatening to shove her out the door until Elmsworth, as chivalrous as any man could be in a saloon, and wearing the whitest hat, made way for her. He grabbed Bellbin by one arm, squeezing him until

35

the bartender knew he was under-matched, and quickly offered to solve the problem judiciously.

"What say we settle this difference, stranger? I ain't no hard man to get along with." Bellbin's sudden conciliatory maneuver made him feel off his general feed and decided he'd try to change the impression the stranger had marked of him already; get forward a bit, he would, a little pushy.

"I see you came in on the stage," he said. "From what folks tell me, you had no saddle with you. That's what I call real strange for a cowboy, no saddle. Did you lose your saddle in a card game or lose it to a road gang or what?" He was trying to get back the upper hand, if he ever had it, with the mean looking stranger whose hand was iron in the clutch, his height stretching into his hat's whiteness.

"Where you from, anyway?" Bellbin shot out at him, as if some odd place would push this upstart back to unenviable roots.

He got his wish when the mouth under the white hat said, without a single qualm, "I'm from the heart of old Mexico where the gods go on their vacations."

Bellbin, grinning widely, jumped at the response. "Ha, a Mex lover. A Spick lover. You won't find any love around here." His eyes bulged in his head, and his forehead came red as a flame in an instant.

"I know that," the white hat said, "for sure, you're not a lover ... of anything."

Without a defense of any sort, Bellbin held mute, waiting for the stranger to reply.

Elmsworth, holding lightly to the girl's hand, giving her a sense of safety for the moment, replied to Bellbin with a voice as hard as his looks. "Lucifer took my saddle for his own, out there on the Crispin Brim. If you happen to see him, if he happens to come into town riding a saddle with JME burned onto it, I'm Jebediah Morgan Elmsworth, and that'd be my saddle." His voice changed when he warned, "But don't try getting it back for me; he'll kill you soon as look at you."

"Who's this gent Lucifer you're talking about?" Bellbin said, looking around the room as if he had uncovered something about the stranger. At least, he wanted to cut into the air of the saloon some kind of doubt about the man; get back at him some way.

Elmsworth looked surprised. "Don't you know any scripture, mister? Lucifer is the Devil himself and he comes on with the Morning Star, drops in for a visit or goes on home like it's the end of a long drive. When he wants a horse or saddle to move among people, he just takes what his hand touches, and no argument coming his way. All the kindred folk know about him up on the Crispin Brim, on the Mollycock, at

36

Tevelas and from here back to the Big River and way off to Kentucky and other places where the Devil himself makes heavy work of fear."

Bellbin wanted to put the stranger on the spot, and said, "No man'd take my horse or my saddle without a fight. That's for damned sure."

"You're right there, mister, when you say 'no man' and 'for damned sure.' Be careful how you tread on your own words."

It was Elmsworth's reach for a double entendre. And he put a cushion of sorts into the situation by saying, "Now were you thinking about a job for the girl. From her looks, from her needs, and from apparently what someone has done to her, she needs a hand. Do you have such a thing? Is it in your power to do such a thing? In your control?"

Bellbin responded, "I never yet hired a newcomer to work here, a baby almost. It wouldn't go for either of us." He shook his head. "It just wouldn't work. The traffic is too heavy, too rough."

From a corner table, one older man stood up and said, "I'll get the kid a job, mister. You bring her with you and follow me. Don't let her work here 'cause Bellbin's right. It wouldn't work out here, not with the crowd that comes in here on some days like they're half exploded firecrackers."

His name was Harry Butler, and he was the coffin maker, funeral director and, as he laughingly called himself, "The last man on the totem pole in Cross Roads." He would only admit much later on that he was not so kindly an old man, but had been spurred by fate, association, or "a sudden sense of some piece of good" that overwhelmed him.

Butler qualified his lead. "I can't think of any place in town where the kid can get a decent break in life other than where I'll show you. At least she'll get her chance. It's no great shucks, but it'll do. Maggie's a special lot in herself. You'll see." He led them down the street of the town to a building with two floors and several windows on each floor.

The threesome entered Maggie Glendenning's boarding house at the edge of town but on the main street. The sign over the front door said, "Maggie's Place – Cheap."

The subsequent discussion took place between the two women, and when it was over, the girl, Dora Glasgow, still in her torn dress, still looking as if she had been beaten up by some animal of a man, had a job at the rooming house ... and a room, small, at the back of the building, but on the second floor, away from terror, threats, or sudden intrusions in her life.

Dora thanked Elmsworth, her head hanging down, but a new light finding a place in her eyes. "Thank you for sticking up for me. I needed it and won't forget it." She held his hand for a long time, afraid to look at him before she went off to get cleaned up, have a dress handed to her by Maggie Glendenning, fix her hair, and go to work.

Maggie said to Elmsworth, "You got to be someone special, Jebediah. The girl told me everything, as Harry did. He's a roomer here. And instead of you hanging your lovely Stetson in the hotel, I've got a room here for you. Are you staying long?" Her eyes showed some measure beyond curiosity, beyond business itself.

She was mid-thirties, clinging to good looks under blonde hair and eyes as pale green as Elmsworth had seen in a long time, and nowhere this side of the big river. He wondered if Harry Butler had seen the same things he had, the ever half-caught smile that lingered always, a shine in her hair that spoke of care, and the way her thin waist flared to an eye-catching span.

Both Maggie and Elmsworth, trail warriors in more than one aspect, were aware of the crackle in the air, the edge of hunger, and the possible resolve of interests. Each one let loose a full smile, as though a pact, unsought, unseen, had been sealed.

From the doorway, not seen, Dora Glasgow understood what she had just seen between a hard looking man in a nice hat and a soft looking woman wearing an endless smile. For a few bare moments in her recent history, she felt a small delight rushing through her veins, saying something all the way.

Elmsworth was unhurried in his response to Maggie's question, enjoying the new sensation working him. "I'll stay to make sure the girl gets a decent start, gets on her way. There's something special about her. I noticed it right off in spite of her dress, her condition. Meanness, for sure, had set itself on her. I don't take to that kind of treatment of women, no woman. The beginning here was not too good for her until things got changed. And I thank you for helping. You're special, too."

Maggie enjoyed his voice and his choice of words despite his hard looks. She knew what his heart was like.

Elmsworth stashed his gear in the corner room she showed him, with two windows, one at each side, a decent look out on the town from one window and from the other he could see the peaks of the High Uintas Range at attention in the distance. He knew firsthand the far places such as Red Knob and Squaw Top and the endless mystery that was No-Man's Knob. The views charmed him with their differences.

It was a few days later when Elmsworth saw a big man, as mean looking as he himself appeared to some people, walk into the general store. From the description Dora Glasgow had given him, he knew this man was her tormentor. Black hat down over eyes that must be set so deep in his head they could touch the back of his brain; a slant to a bulging body reeking of power; and the promise of giving a good horse a hard ride every time up.

He studied the horse tethered at the store rail from the blacksmith's shop where he had just had a shoe repaired on his horse. The roll of a whip curled black as a dead-aim bore on the pommel almost danced its flight for him. He imagined a flash of the whip, the deadly snap and curl at a target, the tearing and rending as it landed, saw sun-red blood let free. He stiffened as he pictured, with eyes closed for a fraction of a second, the girl's red dress torn by the lashes.

A change came over him, somewhere in the order of retribution upon cruelty and evil. It built quickly.

He borrowed a pair of tongs from the blacksmith, took a small piece of formed metal from his vest pocket, heated it in the fire, walked out and put a small brand on the man's saddle. He spit on the burn to cool it off, and walked away as the miniature brand of JME cooled on the right side of the man's saddle, not visible from where he'd mount the horse … if he was to mount that horse again.

At the same time Dora, running errands with Maggie who had gone off to another shop, was alone and stopped dead in her tracks when the big man came out of the door directly across the street from her, the same man Elmsworth had recognized.

Dora could not move another step, feeling the welts coming down on her back, this man's arm lashing out at her, hands tearing at her dress. A rush of the blows and anger and abuse pounded through her body. She became faint and knew she was going to the ground once more. Those pains rushed doubly back on her, the recall full and as livid as the original blows.

She felt it all again when the man looked up to see her, grinned wildly and then lasciviously, and started toward her.

In the middle of the dusty road in Cross Roads, Utah, Dora Glasgow screamed as her knees hit the ground, old pains caught up anew, both knees jabbed by hard impact, her breath stuffed up in her chest as she waited for those hands to grab her again, waited for the sound of the whip.

The man, though, did not rush at her. Instead, spinning about at the edge of the road, he yelled back into the store, "Hey, Paul, didn't I tell you my crazy, run-off wife was around here someplace. Well, here she is, her all messed up in that crazy mind of hers, but someone's dressed her up for me. C'mon out here, Paul, and take a look at a crazy lady in a new dress. Ain't this just perty?"

His laughter hung in the air, the meanness and intent of it almost visible to the eye.

Paul came to the door of his establishment to answer the call, to see what was going on out there that had also been accompanied by some women screaming.

In the middle of the road, kneeling, he saw a woman in a red dress caught up in painful sobs, and another woman, Maggie Glendenning just up in front of the undertaker's, screaming, not in pain, but calling for someone he did not know … Jeb Elmsworth. Paulie had not even heard the name before. But Maggie was screaming out the name: "Jeb, Jeb, where are you? Jeb, Jeb, where are you?"

It was as though Mortimer Clocksdale did not hear Maggie yelling, as he again yelled at the storekeeper; "Ain't that some kind of a messy wife, half gone off somewhere and half of her screamin' here in the middle of the street? Got to teach that woman of mine a lesson for runnin' off on me. Got to beat her back to her own bed."

He spun about and headed for his horse, reached up and grasped the roll of the whip and snapped it in the air. The whip slashed and cracked there loudly and he yelled out, "Nobody comes in between a man and his wife. Nobody in this town or any other town."

The sound was deadly as the whip snapped again and again, as though the man wanted to show off his expertise with it, or his cruelty just getting up to speed.

Dora Glasgow continued to sob in the middle of the street in her new red dress, the sun lighting on her as though she was on stage.

Maggie Glendenning continued to call Jeb Elmsworth until she spotted him coming down the middle of the street, tall as any man she had ever seen in his near-pure white hat, still untrammeled. He walked slowly, steadily, guns holstered on his hips. Maggie knew she was looking at a hero, one way or the other.

Clocksdale continued to snap the whip. "You're gettin' on back to your proper bed, lady, and in one damned hurry or I'll beat the skin off'n your back just like I did it last time."

The whip snapped again. The crack of it was like a rifle shot.

Paulie looked about to see if someone had run off to get the sheriff. All he saw moving was a tall, mean looking man coming down the center of the road, in no great hurry, the sun bouncing off his Stetson.

Clocksdale took a few steps toward Dora, ready to snap the whip, when a deep voice said, "Hey, you with the whip." He didn't believe he was hearing those words. He turned to look where they had come from.

"Yah, you with the whip, woman beater. Put that whip down or I'll take it to you."

40

A tall man, armed, stony-faced, was coming down the street. He looked to be seven feet tall, a white Stetson on his head making him taller than any of the horses tied at the rails along the street.

"Mind your own business," Clocksdale said. "My woman ran off on me and I'm takin' her home. Don't get in my way or you'll get what for. No man comes between a man and his wife. Cut out now."

There came a solemn reply. "She's not your wife. She's not married. She never was married. She works for Maggie at her place. And she's been beat to hell before by some wild ass animal which I now know was you. It stops here."

Clocksdale was now facing Elmsworth straight on, the whip still in his hand. He was thinking if he had to use his gun, he'd have to let go of the whip. Else he'd have to get closer. He stepped toward the stranger who had challenged him.

Dora was still sobbing, Maggie was staring at the whip in Clocksdale's hand, afraid of what it would snap at next. The two men were 40 or 50 feet apart, the dust from a sudden breeze was rising in small swirls from the road, the sun filtering through the dust, the grocer stock still at his door, the rest of the town stiff in its attention.

The distance had closed down, Elmsworth still estimating the variables.

"Put the whip down." Elmsworth had stopped, figuring he was just out of whip's reach, about 30 feet away from Clocksdale. He had included in his estimate the near three feet of Clocksdale's arm, and had remembered the number of coils in the whip as it sat on Clocksdale's saddle, moving numbers in his mind.

"Come take it," Clocksdale threw back at him, burning inside to cut the man's face, slash at his eyes, cut his hands before he could draw a weapon. The man was as tall as any man he'd ever seen, his face like it had been cut out of stone. The man's eyes set on him like a target looking back and his hand hung below his holster on his right side like an idled oar in a boat. Could such long arm, such distant hand, be fast to his weapons?

It had come down to that: he wondered if his brother was close by.

And he'd forgotten Dora Glasgow by this time.

It was now or never. He snapped the whip out and the stranger making crazy demands on him threw up his right arm and the whip caught it as it wrapped around the forearm.

"Got 'im now," thought Clocksdale, as he felt the pull of the whip and let go the now cumbersome handle.

But he was surprised. At the exact moment he went for his gun, the tall stranger flashed his left hand across his waist.

41

"Cross draw," Clocksdale said in amazement as his own gun hand came up and the tall stranger had his pistol leveled at him, the whip handle still flying through the air. He felt the bullet hit him in the chest, spin him sideways, and a second shot take the gun right out of his hand.

With the judge in town, plenty of witnesses on hand, Dora Glasgow making her statement in front of the judge, the jury and the prisoner, Clocksdale was sentenced to the penitentiary for a long stay. And before court was let out the sheriff made a private statement to Clocksdale's brother who left town before sunset, not even bothering to take his brother's horse and saddle.

Dora Glasgow eventually married a rancher and found a good life. Maggie Glendenning bought the saddle marked JME from the sheriff who never noticed the small brand on one side of the saddle, and she kept it as a token of good luck in spite of what Elmsworth had called it.

Elmsworth, for that matter, had never taken one meal at Maggie's Place at her table, all his meals brought to his room, or left there when he was away from the place.

The one time he sat at the table was when Maggie gave a small dinner in honor of Dora's first child, a boy named John.

That day, Elmsworth sat at the table, his hat hanging on a nail in the hallway between the dinner table and the kitchen.

Maggie took the gleaming white hat into the kitchen on one of her trips back and forth, marveled at its pure whiteness after all the time, saw the marking on the inner sweat band, where the cleanly burned letters, as if just placed there the day before yesterday, or sooner, spelled *Emanymsaw Ref.* She memorized it, thinking it was some kind of Mexican or Spanish saying most likely, out of his hidden past "where the gods went on vacation." It was much later, in the dark of a long and majestic night, her heart filled with him, that she saw the white light, knowing what had been turned over in her life, as well as his.

Jebediah Morgan Elmsworth, once a stranger in town, just off the stage, had become a town man, the next sheriff, and had accepted all the favors that Maggie Glendenning sent his way, including eventual marriage a few years later, Maggie well aware all the while that he was very quick in some actions and took slightly less than forever on others, much to her endless satisfaction.

Madame Law

The body was prone in the middle of the dusty street, a late morning sun beating down on it, flies checking their prospects, and silence reigning over the entire town.

Not a soul in Welby Falls had gone to check on him, their sheriff shot in the back, his rifle on the ground beside him, and Lily Bentwell, newest visitor in town, at the lone second floor front window of the Black Saddle Hotel. She believed she was the only person who had seen the shooter from a window, also on the second floor, but in the undertaker's place of business, Longchamp's Last Resort for Redemption and Paradise, which was directly across the street.

The figure of a man, she could see, was still there behind the sheerest drape imaginable. It made her think of the pine box due the sheriff, perhaps the body covered with the same material so sheer that a week in the ground would reduce it to nothing again. She hated pretense and puffery. She hated flimsy. She hated bigotry. She hated backstabbers and bushwhackers and men of unprincipled violence, her father going down at the hands of what she hated most, and her father's weapons, agents of vengeance after endless practice, coming as notable tools in her hands.

Leaving her father's town behind, the place where she had grown up, no more ties there for her, she searched for a new location to settle down. Hopefully she'd find a good man, fall in love, get married, have children, and pass once more into the holy earth where her parents, far apart, were spending all their days of eternity ... unless there was something beyond.

She was not sure.

Welby Falls had promised a new beginning; gorgeous scenery at the foot of the Rockies, two streams merging nearby, the grass rich, and cattle taking the place of thousands of buffaloes gone into history. It made her think of hunger hitting villages on the Plains, thick steaks on dinner plates east of the big river.

Now Welby Falls might lose its newest visitor ... it had lost its newest sheriff, to a bushwhacker, a backstabber, from behind a sheer drapery that promised no hiding. The killer had to be known to someone, she thought.

But not a soul, for nearly a half hour, had walked out to check on the sheriff's body.

Caught up in one sudden thought, she strode from her room, ran down the stairs with disdain for lobby sitters and a marked determination shaking loose from her every step, yanked open the front door, crossed the boardwalk, stepped into the swirling dust, and walked with high purpose and bravery into the middle of the street.

Lily Bentwell, a beautiful young woman of 24, no hat on her head, her hair like a shining moon on wet coal, clad in the work pants of a cowpoke, knelt over the body of Asa Chabley, once a sheriff like her father. The Sharpe's rifle, hung by his side like it was supposed to be an extension of his body, looked out of place at the site of his death.

From all corners off the town people watched her. Only the hotel clerk and the owner knew who she was, and the stage driver sitting down at the livery and getting drunk at the end of his long ride. Way back, at the first station on his ride, the farrier exchanged the team of horses and told him about her.

"She's sumpthin'," he had said, and told him about her father's death and how her life had changed.

That life was crowding her as she knelt beside the dead sheriff. A sudden realization crowned her thinking ... no matter how fast she could run, no matter where she would go, she'd never get away from the vengeful promise that held her together.

The hotel clerk and the owner looked on; and the stage driver, from the livery, looked up with the sun glaring into his eyes, yet he could see the woman who had been a passenger on his last run of the week.

He saw her reach for the badge on the sheriff's chest, simply take it off his shirt, pin it on her pale blue blouse, reach for the rifle at the sheriff's side, stand up and from her hip pour every round in the weapon at the shadow behind the sheer fabric in the window on the second floor of Longchamp's Last Resort for Redemption and Paradise.

Smoke idled upward from the bore of the rifle as she stood in the middle of Welby Falls, sunlight bouncing off the star on her blouse, fate delivered from her hand.

The shots from Lily Bentwell had slammed through the open window. The black-hatted man, broad in the shoulders where two rounds now found resolution, once thick of chest where another round found solitude, had leaned forward to return gunfire at the woman down below. Instead, fatally impacted, he fell halfway through the window, his torso hanging over the windowsill, and his rifle, a killer's rifle, fell to the boardwalk with a thud solid enough to send a rumbling into the air.

The killer's death and the action of the woman in the street made the swearing-in ceremony quite anti-climactic. Lily Bentwell had become the new sheriff of Welby Falls without even raising her hand to say "I do."

She would save those solemn words for a good man.

Odyssey of a French Swordsman

"Who among you will swear to devote his life to country and crown? Stand you then and be appointed."

He had stood up on that solemn occasion, had been counted, and subsequently dishonored and disparaged by his entire country, which quickly had gone under a different rule.

On a night dark as new promises, the year of turmoil 1793, hoof beats announcing organized columns of one belief or another without a known flag borne for identification and loyalty, the air reeking with forebodingness and clandestine alliances, Jacques de Lemoine, 22 years of age, experienced in battle, soldier by profession, horseman by choice, swordsman by desire, bound elsewhere, slipped out of France from an unknown port on a small fishing boat and landed in Spain.

His landing was a serious affair, the boat capsizing in a storm, the others disappearing from view even after a desperate search, yelling out names of comrades, and trying to measure the distance to shore. In one moment of search, self-preservation kicked in and he struck out for the shore. He touched solid earth under his feet, stood up in the sea water, knew Spain underfoot, and strode ashore. His sword was gone, his boots gone, his cape gone, all shed for survival to overcome the pull of the water threatening to drag him down. If he had his choice, he thought, he'd rather be on a steed heading into battle, his weapons at hand as well as the enemy, for he knew what he was capable of, what he had done, where he had been. He was not a man of the sea; he was a horse soldier, a cavalryman, a veteran of wars at a young age, who now needed a new cause; that was his destination, his odyssey.

On the beach, leaning on a wooden bench, an old man stared at him, a decrepit old man, a funny hat on his head, the oddest cane in one hand, wielded as if just torn from a tree, a heavy knob on top that could be used as a weapon. The shaft of the cane exhibited many sharp points where branches had been slashed away, each remaining nub capable of depositing pain upon an enemy. In advanced age the man still looked formidable, able to take care of himself. Lemoine wished himself that formidable after uncountable more decades.

But several times the inquisitive old man looked back over his shoulder, to the chimneys and rooftops of a nearby town set inland less than a half mile away. Lemoine thought him at first to be looking for compatriots, perhaps another coastal watcher at the same duty, but the man was not alarmed at the sight of him; more curious than alarmed.

Then the old man said in Spanish, *"Lo que le trae por aquí?"* ("What brings you here?") They were at the very edge of the ocean, the place called Castro Urdiales behind them showing a few housetops, smoke rising from morning fires, the scent of cooking food in the air, olive oil and the riches of women working in the grand mix of early day. Then he repeated his words in French, *"Ce qui vous amène ici?"*

Lemoine, aware of the furtive looks in the old man's eyes, said, with considered pauses breaking up his words, *"Puede usted hablar inglés, lo cual será más fácil para mí?"* He offered an immediate translation into English: "Can you speak English, which will be easier for me?"

"Yes," the old man replied, a glint in his eye, a look again over his shoulder as if there was another listener hanging about them.

"Our boat was swamped," Lemoine explained. "There are no other survivors that I know of, but I must search along the shore to make sure. They were good men to take me away from my troubles."

"How did you alone survive?" The old man's English was excellent. "I have seen no one else come out of the ocean, no strangers other than you on the beach. I have been here since before the sun came lifted out of Asia." He pointed westward.

"I am a strong swimmer," Lemoine replied, his eyes searching the old man's face for other signs, and then his own look sent off to the nearby community.

"You are French, are you not?" the beach watcher said. "Do you flee the unrest in France? Were you loyal to the crown or to the new ideals?" The look on his face, at the choices mentioned, was neutral at delivery. Age itself, it was easy to see, had a solid grip on him, but his hair was thick on his head under the brim of his strange hat, and flowed down on worn shoulders, gray as a cloudy dawn sky. The tunic he wore was torn in a few places, and dearly in need of cleaning, as were his pants, but his boots were close to shining, as though they had been gifted to him by a generous soul.

"I was a soldier. I was doing my duty."

"Aha," said the old man, "without a king the kingdom goes away and with it goes its army. You must leave here soon. Find a boat going to the new world, to America. Everyone there and everyone going there get a new start with a new government of the people. Think about the new chance in a new land, going to the new place with all your old skills that have proved their value. You may go without baggage but you do not go empty-handed. You have those skills you sharpened in your service and a new chance to use them again."

His delivery sounded like a tutor at work; and Lemoine heard the depths of it.

Back over his shoulder the old man looked, first along the beach and then back to Castro Urdiales, the old one still on guard, using his experience, before he renewed his talk. "It is better than going back. I too was a soldier and was hounded, but have found a place here. It can be treacherous some days, for many factions move among us. From France, too, they have come, like you or those searching for those like you. Just a few days ago such men chained up a few men they found coming in on a small boat, just before dawn. I heard they would have their heads chopped off once they were brought back to the chief city, to Paris, to the guillotine. As for me and my past, it goes away at times. And I am too old to go any other place, but caution should be exercised by you for escape. Some you meet will be wounded by a word before the tip of the sword makes them flinch. Watch for such men. Be alert for such men. Use them ably. They too provide opportunity."

He was imparting as much lesson as warning; again it came home to the Frenchman in flight.

Alertly like the good watchman he had become, the old man scanned the area behind him and then out in front of him. "Go along the coast, on that road there." He pointed to a marked trail along the water. "I have a horse you can buy if you have money, or else you can have him. Wherever you leave him, say he belongs to Armand the Cripple of Castro Urdiales. He will come back to me one way or another." He nodded his head in assurance, as though he was known along the whole coast of Spain. His eyes sparkled with belief, with a clutch at humor.

Lemoine noticed once more the man's leg, how it was bent at a strange angle, how it said pain in a familiar language of the mind. They were brothers in the art of warfare, their memories perhaps the same, but their lingering pains now different.

When he mounted the golden horse, Lemoine said, "I will make somebody promise to bring the horse back to you. I will find an honorable man. As I said, I am sorry I do not have any money for you."

"Aha," said Armand the Cripple, "I have found not only an honest man, but a man of standing, a soldier. We of Spain sent off our horses many, many years ago to the New World with our explorers, gallant men going into the unknown breech of darkness. Some of their horses were the likes of my Carlo, gold as the sun or a full moon above the orchards. He will not make that trip. Do not worry about him. He will come back." His head nodded in affirmation, a smile grasping his whole face.

Quizzically, knowing the old man's tune had suddenly changed, Lemoine asked, "How are you so sure about the horse Carlo coming back? Do you know everybody I will see on the way?"

Armand the Cripple laughed heartily, "Oh, he is one of promise, my Carlo, his name meaning the free one. He always comes home. I have sold him five times," a smile adding, "and he always comes home." He laughed again, "Without fail." He laughed again and added, "Perhaps more than five times."

The two men roared at the edge of the ocean, and Lemoine rode off, on his next leg of the trip to America, laughing at a sudden image of one Spaniard saying to a fellow countryman, "Do not buy the golden horse Carlo, the free one, who belongs to Armand the Cripple of Castro Urdiales, for your money will only call him home again, back to Castro Urdiales and to his one and only master. One bit of gold draws and matches the other. The cripple gathers twice the fee."

In 1803 and again the following year Lemoine thought of going back to France when Napoleon was exerting his influence and crowned as emperor in 1804, but he realized the changes were too dramatic for him.

Time, the way it can leap with the adventurous, to men on various pursuits, brought Lemoine, now 33 years of age, in that latter year of 1804 to a small town in the western part of Ohio, to a saloon that had drawn him by its name, *Le Cheval d'or Saloon*, The Horse of Gold Saloon. Behind the long bar, adorning a good length of the wall, was a painting of a palomino pony in graceful flight across a grassy plain. The golden hue of the horse almost sang out to Lemoine when he first walked in and stared at the palomino, for he thought immediately of Carlo, the horse he had borrowed years ago from the old man at Castro Urdiales, a horse as golden as a new coin.

From the moment of his entry, though, Lemoine wanted to call the saloon The Museum, for much of the walls and the overhead beams were hung with old weapons. He saw lances and shields and swords as well as old matchlock pistols and flintlock blunderbuss rifles with bores like hungry mouths, like angry mouths. He noted familiar dragon pistols, the dragon's head clearly visible around the muzzle that many cavalrymen had carried and had brought about the name of the Dragoons in some cavalry units in Europe. His eyes landed on favored weapons his hand itched for, his past called back again, and it made his gaze move onto all weapons in a twist of memory.

Meanwhile, the long ride he had just accomplished working on him, Lemoine thirsted for a taste of wine. He had in no way lessened that taste in his western stay, and drank it in preference to all other liquors and beers if it was available.

And this was not the first time it had brought about a confrontation with other patrons of a saloon.

One burly cowpoke at the bar, broad in the brow and the shoulders and aware of a difference between him and the slim and handsome Lemoine standing on his right, decided he'd put the differences to a test.

"Say, there, stranger," he said, "are you new around here? I never seen you in here before. You come far?" He had turned to face Lemoine

48

straight on, a silly look on his face, as if he was facing a totally unworthy opponent in a silly grudge match.

Lemoine had seen it all before, the same look, the down-range appreciation of differences between men. He took a deep breath.

The big man continued. "You sure look like you come from some other place." He looked about the saloon and tried to bring others at the bar and at tables to side with him, and nudged the man on the other side of him, urging him to enter the cajolery.

Lemoine, not looking at the man, and holding the glass of wine close to his mouth, only said, "From far enough to appreciate my own habits." He voice was level, moderate, in no manner offensive, except for his crystal clear intention of saying, in other words, "I come from a place where people mind their own business."

But the big man was not sure of what the remark meant. "What does that mean, mister? You pokin' fun at me?"

He nudged the bar patron on his left, saying, "What do think of this foreigner pokin' fun at a real American cowboy? Huh, what do you think of that?"

Turning back to Lemoine he said, "You goin' to answer me, mister, or do I call you out?" His hands dropped to his sides, close to a pair of side arms on his belt.

Still sipping at his glass, Lemoine said, "You mean, am I challenging you to a duel, or is it you challenging me to a duel?"

"You're damned right I'm challengin' you. I don't plain like your attitude. You foreigners always bother me bein' so smug and tricky, like you're better than any of us here, us real Americans. I was born here when this country was born." Pride hung on his voice thick as syrup.

"Then I guess you're challenging me to a duel. Is that what you're saying?" Lemoine had his hand on his sidearm.

The big man smiled and said, "Damned right I am."

Lemoine said, "Then I have my choice of weapons? Is that the art of the west, the way of the west? The way of the new America where I have been for eleven years of my life, working my way toward California and the vineyards there. Is it my choice of the weapons in this challenge?" His hand touched again the pistol on his belt.

"Sure is, pal. It sure is." The big man's smile was as wide as his face.

Lemoine reached overhead and drew down from a beam a sword, a long, tapered sword. Light from lamps in the room reflected off its long, thin shaft. "I choose swords," he said. He leaned his whole long and thin body onto the sword as it touched the floor, the thinness of each as if posed together.

The big man's pal pointed overhead and excitedly said, "Grab that big one up there, Gunther! You can crush him with it! One swing and he's on his butt. Grab the big one looks like a hunk of iron from the blacksmith shop down the street. Smash him, Gunther. Smash him a good one!"

A hint of strange intervention crossed Gunther's face as his expression said, "Oh, oh," but it could not be said aloud. Pride, and the usually blustery nature of the big man, made him reach for the broad sword. It was heavy to his hand, but a strange power in its weight, a sold heft came in its handle. He slapped it into the air, clomped it against the overhead beam, and felt the ominous striking power that had come to his hand as the building shook.

Chairs creaked and scraped on the floor as patrons pushed themselves out of danger that created a wide space in front of the bar, like a small arena bound by the bar on one side and patrons at table on the other sides.

At the back of the saloon, other men, not in the affair from the beginning, stood to get a better view.

One of them said to a table partner, "Looks like Gunther Locumb's at it again. But he ain't got a gun in his hand this time. Got a stupid wide blade sword like he's gonna chop down a tree. Oh, boy, I don't see this starting right for him. That other fella looks like a sword himself. Maybe this is the day we been waitin' for. Better have a look."

The other man at the table stood, a smile on his face, and said, "Think we never been lucky at cards, huh?" Down on the table he threw his hand of cards, "and me with three aces."

In front of the bar, in front of people who had known him for practically all his life, Gunther Locumb hefted the sword again. "How do we do this?" he said. "I ain't ever used these before."

Lemoine said, "Stand in that corner near the bar. I'll stand here. The barkeep says, 'Go,' and then we start. May the best man win." He said the last part in French also, as though it was a prayer: *"Pouvoir la meilleure victoire d'homme."* He held his sword upright in front of his face as a salute to his opponent, the flat of the weapon touching his nose.

It infuriated Gunther Locumb who rushed at Lemoine, not just in distaste and anger, but with vile hatred, the broad sword swinging in crude arc over his head as though he was going to crush Lemoine with the weight of it.

Lemoine was ready. He stepped to his left in a slight feint, saw Locumb lean that way, came back in a swift dance and stepped to the right, saw the broad sword swinging its clumsy arc from high overhead as though to cut him in half. The thin rapier, in the hands of a skilled swordsman, slashed into the air, provided the sleekest cut at the wrist of Gunther Locumb, and the heavy sword fell uselessly to the floor.

Silence, an occasional gasp, filtered in the room as the rapier, like a needle, was at the throat of Gunther Locumb full of the direst threat, a horrible death. Locumb did not move, the point of the sword at his Adam's apple, the way a stiletto might feel, keen, sure, a vile outcome at hand.

Lemoine, with a loud voice, said, "If you swear peace with me, and friendship, it is over and done with at this minute. If not, I will carve you to pieces." The thin blade had not moved, had not quivered once in its position, Lemoine's arm as steady and rigid as a fence pole.

Only Locumb's eyes moved, searching out the room, seeing the moment of truth descending upon the silent audience as though it had been cast on the place from high heavens. He dared not swallow for fear it would signal a movement from either combatant. He wondered what the next drink would taste like … if he got to it. He wanted that drink, but was no longer sure of anything else except that he could die in a hurry, at the hands of the stranger who at one point, only most recently, had not seemed to belong in this hard world of the west.

Desperate, but his mind working against his normal ways, Locumb dropped his weapon, unhitched his belt and all in the saloon watched it slide down his legs, the era of one bully at the end of a long trail. It was as though one universal breath was let go from one chest, the sound coming clear, relief in order.

Locumb's pal turned his back on his one-time pal who stood, harmlessly, at attention, while the slim stranger slowly withdrew his slim blade from Locumb's throat and set it on the bar.

The barkeep spoke first. "You kin have it, mister. You earned it, though I'd begin to tell stories about it if you left it here for us to look at once in a while."

With a quick motion Lemoine hung the sword back on the two nails that held it on the overhead beam. "It's my pleasure to return it to its place." With a slight bow, "Merci," came from his lips, and then Lemoine said to the barkeep, "Please pour a drink for my new friend here, and another glass of wine for me. I'd buy a drink for all present, but I can't afford it."

"Hell, mister, the drinks are on me. We'll celebrate the Day of the Sword from now on. I can just see a match come out of it, a day-long affair, a shivaree for Le Cheval d'or Saloon." He did not offer it in the best French, but all understood.

From one side of the saloon, a heavy-set fellow wearing a wide brimmed and sparkling-clean white sombrero approached Lemoine. "Sir," he said, "I am Augustine Lombard of the Little Italy Ranch that sits along the river ten miles west of here. I ask to whom I am talking and if you're open to offers of employment, I sure could use a man like you. The pay to start with would be three dollars a day and board and keep and one weekend off a month. You appear quick, smart, and possessed of the talent to survive. Have you been a member of the military?" He put out his hand.

Lemoine shook Lombard's hand. "Sir," he said, "I am Jacques de Lemoine, soldier, horseman, swordsman, bound someplace lest a job detains me. I am once of *Colonel-General Cavalry* of the besieged garrison at Lille, France in 1790. We fought among ourselves, the people and the cavalry, and one of us lost his way. I have come to America, perhaps ten years ago, and have worked my way in many places, done many things, and look for the future all the time. I would like to buy you a drink and one more for my new friend here, Gunther, but one apiece, mind you. It is all I can spare at this time."

So it was that three strangers came into diverse roles, friends to each, one an employer, one employed, one still looking on, the way things change in life for one and not for another.

"What do you say to my offer, Mr. Lemoine?" Lombard had his hand out, waiting for the acceptance.

"If you offer Gunther a job, I will take the offer. One needs friends no matter where he is in this world, or what he does. Gunther is now my friend. I am his friend, though I have come from afar. Do we not all come from elsewhere? And now Napoleon is to become Emperor of the French, in my own language *'L'Empereur des Français.'*"

Lombard shook with laughter. "You are right, Mr. Lemoine. We all come from elsewhere, myself from Italy 20 years ago and your new Emperor, the General, has a foothold in my old homeland, too." He turned to Locumb with the origin question on his face.

"I was born here, in Pennsylvania," Locumb said, almost apologetically, "but my folks came from Germany, from the forests of Bavaria. I am the first horseman in our family."

"Now you are hired, Mr. Locumb," Lombard said, "for I have Mr. Lemoine's word of acceptance."

Fate moved swiftly for the three men, tightening the bond from a strange beginning; twice more Lemoine saved Locumb from certain death, once with the sword pulled miraculously from his scabbard when both rifle and pistols had fully discharged all ammunition against a gang of renegades, and once with a deft shot from his rifle at a bear about to tear Locumb apart. The swiftly ascended foreman of Lombard's ranch saved his daughter Alicia, 20, from a kidnapping plot by sheer bravado and trick horsemanship, and Gunther Locumb had in turn saved

Lombard in a mad stampede of cattle, using his brute strength to pull the cattleman from a certain trampling.

A few years later, in 1806, Augustine Lombard stood happily and proudly as his daughter Alicia married her savior with Gunther Locumb standing as best man at the wedding.

A son was born in late 1807, Benjamin Lemoine and Lombard threw a boisterous party at the ranch.

Thereafter, in testimony of events and celebrations, Lombard started a small shrine of sorts with memorabilia in place: Lemoine's sword and his original matchlock pistol, two shoes taken from the horse Locumb rode to save the rancher, Lombard's own pistol that had jammed and did not fire when he aimed at what he thought was an intruder but was only a hungry vagrant that ended up working for him, and Benjamin's birth record handwritten by the local sheriff.

As a separate part of the testimonial wall at one end of the family room, Lemoine started keeping pertinent records of his new family and his old days that had gone anew in France. He used dated events burned into a simple slat of wood that were placed in ascending order, oldest to the newest. This slat method enabled him, when news came much later than the event and oftentimes after other events had been entered earlier, to be posted in proper chronological order.

The notations were by year only, and were maintained faithfully by Lemoine, which began simply as: 1806, Alicia Lombard and Jacques de Lemoine married. (The legend burned with care into the simple wooden slat showing an artful hand.)

That first entry set the tradition off and running, Lemoine looking to his past, his old homeland, his new homeland, his military and family interests, as follows:

1807, Son Benjamin born to this house.
1807, Victory of Friedland over the Russian, and Code Napoléon enacted.
1809, The Emperor moved into the Elysée Palace.
1809 Napoléon departed to rejoin the Grande Armée.
1809, Napoléon's victory at Wagram and at Znaim.
1809, A daughter was born to this house, Mary Elizabeth.
1810: Napoléon married Maria Louisa, Archduchess of Austria, Civil marriage at Palace of Saint-Cloud and a religious marriage in the Louvre.
1811, Son born to Napoléon and Maria Louisa at the Tuileries Palace, with title of King of Rome.
1812, Son Norman born to this house.
1812, French troops entered Prussia.

1812, Napoléon departed for the Russian campaign. Another son was born.

1812, The United States declared war on Britain.

1812, Napoléon victory of Borodino or the Moskova.

1812, Gunther Locumb killed by Indians … (never married, no children)

1812, Napoléon entered Moscow and left, starting retreat from Russia.

1813, Prussia declared war on France.

1813, Augustine Lombard died from drowning.

1814, Benjamin's tutor, Fitzgerald arrives and starts lessons.

1814, Napoleon exiled to Elba (300 days).

1815, Napoleon returned to France.

1815, The battle of Waterloo is lost.

1815, In the Elysée Palace, Napoléon abdicated in favor of his son.

1815, The allies entered Paris - Louis XVIII returned to Paris.

1815, Napoléon tried to reach United States. Instead, as war prisoner, deported to Saint Helena.

1816, Fitzgerald says Benjamin is the best student he has taught.

1821, (Saturday May 5) Napoleon died and I, Jacques de Lemoine, was 50 years old this same day.

1822, Benjamin wrote his first story, The Golden Horse. ("A gift is ours," Lemoine burned into the wooden slat as a post script to this entry.)

Jacques de Lemoine, Jack Lemoine to all his friends, was constantly exclaiming to all those friends about Benjamin's story of a golden horse named Carlo that was sold seventeen times and kept coming back to his master who raised hundreds of golden horses from that sire. "The lad has such a grand imagination to conceive of such a tale and I am sure that this family will see a new hero rising in its midst, a master storyteller, not born to the sword, but born of it. No doubt he has many more stories to tell in his time."

As Lemoine waited to read more stories from his son, he continued to live the legend of his times.

One Night in Calico

Tudor Yarborough III rode into Calico as the first light snapped on in the saloon sitting directly ahead of him. He was as thirsty as he'd ever been and a ponderous sense of dryness came over him. Perhaps a bath at the hotel would do him well. It had been a while since he and his horse had forded the river just below Chico Corners, downriver a dozen miles and escaping the posse for the third day. And none of the posse knew they were on a fruitless mission.

His horse had fought a difficulty in the river, and Yarborough's rifle and lariat were gone, but he had his revolver, a small sum of money in a money belt, and his saddle bag with his earthly remains, which he had tied securely to the saddle. The list of contents of the saddle bag ran through his mind amid his wondering why he'd kept some things and let others go, tossing them away or burning them in several campfires. In a tin that held off water were two pictures of his parents and kid brother and sister, along with the sheriff's badge his father had worn at Willow Bend and a copy of the wanted poster that erroneously claimed he had killed the stage driver and two passengers outside Fremont, Nebraska. There was an extra shirt in the bag and a pair of socks.

The sketch on the poster was a good likeness he knew could be attributed to an old friend and artist, Shannah O'Toole. Shannah had drawn several pictures of him in pencil when they were locked in a quick romance, summarily broken when he was denounced as a killer by an opponent of his father in a previous election, sour grapes of the worst kind.

The sour grapes fact had eluded Shannah, too, as it had a great many people in Willow Bend. She was shamed in her own family and it left Yarborough as cold as a January morning, even as he wondered if he was really as good looking as she made him out to be.

He knew who must be leading the posse on his trail. None other than loathsome Orville McClernon, reptilian backstabber, as yet unproven bushwhacker, but successor to Tudor Yarborough II as sheriff of Willow Bend.

As he settled his horse into the Calico Livery and saw that it was rubbed down and taken care of, Yarborough thought of a bath for his own good and headed for the hotel, a small addition atop the Prince of Wales Saloon, more lights now lit up in the saloon.

He felt the side-tracking influence of a stiff drink and a beer slide into his appreciation; it had an overwhelming acceptance.

8:00 PM

Yarborough heard the music and the laughter and the slow drone of talk from the other side of the Prince of Wales Saloon door, and felt a momentary sense of comfort and security. There'd be the smells of stale beer and floor sawdust, an odor of a hard liquor to whip the nose into hearkening, a burnt steak's scent floating on the air from a late meal as it kept hanging out in a corner, each one of the hard scents like an old welcoming committee. Incense or bouquet didn't matter to him because he'd be safe there for at least a night, the posse way off his trail by now … he'd seen to that with several moves and ruses learned from his father who had learned them from the many wily outlaws he'd chased to bay over his long career with the badge.

"Never refuse a lesson that can help you later on," his father said on returning from several pursuits of outlaws.

"Let me tell you what Dirty Jack did this time," and he'd roar with laughter as honest as a sharp ax and then he'd illustrate a maneuver or ruse Dirty Jack had used. Some of the tricks were novel and intricate. His favorite one from Dirty Jack was to carry a pair of wooden horseshoes in his saddle bag and lead the posse, by hiding his horse someplace and wearing the wooden shoes himself, right to the edge of a cliff beside a river, and try to confuse the posse that him and his horse went right over the edge. "Sometimes it was enough to get them off his trail for a short spell." He'd snicker and laugh and add, "Perhaps it also gave Dirty Jack a laugh or two and made his flight a bit easier to take."

The taste of good liquor and the sound of the music drew Yarborough into the Prince of Wales Saloon, and into the bright lights for the first time in a pell-mell rush of hidden trails, deep mountain passes, constant pushing by the posse riders, scattered fears and warnings, and a dream of escape at every turn.

With his revolver near weightless on one hip, worn for an easy and quick draw, eyes trying to see every face in the room without alerting too many curious patrons about a new customer, he advanced toward an open space at the far end of the bar.

One of the ladies of the saloon smiled at him, and the bartender, a happy looking gent named Jake Thursday, smiled at the lady and Yarborough in turn, and poured a beer, as the lady started to move closer to Yarborough. Her smile had not lessened at all.

Yarborough thought about Shannah's pencil sketch and wondered if the lady recognized him, liked his looks, or was just quick to get down to business. He decided he'd savor a drink before anything else.

That decision sat in his mind as he reached for the beer the bartender shoved his way, and the bartender said, with great surprise to Yarborough, "I think the poster sketch looks just like you."

Surprised and alarmed, Yarborough almost drew his gun, but the bartender said, "Easy now. My name's Jake Thursday, and they were in here today, ahead of you. I've known that rat McClernon for a few years and when he showed me the sketch and gave me the story, I saw the other side of it, him bein' the barn rat he is. I go back a long way with him, even before he got to Willow Bend. He ain't changed none that I can see, so I'm on your side. You best find a place to hide for the night because some others were in here today and saw the poster. McClernon only had one and wanted to hold onto it and wouldn't hang it up. I'd guess you're some lucky on that account 'cause we got some folks here with mouths like clothes on the line on a windy day."

Thursday looked around and said, "She's your best bet and is a square shooter," as he nodded at the girl still looking at Yarborough. "Her name's Coralee, which ain't her real name but a make-up name, but she's a good lady and dependable. She owns the place since her father was killed about a year ago in a crazy shoot-out between two stupid punk gunmen couldn't handle the drink. She almost got killed too, standin' in the middle of it screamin' at them two crazy kids."

Thursday high-signed Coralee, and when she came to the end of the bar, he said, "Coralee, this is Tudor Yarborough and he's a good guy runnin' ahead of a bad lawman, that noisy sheriff who was in here this mornin'. I know you got up a heavy dislike for him in a hurry 'cause of the way he handled the cook and makin' all kinds of demands when you was upstairs. Tudor here needs some quick hidin' in case the sheriff comes back, which is likely what he'll do if he runs out of signs out there. They always come back if only to wet out the dryness. They got a sketch of him on a poster, but didn't hang it up. Tudor's father was the sheriff over there in Willow Bend one time, a good man."

Coralee said, "Did that animal show that poster around? I didn't see much of him except how he acted like he was the king of the hill."

Thursday said, "He showed it to a few people in here then, but I can't remember who saw it, who was here then. This gent needs a spot to duck into for a spell. Believe me, that guy chasing him is a poor excuse for wearing a badge."

Coralee smiled at both of them, looked around the room, and said to Yarborough, "Go into the kitchen and wait for me. Be kind to the cook. She's a good lady."

She spun on her heel and headed for the other end of the room, every eye looking at her as she walked, her movements sliding over her chassis the way a reflection moves on a pond in a gentle breeze.

Yarborough, watching her like he was seeing the sunrise come up after a bad sleep, marveled at the sensation touching him.

9:00 PM

Coralee's room, on the second floor front, looked down on Calico and the river in the distance where it caught a few stars on wet brush along one side of the river. Yarborough thought the stars looked like lamps lighting up another street in the town, a comforting image. Also coming on him was the long day of running ahead of the law as it claimed him. He closed his eyes as he sat on the edge of the bed, thinking to relax only for a few minutes and, with the exhaustion at work, slowly leaned over and fell asleep on the one bed in the room.

11:00 PM

Some sound other than voices woke him. He didn't know what sound it was, and then he heard voices, the first one being Coralee's just outside the door. "I suppose you want to check my room, too, Sheriff. I'm only the owner here. I don't work here, but if you want to see my room, I'll let you in. Don't even breathe in there. Take your quick look and get out of my place. I don't like your attitude or your lack of manners toward proper ladies."

Yarborough was upright in a flash, but made no sound. He had his revolver in hand, his eyes looking out the corner window, guessing the distance to the livery and his horse, and understood Coralee's making a stand in her own place of business. He wondered if she'd turn him over to the sheriff and be done with him and thought she wouldn't.

But he waited for the latch to noisily climb free of its roost and the sheriff enter the room and arrest him.

"Now, now, Coralee," the sheriff said, "don't go jumping too fast. I'm not as bad as you think I am. I'm just an old cowhand trying to do a tough job, and this time I'm chasing down a killer. It's simple. It's him and me and the dead person, the one he shot from behind a rock, just a plain old bushwhacker, that's all he is. That's all that counts. I don't want to look in your room. I trust you. You have too much sitting in your saddle to risk losing it all by going against the law, against the badge I'm wearing." The threat in his tone was easily noticeable. As a further degradation of his elusive prey, he said, "That's just the way someone killed his own father too, so you never know how things go, do you? What makes people spin the cylinder the way they do." He placed one hand over his side arm that showed a bone-white handle.

The sound of several pairs of boots came from the hallway, and the descending movement on stairs made a new sound followed by a heavy silence. Yarborough let out a breath he must have held in his lungs for the whole time of the outside discussion. He went back to bed and rolled over easily in the bed, though sleep did not ensue.

He lay awake for a few hours, not daring to move about too much, all the while searching in his mind for answers, reasons, the immediate past and the immediate future. He had not heard from Coralee after the sheriff and his men departed. They may have gone out of town, he figured, or were put up somewhere local; but he was sure they were not in the hotel.

2:00 AM

The latch was lifted on the door and Yarborough stiffened in the bed, gun in hand.

The door swung open with a slight creak, and the essence of a perfume entered the room. It carried the aura of Coralee.

Yarborough said, "Did he bother you, Coralee? Are you all right? I heard you last night putting him off by saying it was okay to look in your room. You must have been pretty sure of the outcome." He hoped he had correctly interpreted her action.

"Oh, I'm fine," she said. "I knew what I was doing. I've been a gambler before, and I had the good odds." With a sincere smile she said, "Did you get some sleep?" then quickly added, "They're down at the livery, in the loft. The sheriff and five other men. I think they're leaving after breakfast."

"I'm afraid they'll recognize my horse down there. I should have known better than to leave him there."

Coralee replied, with some consideration and care in her voice, "Jake took care of that. Your horse is with a friend and your saddle is in the leather shop, supposedly getting fixed." She smiled a wide smile.

"Why'd you treat me like this? I don't even know you."

Coralee replied, softness revealed in her voice as shallow as a whisper, "I don't like those who pretend when they're wearing a badge. Our own sheriff is a loser too, just like the one chasing you. And Jake Thursday is like an uncle to me, and he tells the truth every time out of the stable. He never lies, unless it's for me."

She looked down from a corner window onto the dark street. "Nothing's moving out there. They're probably sleeping good, getting rid of the long chase you've lead them on for the past few days."

He said, "Please take your bed back, Coralee. I'll sleep in the hall or down in the kitchen."

"No," Coralee replied, "I've been sleeping in another room and a couple of the ladies have doubled up. I'm the boss, you know. You lock the door, go back to sleep, and I'll wake you up when they've gone, but don't come out until I tell you, or Jake does."

She gave him a look that melted him, and for a few more hours he saw it again and again, that look, the look only angels can share.

5:30 AM

The knock was light as an echo in the back end of a cave, and Yarborough was not sure he heard the knock, but he felt he had been summoned from a tossing sleep.

At the door he whispered, "Who is it?"

"Jake Thursday, Tudor. I think they headed out of town, goin' east. They might be back if they don't pick up any sign of you. I've got your horse out back of the kitchen. You can grab some grub on the way. Best to move it and keep Coralee out of trouble with that McClernon. I think she's got a soft place for you."

6:00 AM

Saddling up, putting a bag of grub in his saddle bag, Yarborough headed out of town, also heading east. Now, for a change, he'd track them. A small pleasure engulfed him.

Toward late afternoon, the sun touching most surfaces, no clouds evident to the whole horizon, he finally spotted the posse at a cross-trail water and grub stop that he was very familiar with, and knew the owner. The posse had looped across a few valleys, crisscrossing their own trails a few times, which had raised Yarborough's curiosity.

He'd been to this site several times with his father in years past and remembered fondly the old man who ran the place, Homer Iacobellis, and how difficult it was to first say his name carved on a piece of board.

The old man made it easy on him the first visit. "Just call me Yaco 'cause it's easier to say," he'd said, putting an end to the problem of saying correctly and with respect an old man's name. Yarborough wondered how many times the old gent had gone through the same routine.

Almost aloud, he said, "I wonder if the old one is still around," remembering how he was physically bent over back then, when the old man confirmed had his condition by saying, "I'm closer to the ground now, and getting closer, so it won't hurt too much when I go down."

Yarborough was high on a crag looking down at the posse's horses tied up at a rail and none of the riders in sight. He pictured them at a decent meal and started to munch on the grub Coralee's cook had prepared for him, all the time keeping his eye on the cross-trail stop.

And then, in one sweep of his vision, he saw the reflections, saw them a few times, coming from the same spot at the edge of the small building, tossing off blips of sunlight, and suspected one member of the posse was watching the trail behind them with binoculars, his field of vision sweeping back and forth, and the movements of the spy glass or binoculars catching old sol.

McClernon, it was plain to Yarborough, was expecting him. He had known his father, what he had been like in dire straits and circumstances, and what the son was most likely to do in certain situations.

He'd also count on McClernon's reactions.

The voice of his father came back, re-affirming an off-hand study; "Never forget a lesson that can help you later on." He meant, "You have to use all your skills to catch some bad dude who might be just as smart as you."

McClernon, he figured, was aware of a lot of lessons and was likely clued in to a few others he'd come across. This one might be, "Lure a desperado into your clutches by making him follow you right to the hoosegow."

Yarborough weighed that possibility with deep concern and spent time on a new routine. But he kept thinking about McClernon leaving a wide trail a tenderfoot might follow with ease. Going back over the trail, he recalled the broken twigs, the snapped branches, the deep hoof prints in especially open places, a fire that had been warm to his touch well after a water stop. "Why didn't he leave his name on a hunk of wood and plant it on the trail?" Then, as though brightness slammed into him, he asked, "Why the hell didn't I see it all earlier, him playing with me? I wonder if he suspects Coralee of having any part in it. That's the last thing I want to happen."

A deeper and more malicious thought came to him that McClernon was setting her up for a gigantic fall right into the sheriff's grasp. And he was playing a part in it; what would his father say to this situation?

He kept thinking about Coralee and how she had shaken him up on more than one occasion, his life probably in her hands more often than not during the night at Calico. She didn't deserve any pain from him.

He'd remember that forever, he was sure. Just as he would remember Shannah in their short time together and her quick exit in the face of family embarrassment and ridicule. He was excessively lucky to balance that fact against Coralee's stance with McClernon, and knew the scale was heavily in Coralee's favor ... and thus his.

What further came to him was the possibility he might know some members of the posse. The few times he had them in his view he could not identify any of them. He was looking for that break. It might give him an edge.

Yarborough made a decision on that assumption, that some of them were good acquaintances from his early days in Willow Bend. His friends had always been bouncy, young enough for any adventure, instant volunteers for a posse or a search for a lost soul. They were good kids, young, in love with every new girl, part explosion in their own right.

There was a time, he recalled with clear vision, that his father had great influence on all his close friends; the old man showed them endlessly the difference not just between right and wrong, but winning or losing in the battle for justice and temperance of emotions; "You lose your head and you're dead before your head hits the ground. A quick trigger means a quicker death, yours or his. A wasted bullet can save your life, or someone you love, and only minutes later. These options come as quick as you can deliver bullets. Options are quicker than bullets. Make the difference on your own ground."

The wise sheriff's son slipped down toward the cross-trail stop, making sure the eye glass user would not spot him, found a secure hiding spot, much closer, where he could see some of the men, try to identify them; help could be used no matter where it came from, no matter what side of the badge.

When the posse members came out of the small building, Yarborough was unable to identify anyone though a few seemed somewhat familiar. He decided to wait out their departure and check the proprietor of the place and try to get some answers that way.

The posse rode east again, and disappeared beyond a bald-faced cliff the sun was hitting. They re-appeared later still further down the prairie after coming up out of a dip in the prairie. Then were gone from sight again.

He rode up to the cross-trail stop and old man Iacobellis, still leaning, still hanging on, came out and dumped a small bunch of garbage in a sump hole, two birds overhead swooping low when he turned to leave. Yarborough yelled out, "Yaco, this is an old friend, Tudor Yarborough's son, Tudor III. 'Member me?" He waved his hand as he neared the old man.

"Yah, Yaco remember you and your papa. Bless his name. Bless his journey." Then said, "The men just go out look again for you. I hear them talk. That big man, the sheriff, '*ha la bocca grande bugiardo,*' he big mouth liar. He say wrong thing about your papa."

"I know he is, Yaco. He blames me for killing someone I did not kill, I swear to the Almighty."

"You don't have to swear for Yaco. Yaco know. Yaco know for long time you and good papa are good men, good friends." He blessed all memories with his hand making a cross in the air, his eyes closed, an unknown image seen or brought to mind.

"Did you hear any of the names of the men riding with him?"

"Two names I hear. One, Corsica like island, and one, O'Hara, young man have red hair like fire under hat. Corsica swear in old tongue and tell me he hate big mouth liar. He say he only ride because big mouth liar say he will put friend in jail and beat him, beat his woman. Maybe worse." Then the old man muttered it several times, all in his old language: "*Metterà amico in carcere e picchiato picchiato la sua donna. Forse peggio.*"

Yarborough didn't understand a word of it, but somehow knew what the muttering was all about. He had liked Yako in the past and was fond of him all the more; it was understanding a good man that made it so.

Now, he assented with surety, that Angelo Corsica, the curser, was a good friend from the old days, the younger days, but no more so than Rod O'Hara, who slept in the loft of the barn with him many times, telling stories, of their favorite horses, best hunting adventure, where they'd go if they ever got the chance, what girls smiled at who at the general store or around town at picnics or dances. Even in church.

Both of them, with a chance for an escape from McClernon's clutches, would take a chance to do so and in his favor. He'd have to count on them right from the start. It made him wonder about friendship, how deep it could go, how it made deeper friendships or let them be. Shannah had been locked in by his looks and had sketched him. Then she had departed at the first sign of trouble. He saw distinctions, differences because Coralee on the other hand hung in tight when it really counted. "Now," he said with conviction, "there's a girl of interest." He could count on her if hell was rushing at them.

Advice from Yarborough's father surged back into attention: "The less foes you face might give you an edge in comrades. Change the numbers whenever you can. Spoil their ammunition. Run off their water. Reduce their cover. But don't ever steal their women. It will never pay you back for your troubles."

It was left-over campaign maneuvers the old sheriff had used in years of outlaw pursuits, endless face-offs at the finish of a long journey, the back trail littered with errors and illuminations about the minds of men.

His predicament made him decide in that instant that he'd best use his friends to try to dilute McClernon's forces, reduce the odds. O'Hara, it came evident, would be the one to take a chance with on the first try. The redhead was a good man, reliable in a fight.

He said to his horse as if it was a listener, "It's time to put all those lessons to work, horse, and get on with all of this."

He bid adios to Yaco and headed back up to his previous lookout, hoping the posse would come back.

They appeared later, on the horizon, trail dust making the announcement, and slowly rode back in to Yaco's place. About to search for best ways to approach the cabin while they were there, Yarborough saw two of the posse take saddles off their horses and get them ready for the night. The posse, he realized, was going to spend the night again at Yaco's place.

A plan slipped into his mind. Rummaging in his saddle bag, he pulled out the tin container with the pictures and badge and wanted poster in it, checked the shiny surface and decided it was still shiny enough to reflect morning sunlight. He wrapped the contents in his extra shirt and put them back in his saddle bag. The shiny tin he set on a clear surface of rock where the sun would catch it sometime in the morniing.

He pictured the resultant scene in the morning. With the scene locked into his mind, he found a decent spot to sleep, prepared it, saw to his horse's needs, and went to sleep.

Well before dawn he was downhill in a good surveying position. A lamp glow appeared at one window and was followed minutes later with smell of a new fire filtering in the air. Morning rounds were being done, and coffee aroma soon came after the fire's smoke. Other flavors came on the air, like bacon and burnt bread.

All five riders used the outhouse in a matter of 10 or 15 minutes, and he easily recognized old friends Angelo Corsica and Rod O'Hara, then McClernon. He did not know the others, and Yaco did not come out of the cabin.

While the sun was coming up and touching surfaces with its warmth, the posse members saddled their horses. They were in the middle of mounting when McClernon himself pointed up at the rocky ledge where Yarborough had left the shiny tin.

"Do you see that refection up there, boys? That's him, that's Yarborough. I'll bet on it. Got him right where we want him." He chortled and made sounds in his throat, and said, "Now we got him. Followed like I knew he would, and he's up there and there's only two ways down. So we got him. You three go that way, up the south trail and me and Gabbler'll go up the other trail. We'll have him in a couple of hours. Don't let him slip into a cave on you, and you better shoot at first sight. Knock him down. Get him under cover where we can smoke him out one way or another."

There was a fair amount of glee in his voice that Yarborough, closer than he had been in a long time, heard clearly. And measured.

The posse took off in two directions and Yarborough, after making sure they were out of sight, slipped into the cabin. Yaco was in his cot, his head bloody but unbandaged. "Big mouth hit me when I was going out. Said I had to stay here. Hit me hard. That Gabber one he killed your father. I heard him and big mouth talk. Say they get you and it done." He rubbed his hand in the old gesture.

Yarborough said, "I'll write that down on the back of this piece of the poster and you sign your name to it. Is that okay with you?"

Yaco said, "I sign it I-a-c-o-b-e-l-l-i-s like real way. Yes, I will sign."

Up on the ledge where the tin container had lost some of its shine, it sat on the rock clearly visible to Angelo Corsica, Rod O'Hara and another rider. The two old friends had worried they'd be the ones to find Yarborough, but what they found was a note on the back of half of Yarborough's wanted poster that said:

"To whoever finds this note, the killers of my father, Tudor Yarborough II, Sheriff, and a sidekick named Gabbler are part of the posse that has been chasing me. I will get them before it's over. This is signed by me, in my hand, knowing that the end depends on who finds this note. Signed, Tudor Yarborough III."

O'Hara, in a second, said, "We're getting out of here. I never wanted to find Tudor on this search. I don't believe he killed anyone and the sheriff and his sidekick are in on it. I'm going. You with me, Angelo?"

"Yes, I am, and Harry here's going with us whether he likes it or not." He whipped the gun from the other man's holster and said, "Excuse me, Harry, but just in case."

They went down the mountain, leaving the note in place.

McClernon, finding the note as he came up the other trail, rushed with his sidekick to get down off the mountain, knowing that Yarborough was now down below them and not on the mountain at all.

They found Yarborough, of course, waiting for him. He was standing in front of Yaco Iacobellis's cabin, three riders behind him, each of whom had read Yaco's signed note.

"I know you killed my father, Gabbler, and McClernon sicced you on him and now holds that over you, so you best do one of two things right now, draw on me or draw on the rat who's got a hold on you."

McClernon couldn't wait, feeling the noose coming closer. He drew and shot Gabbler in the back, grabbed him as a shield, and faced Yarborough straight on. He didn't get off a shot, as O'Hara, at a better angle than Yarborough, dropped him with one shot. Gabbler and McClernon fell as one body, lay on the ground as one body, and Yaco Iacobellis knew good old justice had come this far west.

And Tudor Yarborough was sure to give thanks to Coralee back in Calico where he had already spent one long night and hoped for more.

Only the Dead Cry Lonely

Jackson Alsop, sheriff of Dunkirk Falls in the Montana territory, rode back into town as evening settled itself like an October blanket, snow promise sitting in the air, a chill with it, and his horse tired from the long chase. Jeff Lundstedt was still out there in the hills, a fugitive but not a fugitive, an escapee from jail, but cleared of a murder charge just after he broke loose, Sheriff Alsop trying to catch up to him before one of the bounty hunters, out there too, killed him and brought back his body ... trying to collect a reward no longer available.

What else bothered the sheriff was the manner of the reward posting, hung on the door of the saloon by the father of Lundstedt's girlfriend, Gilyard Lansing, owner of the biggest spread in the territory. The reward was posted before the erroneous verdict was announced and within a day reversed by the judge when new evidence came to light. Alsop thought all of it was so damned convenient, and contrived, that he swore he'd get to the root of it.

Alsop had been on the job just shy of a year, and when he was only a month or so wearing the badge it was leaked to him, by the livery man, Max Turner, that he was really appointed by Gil Lansing through the town council that he controlled. "The man wants people owing him, even as big as he is. You can drop half the other ranches on his spread and he'd still have enough left over to take care of you and me and half the town for the next ten years. But he wants people owing him. It's simple as that, and he'll toss it in your saddlebag someday and try not to let you know it's there. But it is."

Then Turner, said, "You know as well as I do, Jackson, that on the coldest day of the year you can still burn your fingers in a fire. If it's there, you can get burned. Lansing's a big man and by now more people owe him than we can guess at and we'll never know who they all are. Only way to tell is how folks move when moving's needed."

Alsop said, "Who owns the livery, Max? Doesn't he own it but fronted by you? Are you owing?"

"My momma made me promise never to owe anybody if I can help it," said Turner. "If Lansing thinks I owe him, let him do so, but I ain't an ower. And I'm telling you what I know 'cause I think you're straight as a gold bar." He stopped talking for a spell, looked at Alsop's horse and suddenly said, "When you gonna need him again. I like that boy too. He's okay in my book. Lansing's daughter likes him too, told me straight out, but I could never tell him, the boy. She said, 'Let him find out by himself. I don't want to guess on anything.' How's that for you, Jackson? Ain't she the number, and like a new flower just budded?"

"I wondered about Terson's testimony that he just about saw the boy shoot Oliver. Terson must owe Lansing, but Terson's wife came to me and told me he was with her and couldn't have seen the shooting. She said she couldn't stand seeing that boy get hung because of a lie and just because he was in love with Ellen Lansing."

"None of it goes back on Lansing, does it?" Turner offered. "I'll have your horse ready to ride the minute the sun comes up. The girl told me once their favorite place was down by the Fox Hill Bridge, but on the other side, in that mess of canyons in there. They picnicked down that way a few times, she said, and didn't worry about having a fire. So, if you haven't looked around in that area, I'd start there."

The sheriff, walking away from the livery, remembered how often that a plain old livery man like Turner could say things that popped up days later, when he might be alone on a ride, with so much clarity or such unreachable deepness that they amazed him and flustered him at the same time. Nobody else in the whole town was like Turner. None of them could bring things to mind the way he could. Now the delivery about burned fingers would stay with him and he'd have to add it to other gems like Turner, after a long pause in a conversation one day at a Boot Hill ceremony, said, "Only the dead cry lonely, Sheriff. Only the dead cry lonely."

That still worked on him and still made the old gent seem like an elder from one of the Nations, all of life's possibilities and realities stuffed in his wampum bag for the choosing in someone's education. He promised himself that he'd pay keen attention to what the old gent had to offer any time they talked.

Indeed! "Only the dead cry lonely." Everyone else has someone to lean on, to cry or wail at or with, to seek help from no matter how far away they are or how deep in their past. But not the dead.

Alsop had his evening drink at the Broken Heart Saloon with the bartender at the far end of the bar. A short while later he slipped out the back door and was at the door of Missy Plourant's rooming house, ate the meal sitting on his bedside table as usual, had another drink and was asleep in minutes.

The sheriff went to sleep thinking that Jeff Lundstedt was a good young fellow with no more and no less promise than the other cowpokes his age, but had shown a touch of the actor when he broke out of jail. He used a ruse on the elderly night jailer, and tied up the jailer in a most considerate manner, and not too tight, so as not to hurt the old gent, whose feelings would be hurt enough by the escape. The young man most certainly knew what he could expect from Lansing and his influence in the town, in the territory.

With the sun not yet burning atop the peaks and hills, a pre-dawn gray lifting from darkness the way dew sometimes rises in a thin vapor on the prairie, Alsop was riding toward the Fox Hill Bridge well out from town. On the other side of the bridge and the arm of the Hoyt Stream it crossed, sat a conglomeration of canyons and serious divides in the rocky terrain. Hiding there, at least on foot, would be easy to do and hard to follow. The sheriff, rarely ever giving up his horse, would still resist that separation as best he could and for as long as he could. He was not a mountain climber, not a mountain man, not one of the young athletic types who could easily manage full days of searching on foot.

But he was not dispirited as he rode along, bringing to mind several of the bounty hunters that Turner told him had set out to capture Lundstedt. They were a determined, serious, and wholly merciless group, with Trigger Bascombe being the meanest and the most successful one in the lot. He shot early and often and was most deadly in his aim. Three times Alsop had seen him come into Dunkirk Falls with a fugitive across the saddle of a horse, the rifle in Bascombe's hand as though he'd use it against anyone threatening to take his bounty from him.

Alsop had the uneasy feeling that it would be Bascombe that he'd have to beat out in this race … and that's just what it was, a race to save a young man from a deadly, but usually lawful, killer.

The sheriff said aloud as he approached Fox Hill Bridge, "I hope Bascombe's still sleeping someplace." Several times that thought crossed his mind, but he had doubts about that edge in the game.

In one of the canyons in the range on the other side of the bridge, Alsop smelled the smoke from a fire, and breakfast remnants in the mix of odors. All smelled burnt … bacon, bread, beans, coffee. The breezes moving around the area were random and seemed without a visible source. The fire, however, was not in the canyon he was in. He saw no smoke, no flames, and no figure moving about, so he backtracked and went into the next canyon.

The smells came stronger, the smoke near visible at the deep end of the canyon, and Alsop saw a figure at that deep end. The size of the man across the shoulders said it was not Lundstedt, and told him it was Bascombe, big and brawny, and sitting as though he expected company. The figure turned around, lifted the coffeepot in the air and waved him onto the fire site.

"Damned bounty hunter knew I was coming," Alsop said to himself. "What else does he expect?"

"C'mon in, sheriff. I knew you'd be here sometime. That's a mighty big reward Lansing's put on the boy, who's somewhere in these canyons. I found sign early this morning. Sit down now and have a hot cup. It'll do you good."

"The boy's innocent, Bascombe. The judge reversed the decision. There's no bounty. Not a dime coming from my office."

"That don't go for Lansing, Sheriff. That was a personal promise to me and I aim to keep my end of the bargain. It's too damned good to turn my back to it. I know Lansing'll follow up his promise. He wants this boy dead for some personal thing and I ain't about to disappoint him."

"That'd be murder, Bascombe, if you kill the boy, and I'd chase you down long as I had breath." He dismounted as he spoke and in that moment Bascombe had his gun trained on him.

"Not if I was never to know the boy was let off from the conviction, Sheriff. Long as I can say I was out here and didn't know, I'll collect from Lansing, and that's for sure. He won't dare refuse me. Man has hunger's bad as me. We know each other too well. I done work for him before."

The gun was steady on the sheriff.

"You kill me and leave me out here and they'll get you, Bascombe. I know that."

"Drop your gun, Sheriff. I ain't playing no games with you. Sit down there on that rock and put your hands behind your back. I'm tying you up, and if I get that boy in my sights, you'll be next. If I don't, you can explain this talk all you want back in town, and to Lansing, and nobody can do anything against me. That you can put in a pipe and smoke up forever. My word against yours."

The rope was knotted on Alsop's wrists, his gun set aside, and Bascombe offered a cup of coffee to his lips. "Drink it now, Sheriff, 'cause I'm going to look for that boy after I tie you to a rock. It might take me the long part of the day, so drink now. If I don't get him, I'll be back much later, but that boy can't fight off me and the thirst and the hunger and the smells of food in the air. I'll get him."

That's when Alsop first noted the burnt mess in the skillet beside the fire, charred ruins of a possible decent breakfast and origin of heavy smells. The man was as cruel as he sounded, and as devious.

He thought, "I hope that boy is a lot stronger, and smarter, than I figured him for. He's going to need it with this gent after him."

Bascombe walked off behind Alsop where he couldn't see him and hid the sheriff's handgun and rifle, came back, offered another sip of coffee and headed into the deeper part of the canyon, his rifle in hand and ready, wide in the saddle as he rode.

Perhaps fifteen minutes later, Bascombe out of sight, Alsop heard scraping sounds behind him, then the skitter of a stone on stone, and a whisper from behind a rock. A voice said, "Don't move, Sheriff. It's me, Jeff Lundstedt. I got your weapons where he hid them and I heard all the talk. Does Ellen know that I didn't kill Oliver?"

"Better untie me quick, Jeff, before he comes back. That man meant every word he said about doing us in. Hurry now. Untie me."

"Oh, I'll do that right away, Sheriff, but he's not coming back in any hurry. I planted enough teasing sign out there, all the way to the end of the canyon, and enough there to keep him guessing where I went from there. I saw him last night set his fire up like he wanted me to try and get to him."

He untied the sheriff. "Does Ellen really know I'm not a killer?"

"The whole town knows it including her father. He's got some deep reason he want you dead."

"It's not very deep, Sheriff. He doesn't want any cowpoke like me, someone real ordinary coming along and getting his daughter and his ranch, which are about the only two things he loves in this world. And all Ellen and I love are each other. That's what bothers him so much. He can't stand that. I don't think the man has a happy thought in his life outside of the ranch and Ellen."

"Well, Jeff, you've done a good deed here today, lots of smart moves, so I'm willing to listen to what you think we should do now."

"That's what I'm thinking about, Sheriff and I think we ought to keep everything the way it was when he went out there. You sitting there like you're tied up, but you're not, and like you don't have a weapon, but you do, and we'll catch him right square. But he took the water with him, and we have to face the day without water."

Alsop looked at the remains of the fire and the burnt breakfast and said, "We still have his coffeepot, Jeff. We can share that. It should be enough."

So they stayed for five or six long hours of the day, sneaking drinks from the coffeepot, Alsop looking as if he was still tied to the rock, his hands behind him, his handgun in one hand, and Jeff Lundstedt, lying behind a large rock with the sheriff's rifle in his hands. He'd been once convicted, once jailed, the conviction overturned after escape from jail, a supposed fugitive to some bounty hunters, but not to the one apparently now in charge of things.

Sunshine in waves poured down on the still pair waiting on the bounty hunter with the supposed upper hand.

The full turn-around was in the making.

The canyon became furnace-like, and a deadly silence hung in the air, most critters around off in hiding from those present, the smell of gun oil possibly cast about by the heat waves. And overhead, riding the unseen thermals, the vultures, ready sometimes to investigate the still figures, kept their distance as one or the other of the "prisoners" made a definite movement saying life still moved in them.

Later in the day, the keen ears of the sheriff at work, he heard sounds from the heart of the canyon. He kept still, but whispered to Lundstedt, "You awake, Jeff?" He had not heard from him for almost an hour.

"I'm awake, Sheriff, and I heard that sound. It's got to be him. I'm not going to move a muscle. The play is all yours. I'm just a back-up."

Alsop entertained the sudden image of him pinning a deputy's badge on Jeff Lundstedt. It would be well-deserved and a note for the future.

Bascombe, in a matter of minutes, appeared about 100 yards away, standing beside his horse, studying the layout of his campfire and his prisoner, still tied to a big rock, the rope still in prominent display about his body, his hands behind him. All else seemed to be the way he left it earlier.

The bounty hunter was slow and deliberate in his approach, walking on the right side of his horse, the reins in his left hand, his rifle in the other hand. He was not going to be surprised if there was a change. He saw the sheriff as though he was sleeping, and figured the heat and thirst had got to the man, and the campfire and the surroundings were exactly as he left them; the fire was out, but the coffeepot sat on a rock at the edge of the fireplace he had made, the sheriff's horse was still tied further away, and all looked to be the same.

Still, he came on slowly, walking and not riding, caution in every step.

Eventually, not twenty feet from the trussed-up sheriff, his curiosity and security now pretty certain to be valid, the big bounty hunter slid his rifle into the scabbard on the saddle, turning his back for a few ticks of the watch. When he swung back, hearing a new sound, reaching for his handgun, the sheriff of Dunkirk Falls had his gun trained on his chest.

"Don't move, Bascombe, or you're dead." He straightened his arm and pointed the handgun even closer to the bounty hunter.

"I ain't moving, Sheriff. Nothing's changed. It's just my word against yours, so there's nothing you can do and Lansing will take care of everything, just like I said. My word against yours."

Bascombe's whole stance and demeanor changed when the sheriff said, "I'll just ask him to speak in my behalf, Bascombe," and he added, "Keep that rifle on him Jeff. We want him to testify with his lies. If he moves one inch, shoot him in the hip."

Jeff Lundstedt, once fugitive, stood up carefully, the aim of the rifle right on the bounty hunter not more than forty feet away from him.

"I'll get him straight on, Sheriff. If I miss, it won't be down, but up along the chest." His aim was steady and on target.

They rode into Dunkirk Falls at dusk, the sheriff, the one-time fugitive and the new prisoner. At the livery, near the head of the town, Max Turner rang the town bell as loud as he could, yelling at the same time, and the townsfolk poured out of the buildings, the saloon, the general store, a few other shops, as the mini-parade neared the sheriff's office.

There was a roar of approval from just about all the townsfolk, except a few Lansing confederates, but some of that changed too as Ellen Lansing rushed form the crowd and repeatedly hugged Jeff Lundstedt, the sheriff's rifle still in his hands.

At the edge of the crowd, tears on her cheeks, a true sense of joy rushing through her, Missy Plourant promised herself that she'd have another surprise for the sheriff when he came back for his night's rest.

Pearl's Diamonds

The train sat at a water stop miles before Humphrey Station on the Dakota-Idaho Line, a rifle jammed in the back of the engineer, the conductor temporarily locked in a caboose closet, the telegraph lines already cut in a few places, and Pearl Weber's gang holding the train for her. She was ten minutes late coming from the hideout, the wires cut after an incoming message addressed to a "Virginia Alexandria" had included the coded line, "Mother is keeping her bed warm at home in Purchase."

Purchase was in Idaho and the message from her brother meant her mother was dying.

Pearl Weber, all beautiful 5'2" of her, curvaceous in a rough outfit, was the leader of a pack of gunmen wholly admiring her precise plans for robbing banks and trains, and her advice on handling the split-up of shares as soon as possible after their generally successful robberies. In line with another of her precepts, she also planned retirement situations for those who would listen. Not many heeded such a credo, the way cowpokes came and went in those days after the Great War, old wounds, long needs and dreams of quick riches usually holding sway. Occasionally one man would plan his old age comfort because he believed Pearl knew what she was talking about, believed she had a hand touching on fate.

She had preached endlessly to those who followed her, "It's nice out here, but it's big time in the Big East for those who get there." She owned an estate in Vermont holding onto the side of a mountain, a cabin nestled under trees beside a lake in the heart of Maine, a beach house in New Hampshire that drew her gaze toward Paris and London, and money in banks in Boston, New York City, and the nation's capital.

One possession on Martha's Vineyard, high on a bluff catching Atlantic changes, was really her dream home, a stately house of a dozen gables and a widow's walk on high, and full of whaler's tales, pirate stories, and sudden romance hanging inside the walls waiting to break loose. All of Spar Hill, once belonging to a sea captain who never returned from his last voyage, was hers. Only there once for a short visit, the wallpaper pattern in the great hallway kept its design in her mind as vivid as an image in a locket. That secret view caused her to say repeatedly, "Spar Hill's where I'll retire when all this is over and done with."

Her arguments on safe and solid retirement continued: "How many real old men do you know?" she'd say to her gang, to those who listened, "and if you know some real old ones, ones who were in our business, what do they have to keep them going now that they can't shoot straight, or ride for a full day, or bust out of jail once in a month of Saturday nights?"

Pearl, with a twist of blonde hair trailing from under her Stetson, presented a highly favorable look for one leading a gang of toughs. The angelic face under that Stetson set her off from many women of the west. She carried the wind, the sun and lengthy days on the run in the saddle better than most women, showing little wear and tear on her looks or in her form. A few former gang members had learned, in a crucial test of wills, that they did not fit in any way romantic with the leader of the pack, who some members referred to as The Alpha Female with the Hot Lips.

Chico Manirez, as good looking as they send up from below the Rio Grande, and a crack shot with any weapon, said, privately of course, "It was no match with Pearl. She knows what she wants and it's not me. That's cut and dried and I leave it there, only to think about it once in a while on a starry night knowing I'll never make a move on her again."

Now once more she had gathered them, the motley crew, and advised them that she needed to get on board the next train west, to Purchase, but dared not board the train from a regular station on the line. She asked them to take care of it, so they did ... at the point of guns. They snuck her aboard, disguised as best she could, released the conductor and the engineer after a fake robbery seemed to have gone astray, and Pearl Weber was on her way home to see her mother confined to her last bed.

The message, as said, had been sent to one Virginia Alexandria, which really was her mother's birth place, at the Pine Hills Station, 60 miles from her mother, her brother, and their home in Idaho. It was a method of communication her brother had used several times, a device Pearl insisted on.

But her brother, in a twist of fate, had sent the message at the point of a gun belonging to Purchase Sheriff Oscar Ridlowe. The sheriff had put together a small chart of facts about Pearl Weber and her Diamonds, a distinctive and highly wanted outlaw gang. When he heard Chester Weber's mother had been ill for a few days, he leaped at the chance to entice Pearl Weber home ... and into his jail.

He had no idea how it would work out, but it was better than sitting and hoping she'd make a big mistake ... like coming home for any reason on the spur of the moment and him unaware of her arrival unless he pulled the strings on it, unless he was on his toes.

When the telegraph lines had gone down after the phony message had been sent, as reported in Purchase, he knew Pearl Weber was on her way home to see and comfort her mother. The next train, due in the dusk of evening, was an obvious opportunity.

Two of the gang, before the water stop, had hailed the train from the tracks, one horse dead beside the tracks, one at a limp not far away, the saddles and equipment subsequently tossed on board the train.

When Pearl had been secreted aboard the train at the fake hold-up, she had company, at a distance, in the next car … apparently two luckless cowpokes off the trail.

Collecting fares from new passengers, the conductor suspected the woman in the heavy make-up and the Mexican-style head veil. He could tell from her bare wrists that she was nearly as white as a prairie acacia and not a darker Latin lady. There was a reason she had come aboard late, as did the two cowpokes, all three of them trying to hide something. He could have discounted the two cowpokes caught out on the trail with no horses, but one and only one woman came to mind needing such a disguise, and that was notorious Pearl Weber, the vaunted leader of Pearl's Diamonds.

He vowed he'd do nothing rash when he was released from the caboose closet, but secretly promised he'd advise the law the first chance he had about his suspicions. When he sent a telegraph to the sheriff of Purchase from Humphrey Station, further on the line from the water stop, he had no idea that the reception at Purchase was already planned and manned.

At the command of Sheriff Oscar Ridlowe, a dozen sworn-in deputies were placed about the station in Purchase, and each man given specific orders. And regular deputy Bruce Maxler, dressed as a sporty gent from back east, with a suitcase to match, stood under a lamp at the station, ready to board the train bound further west. In a shoulder holster under his fancy jacket sat a Colt revolver, snug as a bee in a closed bud. Maxler was an expert marksman, daring, veteran of some successful posse hunts, and as smart as a lead actor.

When Maxler stepped into the second passenger car, the two "stranded cowpokes" laughed at his clothes and his manner of storing his suitcase for the ride. And at the other end of the car, Pearl Weber, catching a full look on the face of the fancy clad newcomer, felt a pull at her heart; he was a most handsome gentleman, nattily attired, setting himself off from the two laughing gang members who had no class at all in their manners, them preparing to leave the train.

When she gave the two gang members a high sign to knock off their current attitude, each man backed off as gracefully as he could, and apologies were delivered and accepted by Maxler who noted the beauty of the lone woman in the car. He hoped against hope she was not Pearl Weber, hoped that the real Pearl Weber was in the next car. But his doubts overrode his high hopes.

Pearl Weber said, in a clear and pleasant voice, not the voice of a gang leader, "Excuse me, sir, but you're obviously from back east because of your good outfit. Where are you from and where are you heading?"

The interest in her voice was as rich as could be, and her eyes, in the light of several gas lamps, echoed the same interest.

"I'm not going very far, Ma'am," Maxler said, the impact of her voice clearly impressed in him.

Pearl said, "I am getting off here, sir, and wish you a good journey." Her smile was illustrious, and her two gang members were awed by the swift change in her manners.

Maxler, caught between several emotions, concerned about the two men who had been direct in their approach and quickly diverted from it, the beauty and the office of command in the voice of the petite woman, and the weight of the revolver pushing on his chest, instantly hated his job ... but realized there was nothing he could do about it.

While the two gang members were caught up in their realizations, Purchase Sheriff Oscar Ridlowe slipped in behind Pearl Weber and had her twisted into manacles that bound the slimmest of wrists. When her supposed escorts saw what happened and tried to make a move, they found themselves staring into the bore of Maxler's Colt held in his steady hand.

Before her trial was to start, several sly moves were made upon the jail at Purchase by some of her men, but Ridlowe was ready, as was his small army of deputies, and they drove off each attempt to free Pearl Weber.

The judge, a noted high bench juror summoned to sit in judgment, was not due in town for a week or more. It would be an interesting case; no person had ever been killed in one of the robberies, Pearl Weber had never been seen by a witness at any of the hold-ups. All information had surfaced as innuendo, a bit of bragging by some outlaws under the influence of drink, and rumors that galloped at times like a runaway horse and wagon.

In the meantime, at Ridlowe's direction, Bruce Maxler was assigned as Pearl Weber's constant jailer. It was a job he grew fond of in a short time as she told him, not about all her holdings back east, but only the stories and tales that came from Spar Hill. She danced the place into his mind with tales that gripped him long after they were told.

Maxler, young, handsome, lively and lusty in imagination from every angle, was captured, captivated, and swung by his heels by his lovely prisoner. When she smiled he melted, gloried when she held his hand, and carried her into his highest fancies. When he slept, in a corner of the jail, Pearl Weber on a cot in her cell, he dreamed of pirates and whalers and sea queens and one beauty who sailed as captain of her own frigate. The fictitious name of Captain Diamond of the Atlantic Treasure Fleet would not leave him.

As it was, possibly seen by Ridlowe, and possibly not, Pearl Weber at last had fallen in love. To address her new feelings she began to include Maxler in all of her stories, and her own person, by name or description or by whatever means she could devise, came along ... with her heart attached in every case.

It was the ultimate of attractions for both parties.

In the dead of night, two days before the judge was due in Purchase, Pearl Weber, prisoner, and Bruce Maxler, jailer and deputy, slipped out of the jail in Purchase and disappeared forever from Idaho.

A small note, pinned to the wanted poster board in the jail, carried a simple message: "It's love that did this." There was no signature on the note.

The pair was never seen again in Idaho or any other western state, as far as Ridlowe knew. The remnants of the gang, wherever they were, or however they got on after their leader disappeared from jail, whether they had retired or not, never once mentioned to any law officer a place they knew of called Spar Hill, an historical estate on far-off Martha's Vineyard, catching all it could hold of the Atlantic Ocean, and its storied walls at last letting go secrets held too long from the living.

Quinn Cosgair's Treasure

Sgt. Quinn Cosgair, two days from the end of his current enlistment, September of 1871, three hash marks earned for his left sleeve, participated in the battle with Comanches at Blanco Canyon, nearly forty miles long, and when the Comanche women and children finally were able to flee the attack, the fighting Comanche braves drifted off into the silence of the Llano Estacado, Palisaded Plains, like high spirits of old, the invisible ones.

Some of the troops said, "Good riddance," to the Comanches, and the wise ones, generally to themselves, said they hoped they'd never see the Comanches again.

Captain Ivan Blundell, the commander of the 5th Cavalry, was glad to see the women and children get away. The inevitable would have haunted him again; he'd known too many sleepless nights after such engagements.

There were some things that Sgt. Quinn Cosgair, a cavalryman for all of his three hitches, might tell his captain, and some things that'd never pass his lips even if Death came calling with its pressures.

Quinn Cosgair had told Blundell at one time while they were on a quiet patrol, "I got tired fighting about my given name, Bréanainn, every place I went, Captain, so I changed it to Quinn. No paperwork, as they say, but the word of the man, Quinn Cosgair. That family name in the old language sounds like Garbhainn."

He let the word hang in the near-Celtic air, an aura upon which the captain dared not intrude lest he stumble.

Cosgair, in conscience and in hope at the end of the Blanco Canyon battle, did not tell Blundell that he had seen one Comanche woman, appearing late in the battle after all the other women had gone with the children, slide sideways, elusive, like a ferret, behind one sheer side of a cliff fall. She obviously was too far behind the other women to catch up.

He kept the spot in mind. If she dared move, she faced torture at the least from many of the men who had lost many comrades to the Comanches in previous engagements. If she remained hidden with water and food, she might wait a few days before attempting a night escape. If she became thirsty or hungry, she might pay for it dearly.

And he had only three days left of his hitch, he looked forward to a number of opportunities; perhaps he could help her, if she wanted help, would take help, had not already been captured, tortured, dead.

At the back of his mind, as if the thought had sat there to be found at the proper time, the words of an old trooper had been revealed; "The Comanche make sure they take as many women prisoners as they can handle on their flight away from a battle or a raid. They take 'em or kill 'em. It's as simple as that."

He made sure he did not appear too anxious in front of the captain. He did not care what the other troopers thought of his observations.

All the wide open parts of Texas were in turmoil from Indian attacks, quick raids, and long and deadly engagements with fierce warriors. Names came across the land from the hidden camps, the villages and the great lodges, names that were developing a continuing history: Bull Elk, Wing Talk, Black Horse, White Robe, Black Mustache, One Wolf, and Three-Crows. The commands seemed endless, the ranks littered with heroes. The Comanche medicine man Isatai constantly pushed for war with the white man … settlers, ranchers, and the whole vast army.

Comanche actions were continuing in the mid-70s and Cosgair was well aware of the consequences for a lone man out there on the Plains. He was aware that the death of one of the chiefs or of their kin would set any hopes of peace far adrift on the Plains. He was also worried about the tribes joining forces, becoming a stronger force.

But when Blundell called him in on the next to the last day of his enlistment, he served him his discharge papers, saying, "You've been a good soldier, Quinn, and I want to wish you the best. I know I can't change your mind. Do you have a horse and saddle at your disposal?"

"Oh, I'm all set there, Captain. I've got a horse my own, from the outside, broke, rid and saddled entire he is. A handsome bay he is, sixteen hands high, eye of the devil in the pasture and he'll do me well." Cosgair could feel that mountain of muscle already moving beneath him.

He didn't want to hang around chewing the fat with the commander. He had someplace to go; something to check out. He was itching to move.

At the livery in Wells, he swapped his army clothes with the owner, part of his deal for a horse he'd previously picked out, a saddle that he especially wanted, a new rifle and side arms, a saddlebag, two blankets, a bed roll rolled up in a canvas. He wore a gray Stetson, gray shirt and dark gray vest, black pants with no stripes down the sides of the legs, a pair of handguns on his belt, the honorable discharge in his shirt pocket. Hope sat so well in his eyes that it was noticeable.

When he left the Wells Horse House run by an old countryman, Padraig Ó Síocháin with the new name of Pat Sheehan, he was shuck of the army all the way. He had bathed, shaved, cut his hair back and was a new man in a new life.

With a brogue thick as mesquite, his curiosity as deep as its hardy roots, Sheehan could not let pass any information in which he was not fully vested.

"What in God's name are ye up to Quinn," he said, "drawin' down the curtain like you were on stage for a drama? Ye look like a banker from Cobh hiding the yield. What are ye up to? And I'll wager a good pound it's to do with a woman. I'm bettin', too, another pound Blundell has not found an inklin' of your leanin'. Am I right on that, Quinn? Am I right?"

The delightful sparkle of old light was in the eyes of the livery man, the village tongue brought to pub.

"Don't let me down, here, Quinn," he continued. "'T'is a woman, isn't it? A real God-blessed woman after me own heart, here, glory be, in the heart of this wasteland of grass and mesquite and so dry me throat's awork at thirst again. What do ye think of that, a woman for me best soljer."

He bowed low, raised his head on high, threw his hands skyward, and said, "Thank ye, Lord, thank ye for such a sign. This world carries on what I left in Cobh." His head shook in joyful and also remorseful memory.

Quinn Cosgair, once a 5th Cavalry sergeant with three hitches to his credit, a dozen battles in his past, rode away from Wells headed for fate, destiny, karma, and drama of an unimaginable sort.

He was ready for anything, having been most places already.

The Blanco Canyon might have appeared to any other man as geography set with peril, hidden peril. The high escarpment shifted and changed as he rode, presenting the unknown reservoirs of secrecy in its walls. But he felt a new comfort, not fooling himself that it was merely a new freedom.

The sun was getting hot, the horse he had named Bullet rode like a gifted mystery of grace and comfort, and the air was set with and edge toward thirst.

Overhead three huge vultures signaled their endless search for carrion of any sort, preferably the bigger the better.

Cosgair thought about the Comanche woman he had seen spirit herself away from capture. He considered, for only a second, that the birds floating above, might have spotted her in a fateful flight to freedom. All his learning said that such a woman would not lose a battle at this point of her life. Much to gain was one promise she faced in her dire straits. She was resourceful. She had been trained to withstand ferocity, hunger, severe cold, endless heat, aridness, thirst, animals of all comings.

In the middle of such reasoning, the back of his mind released another small piece of information that might have been assumed, seen, guessed at, held out for. And then a known assumption, as he actually called it, came upon him from that recess: the skin of the woman, this woman for whom he now searched, had been different from the other women in flight, different from the children in flight, different from the braves who had disappeared from Blanco Valley as if they had never been there in the first place.

That woman now hiding, he continually hoped, in some niche or cave or rupture in a sheer wall, was a captive white woman brought along in her life as a Comanche woman. He had a final duty.

As he rode close to a long stretch of palisade walls, the vultures wheeled away in their search, the thermals lifting them and escorting them in easy pursuit. He did fear that he'd miss the signs he had set at the end of the battle, but he kept his eye alternating on the ground before him and at the land all around him, alert to any other Comanche who had hidden from capture.

The horse Bullet was a distinctive animal, and exhibited traits that leaders of wild packs learn with success or they do not make any headway in procreation. Bullet made him aware of a snake on two occasions, disturbed a peccary at another point, and seemed to adjust to the vultures overhead. He gave Cosgair a sense of security that was significant to a lone man; the horse would also advise him, he was sure, of any other people in proximity.

Ahead, as if there by precision of planning, loomed the first key he had set, a strange mound on the grass, as if long in the past a body had been interred. Then came a second such mound, but slightly higher, and a sheer wall of the palisade where one crack ran down into the earth as if it was a lightning bolt from pre-history.

The Comanches, he figured, must have known of this place, this split in the palisade, these seeming burial mounds, this singular escape hatch.

He approached the site.

A sheaf of one wall, like a page of a book, had fallen away from its binding. It was as large as the side of a barn. He was able to slide behind it still on horseback. A crack in the wall behind it was nearly twelve feet high, widened near the bottom so that he could walk into the palisade beside his horse.

He walked into the break, the reins on one hand, and a revolver in the other. He had passed nearly 25 feet into the break when he became conscious of another person in the niche.

Cosgair called out, "I mean no harm to you. I saw you come in here a few days ago at the end of the battle. I did not report you. I mean you no harm. I have left the army. I am a civilian now. I hate war. I am sorry you were captured by the Comanche. I believe you are a white woman who had been held against her will. I wait until you speak to me. I will leave water and food here in front of me, but I cannot leave. I do not want others to see me come out of this place."

He set down a canteen and some food on a rock. "I will not hurt you, believe me. I know you have gone through a hard time, perhaps through a kind of Hell. Let me help you."

He stepped back, watered his horse with water spilled into his hat, sat on the ground.

Twenty minutes it took her to move. Stealthily at first she moved, hardly making a sound, but approaching the water and the food on the rock. Out of darkness she came and a piece of light suddenly fell across her face. Her saw a glimpse of hard beauty, hurt beauty, but marks of beauty remaining upon her.

His heart nearly broke. A pain rushed through him. He thought of his mother, his sister dying in her bed in Roscommon, not many years younger than this woman.

She drank first. Then drank again, slowly, no rush to it, as though she had learned this behavior from life's hard teaching. Finally, she took pieces of the food, chewed slowly, savoring perhaps not taste but salvation, her body making a statement to her.

Gradually, the sun moving its degrees, more sunrays slipped across her face. She did not shy from them, or try to hide herself, and Cosgair saw evidence of beauty about and within her. The highlights came in abundance, at first the long lashes and then the blue eyes like homeland eyes, and lips, now prim and somewhat severe, but promising softness that could melt him. Her cheekbones shone with her original paleness, a gloss, perhaps a touch of gold. His heart, the heart of an old trooper, had moved without even hearing her voice.

Her hair, though unkempt, was as bright as a golden finch he had seen once sitting at the end of his blanket out on the prairie. He remembered the bird studying him as he pretended to sleep, and kept as still as a log. He remembered, with a sudden panic, the color of his sister's hair and her on her death bed.

At length, after drinking slowly, chewing just as slowly, she looked up, the sun's rays still finding the tired and marked beauty in her face, and spoke.

Her voice was serious, but contained some melody of tone, the way one is impressed after a song is sung or played, and she said, "You have found me at last. They call me Woman-Who-Looks-Pale, Eck'a-wi'pe To'sa-woonit. Big Elk took me some years ago as his woman. My name, my real name, is Evelyn Stocker. All my family is dead. I had no child with Big Elk. He beats me for that, but only so the others will see him do so."

She chewed some more food, took another sip from his canteen, and said, "You are not an army man? But you saw me hide here? What is your name? Did you come just to find me?"

"I was in the army until two days ago. I am now out of the army. My name is Quinn Cosgair. I am from Ireland in the beginning. I was Bréanainn Garbhainn back there in a life of hunger. Now I am no longer in the army. Now I am Quinn Cosgair and I have come to rescue you. We will wait until dark and then leave this place."

He let that sink into her awareness, and made other promises that came easy in his saying. "If you want, I will take you to St. Louis or Chicago or all the way back to lovely Vermont and the greenest mountains you'll ever see either side of the Great River. I will not rush you. I will get you the new freedom you deserve. I cannot atone for what has happened to you, but I will make it easier for you. That's my promise."

He did not move any closer, and his horse kept silent. The sun rays continued to highlight more of her beauty.

She moved closer.

"I know I must trust you. You have been where I have been."

She stood up, more of her beauty showing, and made a final declaration that touched him with simplicity and promise: "And I will leave here in this place, as you did in your turn, the name they gave me, Woman-Who-Looks-Pale, Eck'a-wi'pe To'sa-woonit."

Her hand found his hand.

Revenge for Garret Byrnes

(A note must be inserted here to testify that most of the information appearing in this chronicle was delivered to me in one hand-written, unbound document found in the attic of an old home in Crown Point, Indiana, through an intermediary, a former comrade in the 31ˢᵗ Infantry Regiment, 7ᵗʰ Infantry Division, Korea, 1951, Sgt. Stan Kujawski, of "Automatic Wrist" and Chicago industrial league softball fame.)

On the gray, dull morning of April 6, 1878, in the Wyoming town of Westlynne on a crude gallows made overnight by a couple of drinking patrons pulled from the Wild Horse Saloon by the sheriff, young Garret Byrnes was hung and left on the rope until the coffin maker finished his assigned task. It took several hours for that job to get completed.

The sheriff, Corpus Chrysler, had arrested Byrnes the week before for the murder of a young lady Byrnes had been seeing against her father's wishes. The case was presented to a hastily drawn court and a most curious judge who had been en route to another town, evidence presented, and the jury of townsfolk, in a rapid decision, declared him guilty on the basis of the father's evidence, and other supposed eye witness accounts.

All participants, except Byrnes, retired immediately to the saloon and spent the latter part of the day with free drinks provided by the girl's father, celebrating the verdict as the chief witness in the case.

Byrnes did not kill his sweetheart, which you all must understand from this moment, from here at the outset of this chronicle. The young man had never aimed a gun at any man, or woman, in his life, never mind pulling the trigger on them. He was as innocent as a babe on an Indian cradle board.

In his last words, speaking after the verdict was delivered, Byrnes said, "I admit I only did two good things in my life. One was to break the wildest horses you can imagine, the whole lot of you," said as he looked directly at the jury and then at the rest of the congregation from the town, "and I loved MaryGrace Bartlett as she will never be loved again in this poor life."

It seemed it was all over at that point, records show, except he had one more thing to add to his last words. At that particular moment few of those in attendance were paying much attention to him; it was over and done with and he might cry and wail all the way to the rope, but they'd be busy otherwise.

Byrnes, in a subdued voice that the judge heard clearly along with a few of the jurors and the sheriff himself, said, "My brothers will come

looking for me. You will answer to them, for me and for MaryGrace."
Those last words were delivered directly to Mel Bartlett, sitting in the
first row between two of his hired hands. The man had shown little
remorse for the death of his daughter.

A long time after Garret Byrnes was hung, left for hours on the
rope, and buried outside town, and long after his final words had been
swept into far yesterday, a rider came into town on a gray stallion that
was as big as any horse in town. The man, perhaps in his mid-30s, a
decent looking man with a chiseled face, cheeks that seemed to wear the
sun in them, and a soft but steady voice, rented a room for a week at the
Harmony Hotel above the Wild Horse Saloon. The room looked out over
much of Westlynne and presented a view of the white capped peaks in
the distant range where the morning sun would rise in stark contrast.

The rider said he was an advance man for the railroad company.

All that late afternoon a handful of townsfolk noticed him sitting
at the window of his room, looking down on the town, and then looking
off to the mountains in the distance, as though he was committing both
scenes to memory, possibly setting up a route of railroad tracks firmly in
his mind ... around a rim of the mountains, down along the river, and
out onto the wide grass coming up against Westlynne.

In reality, Corbett Wilson, as he had registered in the hotel book,
was getting a feeling about the town that had hung his kid brother.

Two nights later, after several incidents in the town and at the
Wild Horse Saloon, the sheriff said to him. "You come with a lot of
trouble in your saddle bags, mister. You're running the plow low and the
land's all gone dry around you."

Wilson, who had raised some agitation with certain people over
past incidents, said, "This is a town born for trouble, Sheriff, and most of
it hasn't come by yet."

Sheriff Chrysler realized it was more a threat than an off-hand
remark; he'd found a load of sincerity in Wilson's tone and in his eyes
when they closed down. They made him wonder what the young man
was seeing in the back of his mind, what images clawed for attention.

"How come you keep asking questions all over town, Wilson,
getting people upset about old stuff? Let's face it, we grow so fast here,
like your railroad coming along some day, that history gets left behind in
a big hurry. Nothing much in the past can help us today. We got to ride
and rope and dig our way every day. It's dirty work. It's hard work."

"You're not kidding it's dirty work, Sheriff, and there's a whole
lot more coming this way. There's more than a loud steam engine
coming down the line. You can bet the pot on that." It wasn't the image
that had collared Wilson's mind, for there had come to him the words
spoken at a line camp not more than a month earlier:

The day's work was done. Loose cattle run into a box canyon. Breaks in a fence fixed. A fire lit outside the canyon as the stars began to appear, the brightest one coming first and low on the horizon. The hired cowpokes talking around the fire, the coffee pot set for pouring. Corporal Jameson, an old hand for the ranch, said, "This is the end of it. The boss is makin' one more drive and then sellin' out to Purdy. He's going back to Chicago before they have to ship him back, like that kid I heard of up in Westlynne who got hung for killin' the girl he loved, but some people I know don't think he did it. They buried him on boot hill 'cause they didn't know where he was from. Was kinda close-mouthed, as I heard it. They left him for a couple of hours hangin' there, on the rope, like he was a bounty critter. Could have been all day for that matter, far as I know. 'Magine that, hangin' like a pelt in the sun and no one to cut him down, them folks all drinkin' in the saloon. Don't say much for dyin' there, even if no place is good for dyin'."

"You hear the kid's name?"

"All I heard was 'Garret' and don't know anything else, like if it was first name or last, but maybe he was about 22. Yup, maybe 22 and a good looking kid the girl loved. Oh, yuh," he added, "they said he could break horses like he was born for it."

He had summed up a life.

"No," the other man had quickly said. "Not 22. Only 20." And he left the fire and got his saddle and his horse and left the fire at the line camp.

All the events of that sad and gruesome day of the past had been relayed to him by a few more friends at the ranch and out on the trail. He had started out for Westlynne in the early hours of the following morning.

On the way he turned over a lot of things on his mind, and recollected the special ones, all the way back to his early days.

"There's always tendin' to be done," their father had said. He'd said it at a hundred campfires on the drives, a hundred times in the kitchen around the old iron stove or the stone fireplace, both giving off the crackling sounds of wood popping and splitting from its own heat.

"There's always tendin' to be done. You always owe somebody in this life, from your mother's first pains, to those who ran you right into this day." He was a big man, raised on hard work, his hands and shoulders and forearms showing what they had reaped from his labors. A hard, square firmness sat about him as he talked, as if to say, "You better believe what I'm sayin', 'cause I've been where you're goin' and it ain't easy gettin' there."

He'd pause to look into the eyes of his sons, like a doom master was afoot in the firelight, and carry on with his message.

"Don't forget who gave you a hand, who gave you a lift when it was needed. They could've kept goin' wherever and left you lookin', so don't forget none of them when it comes to tendin'. They made the difference. And it binds us like the best leather made, like the best rope we can twist."

Once arrived in Westlynne the first move Corbett Wilson had decided on was to take a look at Mel Bartlett's ranch, and make Bartlett and those around him think the railroad was coming across their grass. The land was already changing; and it would change some more. The railroads were seeing to that all over the country, and heading all the way to the Pacific and the coastal states beyond the mountains.

Bartlett, being introduced, said, "My foreman says you want to look over my ranch. That you're a railroad man coming ahead of the tracks, looking for the best place to put them down. We've been waiting a long time for some railroad action out this way. We knew it was coming sometime after we heard rumors and whispers coming down the range. Just had to come. Glad you came by. I'll be very interested if the proposition is right." His smile was a thorough one, coming on like it was lard in the skillet, setting the pace for cooking.

Wilson, still in the saddle, his face posed at quizzical, said, "Are all your papers in good order? Your claim? The land office records you're supposed to have on hand? I can't work without them being in good order. I can't make an offer if there's any doubt. Too many places around here are looking for a chance to get the railroad across their spread. They know what changes will come to them. I'm sure you understand that."

"No problem," Bartlett said. "Everything is tight as a noose. No loop holes. Cinched true and tight. All the signatures in place and been there for a spell." There was an instant pause in his voice. "Or the one signature that's really needed, my daughter's when she signed the place over to me. It had been her mother's place."

"Oh," Wilson said, more puzzled than before. "How did she get it? Inherit it? Buy it? Win it in a card game?"

"Hell, no," Bartlett said. "That woman was a damned Apache I had to take the strap to a few times. Straighten her out. Get her in order. But she'd been married before." He shook his head with a quizzical shake. "Why I married that woman I'll never know. Well, I can say she was the most beautiful woman I ever saw, Indian or no Indian. Apache or no Apache. As beautiful as they can come to a tribe. And I stole her from some kind of chief, from what I heard. Always wagging that in front of me, and trouble from the first day."

His smile was a rudimentary clue in giving away inside information, and Wilson would like nothing better than to play poker against him.

"Why'd your daughter sign them over? She sick or generous or with the family's best interests? I'd like to meet her sometime."

Bartlett wasn't about to be knocked off his stride. "She's dead," he said. "Some saddle tramp shot her one night. I never did like that prairie rat, sneaking in here at night to see her, or getting her to sneak out, but I caught them and scared him off. But he came back one night and she was out in the barn to meet him and he must have thought she was someone else and plain killed her on the spot. We grabbed him and his smoking pistol and stood up against him in court and he was hung the way he ought to be."

Wilson, showing great interest in the events, said, "You gents were right on the spot, ready to protect the ranch and all your possessions, from what I can see. That's real interesting, and you got the murderer's gun for evidence. You should be a detective or at least the sheriff. I can see that you'll protect the railroad interests out this way. I'll make sure that information gets sent along to my boss who's the one that'll make the decision on where the new tracks'll go. And he'll handle the money side of things too."

The curious railroad man said, "What does the law do with a weapon that's used in a crime, and is solid evidence? Do they put it on display? Hang it up for the whole town and any new potential killers to take a gander at and think things over before pulling the trigger? Do they make sure it gets sent to the family of the killer or sold off or what? That kind of stuff is real interesting to me."

"Oh, no," Bartlett said. "The sheriff gave it to me and I have it inside to remind me of a real bad night around here."

Wilson said, "A regular Peacemaker, I'd guess. Can always be used by someone."

"Not a Colt. No sir. It's a Remington, Army model. Sits on the shelf in the house. Keeps me aware of what's all around us."

"The killer's gun, huh?"

"That's it. That's what we call it, me and my boys."

Riding back to town, Wilson kept thinking of all the things Bartlett had said. The first one he'd talk to would be the sheriff again, but from a new angle. In town, he went right to the sheriff's office.

Corpus Chrysler, sheriff, saw Wilson coming down the street, and didn't like the feeling that had come over him since Wilson came into town. The feeling mounted as Wilson reined up in front of his office.

"I've been out to the Bartlett place, giving it the look-over and discussing the possibilities of a purchase with Bartlett. I had a good talk with him about things in general."

Wilson sat on the edge of the sheriff's desk, as much an intruder as a visitor.

Chrysler felt his nerves and muscles tighten and a ball of doubt sink low in his gut. The room seemed smaller, the walls closer than he thought. His breathing pattern unveiled a change in him and he spoke haltingly. "He tell you how they caught the killer red-handed, that Byrnes kid, a saddle tramp."

"Sure did. And he told me you gave the killer's gun to him, like a souvenir. But it was a Remington Army model and not a Colt Peacemaker, which most cowpokes carry these days."

"Yup. Least I could do with the gun that killed his girl. Besides, Byrnes had no family around here. Like I said, just a saddle tramp trying to get closer to a good grub stake for the future."

"Ever think the kid might be a relative of those Byrneses down by Cavalry Valley, the ones who own the whole valley almost? If he was he sure wouldn't need any grub stake." He shook his head in mock disgust and put another round in his irony. "You give him the killer's belt and holster, too? Those are nice presents." The facetious remark went right over the sheriff's head.

"No," Chrysler said, "not the holster or the belt. They're still hanging right there on the hook." He pointed to a belt and holster hanging on an iron hook beside a rifle rack. "Been there ever since they brought the kid in for trial. Ain't been moved."

"You sure they're the ones they brought in?"

"Damned sure. Why do you ask?"

"I can see from here, Sheriff, that that holster ain't no holster for a Remington. That's a Peacemaker holster, and that belt was made by Fitzpatrick down in Chilchester. I can tell from the work done on it."

He smiled an insider's smile, and said, "Looks just like mine, don't it?"

Standing beside the desk, he showed Chrysler his belt that was near identical to the one hanging on the iron hook. Then he turned sideways and showed him his holster. It too was a twin to the one hanging with the belt.

The air in the room changed further; it had cooled down, getting icy, but heat was rising in the sheriff's gut. It was like a branding iron had been applied to his stomach. He was slowly coming apart, for all this time he had had questions, but couldn't face up to them. Couldn't bring them to light. Now, he knew, it was all catching up to him, him and his soft stance on the murder of Bartlett's daughter. And him knowing all the time she was not Bartlett's real daughter. That fact had drawn up his interest in the beginning, but he'd let it fall to the side; it would have certainly lead to dangerous and highly unthinkable grounds.

Chrysler said, "You know more than you're letting on, don't you? You're playing with me now. I don't know a whole lot, only what was told me and said in court under oath. In front of the judge and the jury."

Wilson came right after him. "What did the kid say at the trial?"

"Said a shot came from behind him. She got hit. He yelled out that she was dead."

Wilson continued, "Then they come up behind him? Grabbed him? Called him a murderer? Said he murdered the girl he loved? That it?"

"That's the whole of it. There were three of 'em that swore to it. Bartlett and two of his hands."

"What are their names?" Wilson's voice, the sheriff was sure, carried a threat in it if answers were not forthcoming.

"Chad Burling's the foreman," the sheriff said convincingly, like he was prodded or whipped into line. "And the other was his regular saloon sidekick with him, Hank Waitte, a big redhead and mean as they come. Appears to me to be Burling's watchdog. One of 'em's got the voice, that's Burling, but the other's got the gun, the fast gun. I seen him once on a posse, being mean as they come."

His face showed what was mounting in his stomach, coming along the route of all his nerves. And his eyes began to twitch, with the expression on his face undergoing changes, rapid changes.

Wilson read him easily, as though his cards were dealt face up, and pressure could be applied in a number of ways. He went right at him again. "You're part of it now, Sheriff. Have been since the first, but now I know, too. You're not alone in this anymore. It's just like you finally got it figured out, ain't it? And there's going to be a few trade-offs made here, between you and me."

There had come the revelation, the opening. The wedge had been slipped into place, presenting the chance to wipe the slate. The sheriff felt better.

Not yet done and as smooth as an old prison interrogator, Wilson jumped in with the clincher, "Now's your chance to get back on the good side, Sheriff, where you should have been all the time. Both of us know the Byrnes kid didn't kill the girl he loved, but someone did and made him the only suspect. You can see now how that was arranged, can't you?"

In a move as old as forever, Wilson dropped a condescending hand on the sheriff's shoulder, locking up the new union. He made it as tight as an Indian drum when he said, "We would have been a great team right from the beginning, Sheriff, if we started out from the same stall. That's my solemn word on it."

The new tandem in the cause of Garret Byrnes cornered their first suspect in the case at the Wild Horse Saloon that evening when Hank Waitte entered and they ran him into a back room before his drinking pal showed up. Hank Waitte's bravado soon disappeared when the sheriff introduced Wilson.

"This gent's real name is Gavin Byrnes, the oldest brother of the kid who was hung for a murder he didn't commit and which was arranged by you-know-who. He's got all this written down in those papers he's writing in now. It's the whole story right up to now with only a few pieces missing and you got one chance to get a break in the whole thing. All we want to know is who planned it, who said it first, who set it up, who pulled the trigger on the Remington that was supposed to be the kid's gun, but really wasn't. And by the way, where's the kid's Peacemaker? Who took that? Where's it at now?"

Chrysler turned to Gavin Byrnes and said, "You got all that written down 'cause now we're going to get some real answers?"

The steel in Byrnes' eyes was enough for the disarmed Hank Waitte.

"Bartlett planned the whole thing," Waitte said. "Faked the girl's signature on those papers of his, said he hated her and she wasn't his real daughter and knew some Indian used to slip into the barn when he wasn't around. Figured that Indian was the father, so it didn't bother him none until the railroad thing came up. And she owned the land from her mother from way back and he killed her, the mother, maybe five years ago. Got her caught in a rock fall that he rigged on his own. He faked the girl's signature right after she died from that shot."

Waitte was unloading years of dirty work, and Gavin Byrnes was writing it all down.

He let Waitte run his mouth.

"Bartlett knew the kid was sneaking in to visit the girl, at night, like maybe the mother's Indian friend was doing for who knows how long, and we caught them in the middle of you-know-what, in the barn. Burling shot her with a gun that Bartlett gave him, the Remington, his gun. Now Bartlett's got the kid's gun. Wears it on his own belt."

Byrnes hadn't stopped writing in the papers he had put down on a table, the lamp shining on them, where Waitte could see the load of evidence piling up, and the penitentiary coming down the line for him if he didn't get a break.

"What happens now?" Waitte said.

Gavin Byrnes said, "There's a few of the kid's brothers coming this way to straighten things out. We're going to take Garret Byrnes home after we get everything squared away. We're going to do more for this town than any railroad that might come along, but the railroad isn't coming near here anytime in the near future.

He stuffed the papers under his shirt, ready to meet his brothers and finish up some "business that needs tendin'."

You know the rest, all the way from Crown Point, Indiana and Sgt. Stan Kujawski, once of the First Cavalry in the Pacific and the 31st Infantry Regiment in Korea, and known as The Automatic Wrist from call sign Easy Street Six at Lake Hwachon in the Iron Triangle, 1951.

The Ace of Jacks

John Bevans Tailback came on the scene in lower Wyoming Territory when he was fifteen years old, riding into the town of Looping Wells, looking for the two men who murdered his mother and father in cold blood over the last loaf of bread in her oven. He told the sheriff what had happened, all the details including the descriptions of the two men he had seen on that unforgettable day four years earlier.

He had grown well.

"I have not forgotten their faces, their deeds, or their hunger at eating my mother's last loaf of bread while she and my father lay dead on the floor and I was under the curtain on the sink where my mother had shoved me when she saw one of the men sneak up on my father from inside the barn, hit him on the head and drag him into our cabin."

The sheriff studied the boy, saw him a determined, though young man who had been range-bred. He had sturdiness about him, and a good deal of confidence. His eyes, the sheriff additionally thought, were a serious matter, appearing as though they held the answer to many questions before they were asked. He was sure that was true of some searches, this current one to be resolved by the young one most likely on his own. He was as dark-haired as the ace of spades, with blue-green eyes that might toy with a girl, or even a lady, and two walnut-handle pistols hung loose on his belt.

To the sheriff, on a second look, Jack Tailback emerged older than he gave evidence.

"Son," the sheriff said, "you leave this to the law. I'll try to have some kind of poster made up and have it hung proper and move it around the territory. I want you to go off and let us work on it. Tell me where you'll be so I can contact you." Then sipped at his beer, shrugged his shoulders with either disdain or futility. The boy was sure his words had fallen on the deaf ears of a man too busy to pay him any mind.

"Well," said Tailback, "if you're about chasing them gents, you're bound to come across me 'cause I'm starting now to really look for them. I'll travel the whole territory for them, inside and outside, making the great circle of towns around Looping Wells until they're dead, hanged, shot or run down by a cattle stampede, whatever comes first. If I'm there first, they'll be dead."

"You go killing anybody without a trial and we'll rig one on you, son. You be careful."

"They'll draw on me first, sheriff," he said, "so it'll be self-defense." With that no sooner out of his mouth, he whipped one of his guns from its holster and fired a round the full length of the saloon and hit smack dead in the middle of a picture of a singer scheduled to come into town in a few weeks.

The law was impressed, and the young man left Looping Wells, heading west.

Tailback, en route to the next town on his list, reflected on the things he had told the sheriff and those that he hadn't even mentioned, letting them sit back there in his mind like secrets of the dead. One of them came at him often. Unmistakably he kept hearing the words, "Clean sleeves, clean sleeves," and wondered why they were so important and yet so irregular an expression in cow country where every horseman worked long and hard and unworried about clean sleeves except when coming out of a mountain spring as the year warmed up. Those men were the drovers, ranch owners, stage drivers, freighters, sheriffs, marshals and just about every deputy they might have dropped a swearing-in ceremony on. Others, like bank tellers, whose hands and wrists were constantly in sight of customers, like gentle women, ladies of a town, perhaps would be the only ones who cared for "clean sleeves."

One other sign struck his eyes on a boot no more than a foot from his face as he tried not to breathe too heavily under the sink where his mother had hidden him. It was on one boot, no spur attached, but a small quarter moon with an arrow through it. That sign he burned itself into his mind.

"Things to lead me," he said as he rode. "Things to lead me, to keep in mind." He'd slap his gun at such moments, feeling the shot of energy and revenge as it flashed through him. His mother's face he had seen often, but such times as these, with the revenge running amuck inside him, his hand slapping the butt of his pistol, he saw, almost clearly, the full face of his father; the stitched, curved lip where a cow had kicked him, the slight mound over one eye from another accident, the wide ears that seemed to shoot out under his sombrero, the near-flat ridge on his nose, and the kindest, warmest and saddest eyes he had ever seen on a man.

He wondered why and could not figure it out.

In Benton's Mark, a small settlement on his route, he stayed a full day, right through to when the quiet hours came around at last in the Gray Dog Saloon. That stay included a talk with the sheriff that revealed nothing but a "Good luck, kid."

After a decent sleep in the livery, courtesy of the owner, he started anew on his search. The next in line, Wilford Springs, sat on the widening circle of towns he had marked out. The little town sat pretty as a picture as he looked down from a good-sized hill that broke up the trail. The sun, well before noon, sat on the town like an embrace, pulling

94

all its parts into the one golden sweep of the sun. Light glistened on some windows, shot away on others at different angles, almost said hello to him from others.

From his view he saw a single rider alone on the wide grass, not too far from the town, like a daily ride for exercise. After watching the rider, he sensed it was a girl from some unexplainable quarter telling him it was obvious. She rode lightly, now and then spurred the horse into a flat-out stretch of speed, and seeming satisfied with some exhilaration, like waving her hat and letting out a yell, she'd rein the horse to a slow trot.

She looked like she was having herself a fun day. She drew his curiosity.

Slowly he rode down toward her, and kept waving his hat to get her attention. He did so and she drew her horse to a stand-still, eyeing him all the way, but not showing any fright ... not in the peak of the day, in the middle of the grass, the sun behaving too good for her, the breeze as tender as new buds, her horse able to run with full speed to evade any problems on such a nice day.

"Hi," he said, quickly adding, "you look like you're having a whole bale of fun so early in the day, and that horse goes pretty fast when you want him to, doesn't he?"

"Sure does," she said, her face a beauty of a face with full-up blue eyes, lips so pretty like they were begging for a kiss, and her complexion not a beaten-down, wind-worn, sunburned layer of flesh. She appeared slim, young, of his age, friendly, but could bolt seriously if she had to in a second. "Where are you coming from? You going to Wilford Springs?" she said and quickly added, "'cause if you ain't, you're sure going to bump into it."

Her smile lit up the prairie even brighter than he had first determined it to be.

He decided not to hold back anything because he did not want to spend it uselessly. He had no time for romance, or its approach he had decided earlier, though she had started a warm buzz inside him.

"Well, my name's Jack Tailback and I'm on a search for two murderers, and I aim to sweep the whole territory for the next ten years, or forever, looking for them but it's not going to take that long, I just feel it."

"What did they do?" There was real interest in her voice, and her eyes said the same thing.

"They killed my Mom and Dad about four years ago. My Mom hid me under the sink and told me to keep quiet and not move. Next thing one of them brings my Pa inside and drops him on the floor, my Ma screams and they shoot her and eat the last loaf of bread she had in

95

the oven, stuffing themselves and going off and leaving my folks on the floor. I haven't forgotten it. Not for one minute, though I feel guilty as hell about not doing anything then, that's why I'm doing it now."

"What could you do when you were so young? How old are you?" Her face stood forth as the saddest he had seen since he began telling his own sad tale.

"I'm going on sixteen, in a few weeks."

"Oh," she said, "I'll be sixteen, too, in about three weeks. My name is Eva Valley Phillips. That's horrid what they did. I hope you catch them and see them strung up by the neck."

She dwelled a moment on his lashes; curling and black as the ace of spades, she thought.

"I might shoot them first, if I run into them. Only reason I'm out here is to look for them. Find one at a time or both at once."

"So you must know what they look like, if you peeked out from under that curtain your Ma had around the sink."

"I know them right to some of their scars, what they wear, stuff like that. How one's eyes are set on the side of his nose like they were dropped from someplace up high in a close grip, but not heaven, for sure." He paused, looked at her with a tender look, and asked, "What do you do out here alone besides running around and having fun?"

"I like to get some of the good air, get some exercise for me and my horse, and see nice things growing out here. The nice scenery. So I'm always looking for a nice scene or a nice flower to sketch. I really like to sketch. I can fill up a book with some things. My Pa says I'm a natural and can't imagine where it comes from." She laughed at some inside joke she did not share.

"That sounds like fun," he said. "I'd like to see some of that sometime."

"I'll show you if you really want to see them." She was pink in the face as she said it.

Then a single thought must have hit both of them.

Tailback asked, "Do you draw faces?"

She said, "Oh, I've done my folks several times. My father always says that's how he looks, but my mom says she looks different than I sketch her. Says she's younger looking, and I think she says that to please my father, and my father says what he says to please me."

And her face widened in sudden amazement as she said, "Oh, my goodness, I just had the same thought you did. You tell me what they look like and I'll sketch them, both of them, those horrid men, until you're sure I've done them right."

She shivered slightly, closed her eyes, and uttered slowly, "I'd love to do it. I really, really would." She looked at his black lashes again, but not so as he could notice.

A bond had been impressed on young souls.

Eva's parents, as part of their western code, invited to dinner the young man when their daughter explained all the circumstances.

Eva's father, Barney Phillips, said, "If you met up with either one of those scoundrels, Jack, could you handle the situation?"

"Yes, sir," said Jack. "Both of them together or one at a time, makes no difference to me."

"But it might to them," Eva said, and Tailback knew exactly how she meant that observation. He felt warm all over all over again.

There came some discussion of his problems in life, but the parents managed to skirt much of the murder, only hoping the fiends would be caught and be treated as they had acted. After dinner, the two young ones sat on the front porch, Eva with a board in her lap, pencils at hand, and a bubble of energy to get on with the task.

"Tell me again, Jack," she said, "about the one with the eyes dropped from on high." She added a humorous look to her countenance and let it speak for her knowledge that it did not issue from a holy throne. "Tell me what else they looked like, and the color of the pupils and the eyelashes and eyebrows and every single thing you can remember. If we get the eyes down right, I think all the rest will come after a few different views, and mostly about nose and chin and how the lips looked when he made a face or cursed or whatever."

They sat on the porch for a few hours, by themselves, her father coming out only once to bring a lamp as evening thickened, but never once looking at what his daughter so far had sketched.

Once, in the middle of things, he said, "Make this happen in the sketch; make his sleeves clean or neat or how they might bother a gunman if his sleeves are messy or his cuffs might get tangled in his gun play. I don't know why I remember that, but he kept saying he had to get another shirt, his sleeves were messy. He looked in my father's clothes and there weren't any with sleeves clean enough to steal. It might mean something and it might not, but I'll keep my eyes open."

And with the darkness descending on top of a series of descriptions of chin and mouth and lips and ears from Jack's memory, and how one scar made a left cheek stick out like a signboard all on its own, and one arm drawn under the face as it might have been folded, the sleeve of the shirt neat and trimmed, Jack suddenly leaped up and shouted, "Oh, Eva, Eva, that's him! That's him!"

He held the sketch out in front of him, admired it as if he was in a museum, and kept exclaiming, "You did it! You did it."

The shouting and commotion brought Eva's parents out to check on them.

Young Jack first showed Mrs. Phillips the sketch, which brought a vile look of hate across her face.

When Eva held out the sketch to her father, he sat down, studied it for a few serious minutes and then said, quite loudly and with definite affirmation, "Jack, I know him. I know him, I'm sure. He's a hand at Thornwell's ranch, the Daisy D. It's in the next valley. He's been there over a year that I know of. Jake Thornwell says he's a decent worker, but not social at all and hardly liked by the rest of the boys. His name is Bouncer Ditson. At least that's what they call him. Some of them said he's mean as hell. Had some trouble once, I remember, about not going into town with the boys. Doesn't drink with them, they say, but goes off with a fellow from another ranch, just a guy named Londo and no other name, to see some Indian girls in the hills any chance they get. I guess that doesn't set well with some of their pards who have fought off some wild renegade Indians on several drives."

Tailback, standing as if at attention in the ranks, said, "I want to thank you folks for giving me a hand and letting Eva sit around with a complete stranger after having had supper at your table." He talked as if he was suddenly a lot older than "nearly sixteen."

A bit of difficulty came into his voice, but it wasn't indecision. "This day is the finest thing that's happened to me in a long while. I can't thank you enough, but I'll be leaving now."

He stood tall, and Eva thought handsome as he turned to her and said, "I'm so happy that I met you. You're a great rider, a great drawer of faces and the prettiest thing I about ever saw."

He shook her hand.

She kissed him on the cheek.

Her mother smiled in memory.

Her father said, "I can send a few of my boys with you, Jack. This might be a tough swing for you."

"No, thank you, sir. I've been this long hating a few people so I have to take care of it all at once, and alone, as best I can. I would like to come back and say hello again before I go on to wherever."

There arose a distinctive pause, and pre-announcement in his voice, as he said, "I've got to get shuck of this feeling of hatred. It sure doesn't help me here."

Eva said, "Wherever you're headed sure is not going to be far from here."

Both women, at that moment, loved the boy-man, Jack Tailback, for different reasons, as they would be perceived to a regular on-looker.

In a short time, Tailback learned a few things:

He sat for two days in the hills above the Daisy-D Ranch in the next valley, and prepared to leave as the sun started to set when he saw two riders leave the ranch and proceed not toward town, but into the foothills on his side of the valley. He had chosen a fairly secure position to keep watch on the valley; his horse was tied up nearby, hidden from just about all other vantage points, and provided free passage for him to travel in different directions.

The two men rode directly up into the lower hills and Tailback was able to see the trail they had chosen. The trail was now known to him as he had familiarized himself with the trails leading into a few Indian dwellings spotted in the hills. His observation of the riders provided him a view of the bulging saddlebags slung on their horses. He figured the bags contained presents or pay-off goods for the squaws they were bent on visiting.

The men rode slowly but steadily and Tailback followed them at a discrete distance, keeping back at turns in the trail, avoiding rises now and then by slowing down, assuming at one point where the trail split, that they were going to one small group of tepees he had seen earlier. It was situated in a corner of a small canyon protected on three sides by high cliffs.

Tailback kept patting his horse on the neck, saying, "Good boy, Pancho. Nice and easy, boy." They had been partners in this affair and he felt bound and bidden to treat him well. His thoughts were interrupted by Eva and her talent; she had captured the characteristics of both men quicker than expected. He thought her to be a genius, able to plumb his mind in such short order.

More than four years of hate and immediate revenge were near at hand; he could feel them rising in him, just as strong as they had risen years before.

The two killers, seemingly at ease in the small gathering of tipis, tied their horses off on a small tree, removed the saddle bags and advanced to two of the tipis, each one entering one of them. Nothing moved around the tipis, but off on a corner he saw older squaws at work on furs or hides of one sort or another.

From a new vantage point, closer than he had ever been to his parents' killers, he sat on a rock and thought over the situation. Eva kept intruding, and he figured she was telling him to be careful, to be sure, to come back to her. It helped him with some of the decisions bound in his prospects.

The evening wore on, drinking noises and hell-raising sounds came to him from both tipis, and eventually the shrill cries of women being abused swept across the clearing. What saddlebag contents could pay for abuse? What were the trade-offs? He could not imagine, but there lingered the way these two men had gulped down his mother's last loaf of bread from her oven, and her and his father dead at their feet.

Bouncer Ditson and Londo, the pair of them, at last were at hand.

Young Jack Tailback walked into the small group of tipis, the noise still audible, nobody moving to help anybody in pain or in trouble, the names Bouncer Ditson and Londo sitting like poison in his throat, on his tongue, held back from his lips lest he be further cursed.

The weight of the names held him back only for a short time.

Then he let it all go:

"Hey, you murderers. Hey, Bouncer Ditson, hey Londo. You pokes remember you killed my parents and ate the last loaf of bread from her oven while her and my Pa lay dead on the floor, right at your feet?"

He waited, his hands loose, his heart eager.

No response reached him.

He stepped to the side, behind a rock, and the silence continued.

"Hey," he yelled. "You guys afraid of a kid? C'mon out and face me and my guns. C'mon cowards. C'mon." He had stepped forward, both guns in his hands.

Still no answer.

He walked deeper into the area, waiting for one or the other to make a move, shoot from one of the tipis, and try to slip out through an open flap while shooting all the way.

Nobody moved, so he shot at the top of one tipi. The bullet shattered the tip of a pole. Debris flew apart from the pole.

"No shoot! No shoot!" It was a female voice from one tipi, and was immediately followed by the same words from the second tipi.

"No shoot! No shoot!" came again from the first tipi. "They are dead. We have seen you. We know you are not friends. We have killed them. Both cruel. Both mean. It was time for death. This one here die changing his shirt, looking away from me."

Two young females, of rare beauty, slipped out of the tipis, their hands thrown out in front of them seeking supplication.

Tailback said, "Are they both dead?"

"They are dead," each one confirmed.

As though a kite was lifted on high, Jack Tailback felt a fierce energy leaving him, fleeing upward. And he discerned a note of freedom on the faces of the young Indians, two maidens finally cut loose from their terrors.

There was an undeniable understanding struck between the three of them, and with the two dead men hauled out of the tipis and identified by Jack Tailback as the killers of his parents without a single doubt: the faces he remembered, the half-donned shirt on one man telling a story, along with eyes so close to his nose they might have come from one place in one grasp. Each of his boots carried a small crescent moon with an arrow through it.

The signs all falling in place.

A sudden flare of intelligence hit him; since he met Eva, since she committed her talent and drawn the sketches, he no longer needed to clutch at bad memories.

In a twist of justice he quietly ignored the apparent deep wounds that had killed the men and did not see the weapons of mercy that had been employed. Nor did he bother to search for them.

He couldn't wait to tell Eva what had happened. And he didn't have to tell the sheriff at Looping Wells where he was or what he was up to.

Not at all.

He might say his search was over.

The Barkeep and the Kid

He had been there, under the bar in the Dead Horse Saloon, in Fairly, Nevada, for six days on his hands and knees, resting occasionally on his butt. Sleep came to him fitfully at times, hunger soon assuaged, thirst tended, while anger and revenge sat on his plate like a sirloin steak. He would not leave, and Max Turcotte, the bartender, for the kid's revenge, had run an auger through the bar front so he could see through to the front door when anybody entered. The boy could remain hidden while he watched for the man who had killed his parents.

Turcotte, at odd turns and idle times at the spigot, slipped food to Alfie Briscomb, just turned eight years old, a drink of water once an hour as soon as the evening came on. And once, on a dare from under the bar and thinking he might put the kid to sleep, slyly offered him a half glass of beer. The boy sipped on it for half the night.

At the finish of the third day, when the door was closed and all the cowpokes had disappeared and the card shark had no players at his table, Turcotte again lifted the boy in his arms and carried him, sound asleep, to Turcotte's room in the back of the saloon. Something down in Turcotte's gut rooted for the kid, saw him victorious in some rare occurrence, like a duel out front and the whole town looking on as the murderer of the kid's parents went down from the cleanest shot the town had ever seen. Turcotte wasn't a praying man, as he would allow, but the High Name started to cross his lips late at night.

Alfred Briscomb and his wife Nonnie had purchased a small spread from the local hustler of all opportunities, Drew Bantry, and immediately felt the threats to safekeeping coming from many directions; cattle were rustled or plain shot dead in the far end of the ranch, old fences broken down, a small garden of vegetables trampled in darkness, and Alfred Briscomb, late at night on guard, shot one of three men from his saddle as they came too close for comfort with flaming torches.

All might appear as unwritten parts of the sale agreement.

The death of the man, commonly thought to be one of Bantry's hired guns, did not slow things down, but brought a gang of riders back on another night in which Briscomb and his wife were killed, both of them from gunfire as they fought back from the front of their small ranch house. Young Alfie, safe underground in a place where his father had made the boy hide, saw through a slim opening in his hiding place the man who shot his father and then his mother, the man yelling at the other riders, "Bantry says there's a kid around here some'eres. Find him. Tear the place apart and find him." Riding wildly about the ranch house, he kicked over garden partitions and other obstacles in his way. Some of the riders had gone into the house and said nobody else was inside.

The obvious boss of the blackguards was an angry looking man, with a mustache as black as crow feathers on his mouth, a hat that was neither Stetson nor derby on his head but looking like a box, and a wide gun belt across his middle with a pair of white-handled pistols sitting prominent in their holsters. The man's gray shirt and black vest stretched across his chest, swelled by muscle and a large physique, and his horse was a large gray, a grand looking stallion, the boy thought, but carrying an ugly beast of a man.

Alfie, in one horrible breath, swore he'd recognize him the next time he saw him no matter where it was. He'd run for the sheriff or a deputy, get the man arrested, get him what was coming to him … capping it all off by saying, in a determined tone, "Or I'll shoot that barn rat down like a crazy dog or a horse with all his legs broke."

The promise burned in him strong as an ache, the kind of ache he had when his arm was broken by the mule with a vicious kick. "That, too, I'll remember forever." Both images stayed alive in the back of his head, "in my heart of memories," he'd said, and him knowing the improbable comparison.

This morning, when he woke up in Turcotte's room in a cot he had graduated to from a corner of the floor on the first night, the friendly bartender out and about business, he spotted the breakfast that had been left for him. Alfie ate it ravenously after the long night before under the bar, wondering if he would be here for a year or more waiting for the man with the funny hat, the mustache, and the white-handled pistols. How long would the bartender put up with him? Would both of them age here and the killer never show up? He shut his mind to such thoughts as quickly as he could, washed up in the bowl on the chest of drawers, and left on his morning ritual; the continual, day-long walk about the town, his eyes searching for the known and hated face under the funny hat.

Those were his days, like all his days.

But his nights belonged under the bar, peeking through the hole that Turcotte with the auger had drilled, every time a customer came into the saloon, every time new boots sounded out arrival, each new demand for whiskey waking him if he had dozed off.

Some men he knew by heart, the ones that came every night after work at some hard job to wet their throats. They had the same sound to their boots, now and then a click of expectancy as they might have pre-celebrated the first drink of the day, or a familiar yell, in the same tone, to Turcotte behind the bar, his smile a welcome for all thirsty men.

Now and then there'd be a strange face that he would ignore as soon as he identified it as uninteresting; unknown strangers had no place in his life, not from where he sat under the bar, not from what seized his mind every time the door opened.

So he was now eight days there, in that secret lookout spot, his routine the same with each day and each night, with his continued dependence on Turcotte for unflinching support, when he stiffened under the bar just as Turcotte was about to hand him a drink of water. The bartender, alert every moment, saw the reaction and looked up to see the man that Alfie had described several times, though the description might fit many men that Turcotte had seen while behind the bar.

Alfie started to scramble out from under the bar and Turcotte thrust his open hand down and pushed him back under the bar. "Stay there, Alfie, lest he shoots me, then run like hell."

The boy froze in his place, and Turcotte said in his usual voice, "What'll it be, stranger?"

The stranger dropped his hands on the bar, thrust his chest as if making a statement of stature, and said, "Top shelf for a thirsty dog. It's been hell out there."

"Comin' right up," Turcotte said as he swung his hand under the bar and selected a special bottle of his best stuff, hardly cut at all. "Drivin' cows makes any man dry in the throat."

He poured the drink and was about to put the bottle back when the stranger said, "Best leave it there. I got a good thirst from the road. No cows for me. All road stuff." He winked at the bartender.

"I figure you never been here before 'cause I remember my customers and 'specially what they like to drink." He tapped the bottle. "That's good stuff for a dry man. Where you been? New here, I'd guess. Seen any of the country hereabouts?"

Alfie understood what Turcotte was up to, and still wanted to get up and run for the sheriff. But Turcotte's hand was still splayed wide against his face, urging him to stay in place. Then Turcotte said, "You got interest in property hereabouts?"

"I sure do," the stranger said, "'n' more than you can guess."

Somehow Alfie knew what the stranger really was saying, and really wanted to get the sheriff in a hurry. But Turcotte still had his hand on him, holding him back.

The door swung open and another man entered and walked directly to the bar and said to the stranger, "I walked around like you said I should and ain't seen no kid yet. You sure you heard right about him, Edger?" To Turcotte he said, "Give me a glass of that stuff."

The stranger, now known as Edger, issued a hard order to the newcomer. "You finish that drink and get lookin' again. He's abouts, that I was told straight out by Bantry. Don't want them other fellas gettin' us into somethin' we don't need. We get done what we come to do, then we'll get outta here."

The door opened and a gang of men entered and Turcotte said, "C'mon and belly up, Sheriff, you gents must be plumb dried out after your posse run. You catch them critters yet?"

He pushed the bottle toward the sheriff as the members of the posse lined up at the bar. "I'll get glasses for the lot of you."

The sheriff replied to Turcotte's query in a tired voice. "We ain't caught sight of 'em yet, Max. Like they disappeared right in front of us and left a trail that's still goin' a hundred ways."

Turcotte, in his years behind the bar, had seen arrests made in front of him on many occasions, but usually from a bandit too drunk to know that he was giving himself away to the law. This was different, and he was standing right behind the lone witness to a double murder. He recalled old Dutch Haggar standing directly in front of him, saying in a loud whisper, "That damned bank man was makin' too much noise for me, so I just whacked him on the head with my gun and he went crashin' over like he was a tree axed down. Poor fella hit his head on the way down and that was all we needed to get away, but hardly worth it, all that trouble." And Turcotte saw him hung the next day after the trial.

But this Edger fellow in front of him, standing almost in the sheriff's lap, wasn't about to say what he had done to the Briscombs, man and wife and Alfie's folks. Turcotte had to arrange what he could to keep Alfie, the only witness, off the front end of a gun.

He poured drinks for the posse and replied to the sheriff in an off-handed manner, as though he was really telling a lie to liven up the party, like it was Tell-a-Lie night at the Dead Horse Saloon. "Sheriff, I ever tell you about the last posse I was on, chasin' down Lucas Smacker and his boys who had killed them folks at the Hart Ranch down old Tuscalla way, shot them plain an' dirty and them just asettin' on their porch? Why, we chased them fellas like they was on a damned merry-go-whirly contraption and they crossed their trails so many times we got dizzier than 'em and lost 'em and found 'em so many times we couldn't say if they was them or us."

The sheriff laughed and the posse laughed and Edger and his pard laughed and Turcotte laughed loudest at his own story and made sly eyes at the sheriff and looked at Edger as he did so, and said, "Yes, sir, we didn't know who we was and who they was and for all we couldn't know we might have been havin' a damned drink with 'em and not even knowin' it at the end of our ride. Course, we came in not catchin' the damned outlaws we was lookin' for all the time, bein' so dumb as we was."

The sheriff, at some moment in his tired wisdom, the whiskey making him suddenly alive, feeling a thought being born where it had not been, figured he was being told some fact he ought to give heed to. He slid a solitary, careless, quick-glancing look at the two other men at the bar, looked back at Turcotte who winked the slyest wink he had ever let go.

The sheriff said, partly in his own gaiety of the story, "Well, for all of that, Mr. Turcotte, we'd still need the witness or witnesses to the affair to finish off the work in a most proper manner. Did you folks have that kind of luck in your story?" And he emitted a loud and uproarious laugh that collected all the others into it; Tell-a-Lie-Night at The Dead Horse Saloon in full gallop.

And when the laughter quieted down, and drinking began again in its way, Turcotte said, "Why, of course we did, Sheriff. We had that witness right at my feet and we ran the trial and the jury and the judge right into proper speed and them two killers was hung the next day."

The sheriff, now aware of what Turcotte was saying, and seeing the wave of a single small hand from down under the bar, as if some young one was saying, "I'm right down here and I swear to tell the truth," drew his revolver, stuck it in the face of the stranger called Edger, and said, "Don't move, Mister, or you're dead."

Alfie Briscomb leaped up from under the bar and said, in his loudest voice, "That's the man what killed my Ma and Pa, Sheriff, and I been waitin' here for him to come in so he could be arrested and hung for what he done to Ma and Pa."

And long-time bartender Max Turcotte, for the first time in his life, felt like a proud father.

The Colonel's Chagrin

In a dark room of his home, in Beverly, Massachusetts in the year of Our Lord 1908, a man died alone. The house, silent and chilly, had wrapped its cool arms about the man breathing slowly and labored, no caretakers immediately at hand, and none frankly wanted. His name was Edgar Charbonneau, retired colonel of the 4th Cavalry of the U. S. Army, last day of duty on the plains of Texas in 1885, after 37 years of service.

He was the saddest man in the world the day of his death, and the happiest that he was about to pay amends for all his bad deeds.

He had said, prayed, depended on a last statement: "Give me one day to make amends, Lord. I'll take an hour if that's all You have, or a minute to be spared this soul." It was as if an echo had been allowed to enter the room of his death.

For all we know at this point, he might have gotten his wish, or his wishes, but Charbonneau was remembered for a long time after his retirement, and quite often beforehand; some people of northwest Texas called him the Mad Dog of Llano Estacado, The Earl of Death at Blanco Canyon, The Red River Rogue. The castigation of names was endless, the meanings intentional and pointblank, extra weight for the hardiest soul, but especially for an old cavalryman from the Indian Wars of the Plains.

Edgar Charbonneau was a major at the Battle of the North Fork of the Red River in September of 1872, a battle between Comanche Indians and a unit of the U.S. Army's 4th Cavalry. Charbonneau's opponents were led by chiefs of the Comanche; Mow-way (Hand-shaker or One-Who-Shakes-Hands), along with sub-chiefs Tosawi (Silver Brooch) and Bowahquasuh (Iron Shirt). It was the army's first big hit at the fearful Comanche in the western panhandle of Texas, in a stretch of land about 40 miles long called Llano Estacado (the staked plain).

That singular campaign still resounds with the death of many women, children and old men, a mark that Charbonneau, to his last days, could not erase, his commiseration long and noteworthy for a decorated officer. Some observers at the time of the campaign voiced the concern that the battle was "only dredged up and carried out to bring a massacre down on the Comanche savages." The observations, from both military types and non-military types, weighed heavier on Charbonneau's chest than the cluster of medals and ribbons bestowed on him during his long service. It was reported that he quashed a commendation that he be awarded the Medal of Honor, berating a junior officer who had written a commendation, though two cavalrymen from the ranks were so awarded for actions in the same battle.

The long haunting in him all those years was cemented in place one fateful day when fighting slipped away from the edge of his command, and a mother and child, Comanche of course, were not only shot, but their bloods mixed by the end of a bayonet penetrating both souls as the mother tried to flee the battle scene. A drunken sergeant, nearly falling from his mount throughout the attack, stabbed them with one maddening trust and struggled to free the weapon. In anger, sadness, embarrassment, Charbonneau almost shot the man. The only thing saving him was the idea of losing his commission. Never forgotten was the quick and insidious bearing of the inner turmoil that wracked him then and all through his coming days, all of them.

Years after the battle, and after he retired, he went again with a son to visit the Llano Estacado. The son had refused too long making the visit, until it was obvious his father was bound to go alone, driven by an emotion he had not let go of.

The son had repeatedly denied his father, saying, "They were only savage Indians, Pa, sworn enemies who had killed many of your own comrades. You can't be sorry for them. Not now. Not ever."

"Don't you understand, Eric," Charbonneau replied, "I'm not sorry for them. I'm sorry for myself."

Such reasoning had not penetrated the son's thinking ... until that moment. It was July 17, 1900, in Llano Estacado, the temperature was 56°. Charbonneau felt the chill running through his body because the day before had been much hotter. At least he thought he'd found the reason; so did his son, until they both realized that many of the visitors to memorials in the area were staring at Charbonneau, not that they recognized him, but might have.

Those staring at him were, to a man, Indians of the Comanche nation.

One elderly Indian, in a wheelchair being pushed by a look-alike daughter or a granddaughter, asked him if he had ever been to Llano Estacado before. The Indian, wearing a scar across one cheek that he touched several times, showed no other battle reminders, though an aura, deeply perplexing, sat about him fully known but as hidden as heat from an iron stove.

Charbonneau was hard put to answer at first, until the Indian said to his daughter, calling her Yellow Moon Walking but in the old tongue, "He will answer when he's ready, Yellow Moon Walking, because he has the old eyes that I have. We have seen the Llano Estacado in the bad times. All strangers who are not strangers to Llano Estacado say so with their eyes."

His eyes had not moved from Charbonneau and had not even looked at Charbonneau's son.

The old Indian shifted in his seat, kept a stone face though his body was saying it harbored pain, and said, "I am called Bear Claw, and you are a cavalryman. Is that not so?" He held up an open hand, thumb tucked into his palm, showing the spread of just four fingers and Charbonneau understood him to be saying, and recognizing, the 4th Cavalry, the infamous enemy of the battle near McClellan Creek.

"I came here with the 4th Cavalry," Charbonneau said, his eyes again saying the words that were difficult to say. In a stiff moment of gathering himself, pulling harsh memory into place, the retired major and plains fighter said, "and I have carried the pain of those days with me as my personal baggage for all these years. I have kept the scenes of that time in my mind, and at night the pain comes back with each image."

His son's hand, in a subtle gesture, touched the shoulder of his father, and Bear Claw, in recognition of something hidden, said, "I have Yellow Moon Walking to help me with the pain as you have your son at this time." It was a revelation.

Bear Claw, aware of signs emanating from different sources about them, said, "I saw Chief Kai-Wotche and his wife at their dying. I escape with Mow-way, Shaking Hand way you say it, and he die long ago, fighting bear in mountains. His heart carry biggest wound before he meet bear on two legs. How did other cavalry riders manage getting old, those who ride off with you?"

The question was not perceived by Charbonneau to be a rebuking or castigating his old comrades. It was the way Bear Claw came at people, and it must have been the way, he thought, that Bear Claw fought his battles, straight on, heedless of danger and the ultimate that comes to warriors.

Though he saw that Bear Claw wore signs of battle, of age, he also noticed the Indian exhibited an unquestionable sense of awareness for an old man, Charbonneau figuring him to be older than he himself was. They had met again on the battlefield where they had brought arms to bear against the sworn foe, one believing in his war and the other not believing in his war.

Through the long afternoon on July 17, 1900, the new century picking them up and putting them together, a chill in the air that touched each of them in the same degree but not in the same manner, they talked. But after the early conversation, they talked no more of death, of pains that lingered, of the comrades who had long departed them, the battles, this life, until the evening crawled up to the edge of them.

When an owl made announcements, Bear Claw asked that they meet the next day, but earlier. "The owl says we old ones must prepare for night. Can we meet when the owl sleeps tomorrow?"

Colonel Charbonneau and Bear Claw departed with their escorts, the chill coming anew, owls calling around, and the moon standing still on a mountain top.

Eric Charbonneau said, in the comfort of their motel room, "That old Indian, that Bear Claw, does not seem to be a hated enemy. And he seems so bright for an old man, too."

"He's not an enemy any longer," Charbonneau said, "and perhaps he never was. Perhaps I am the only enemy in this affair, and I am trying to let it go."

Young Eric Charbonneau said, "He is so much aware of things that I do not see, cannot see, and might never see. I can say I am glad I never had to face him in a battle. Is he really that fearsome? Like he is a seer or a shaman or a medicine man from that other time and can pull tricks out of a hat. Does he possess something that we do not have? Can you find that in him, how he sees things we do not see?"

Charbonneau thought about his son's questions and his observations. "You must be right about him, Eric. I feel those things, though I wonder if my guilt brings them upon me."

Yellow Moon Walking, talking to her grandfather in a room with friends that evening, said, "The old colonel bears great guilt in his soul, and he exposed it all today. What will he say tomorrow when we meet again. We will meet again, won't we?"

"Yes, Yellow Moon Walking, we will meet again. The colonel is not relieved of all that he bears. He will meet us whenever he can as long as the guilt hangs upon him."

"I think you are right again, Grandfather, as always." The great smile crossed her face the way the moon first touched her. A light bronze beauty rode on her skin and her eyes, pale as a new shrub, a green shrub, also carried a glow.

The old warrior, wondering what the old cavalryman was doing at that very moment, found an inkling of it in his mind and knew it came from late images belonging to Llano Estacado.

The two old warriors, with their personal escorts and ready hands, came again for a few days of Eric Charbonneau's vacation before the trek by train was again undertaken to cross the whole country, back to the edge of the ocean where Atlantic mist rose each day, the old colonel hoping always it was trying to wash his soul, to cleanse it.

Bear Claw admitted he himself came each day to Llano Estacado memorials, the seen and unseen ones, to appease the spirits of the lost who might wander forever if not thought about, recalled in personal demands by the living, and brought out of the lost world for at least a few minutes of each day. "They are caught up in a strange world, and I am pledged to assist their journeys through time. That is my weight."

Charbonneau said, "Is it demanded of all your days without peace within, the same as within me?"

"Ah," Bear Claw replied, "it is said that if one man for one minute can clear worries, sins, guilt, and all the ponderous enemies from his soul, then for that one minute he has an edge on an hour. That is all one needs, an edge on an hour; and think what it promises for that man."

One old warrior shook his head again. "How do you know everything there is to know? Who taught you? The elders of your tribe?"

Bear Claw was silent for a few moments and then replied, "If I knew everything, I would have a place up beyond and would show you what is coming, for I do know the weight that lies on you. Is not for us to escape, but to endure for all others as long as we can, only then would we know everything there is to know, what comes at us in the end or," and he paused to look out over the sea of grass before he continued, "in the beginning."

Charbonneau, with a shrug of his shoulders, said, "But the punishment …?"

"You are right. We are prisoners, but we look for that one minute with an edge."

And so it was, in the mist of a morning beside the cleansing Atlantic, in a room in a house in Beverly, Massachusetts, on July 17, 1908, the retired colonel of the 4th Cavalry caught again the full words of Bear Claw, dead now for half a dozen years.

Neither old warrior had seen what had been coming around them. Or what was happening right in front of them. But it came now in the one clean minute prayed for and promised, the edge also being made on lifetimes with the unexpected but happy union of Yellow Moon Walking and Eric Charbonneau, both consigned to love, raising their children, paying continual homage to lost souls of Llano Estacado.

The Great Brunswick Relic Raid

The host of them, after a great fire destroyed much of their property in Wellesley, Massachusetts, headed west, for open spaces, free land and a new life. Joshua Weddles, a young 50, strong, adventurous, industrious, eventually led the seven wagons out of Missouri bound for the setting sun. They had taken a boat to New Orleans from Boston, gone up the Mississippi River to St. Louis, added some more river travel on the Missouri River to their land mileage, and arrived at Sedalia and a contact there for supplies, information, experience, living almost a year on the Osage Plain learning new ways of the new life.

Adaptation, Weddles knew, was a key to success in the new world.

Weddles was preparing them for their next life, in the far west, a life he envisioned would be a long struggle against their clutch at land, their good promises at work, their past to lend much to the future, both learned as well as lost. And a wish for new riches filled his mind, a shot at making the family a new dynasty.

The handsome elder of the family, dreams as well as hard work part of his vision, enjoyed the leadership responsibilities for the whole entourage. He could bribe with a smile or a slap on the back, and snap a whip at laggards, if any dared disrupt the aim of each day.

They ended up, seven wagons of them and their supplies, near the small town of Great Brunswick in Nevada, which was Spanish for "snowcapped Sierra Mountains," standing over them like sentinels.

"That's Nikninisht-ta Peak you're looking at," said the livery man, T. Collins, at the first stop on their arrival. The lot of them had been looking at the peak for a few days on their way in, and in a town that might be their destination they were still staring at the spectacle of it.

T. Collins went on relating. "They say, the Indians, that La-Tontinsht or Eagle's Face burned his woman up there when he caught her with a white man, a mountain man named Long Tom something or other, hauled wood through the snow to burn both of them. Nobody's ever found any sign, not that they went looking, but some of the mountain men have been up that way more than once. Hear them tell about it when they come down to civilize a while, catch up a clear throat, whomp the belly good."

Weddles, a thorough listener, a learner from any source showing signs of knowledge, paid heed to every word T. Collins said, and he had not yet completed his usual spiel. "That other one," and T. Collins pointed to the left of Nikninisht-ta Peak, "is Barren Widow's Plight but I can't say it the way the Indians do, them being Paiute or Sierra Miwok or some such. You can't hardly tell 'em apart except by the way they wear their hair or the way they dress. But it don't make no difference anyway 'cause they're still Indians no matter how they look, and I do admit Barren Widow's Plight does tell a story in itself that you can imagine all on your own," which meant to Weddles that T. Collins did not know it.

"I suppose that the Indians hereabouts," Weddles tossed into the conversation, "have a physical history attached to their long habitat here, like precious trophies you might call them, or souvenirs or relics that reveals more of their history, more definite evidence than mere talk. Sort of a lasting memory. Maybe a made-up museum of sorts, a collector's place. Something like that makes for special reverence, a true note on history on their tribe."

T. Collins nodded, aware that he knew more than any of the other folks in Great Brunswick about the Indians and their ways. He searched for the word and found it ... he was like a curator of their lore and now and then collared a lead on to a hidden portion of their past. He'd always promised himself that he'd get up there someday, take a good look.

"If you mean hidden treasure or sacred pieces from their past, I'd say yes in a minute. I've heard many stories about some hidden cache up in the mountains that no Indian would ever reveal lest some god swoop down on him and take his soul to hell or wherever the other place is for them. I suppose they're old squaw tales they entertain the young with, make them tribe proud and curious at the same time, but you never know the whip from the lash with them."

"Oh," Weddles queried, offhandedly, his eyes leveled in pure innocence as though he was no smarter than any others in town, "you mean you believe there really are relics or some kind of mementos, Indian-style, locked away up there someplace?"

His smile was the put-on smile of the salesman, the arguer, the manipulator stretching for a gain. He looked at Nikninisht-ta Peak first, the closest, then at Barren Widow's Plight and nodded his head wondering and doubtful at the same time, as if waiting for an answer, for the honest truth in the matter, if it was available, if it could find he revealed.

T. Collins came right back. "Not at Nikninisht-ta Peak. No siree. Not on a bet. They don't go near there at all, just in case Eagle's Face wouldn't like it. They're scared hell of his spirit hanging around up there waiting for people looking for reasons other than the truth about his woman and Long Tom. From what I understand he ain't never let go the anger he had that time, like there'd be no peace ever for him on her account and the mountain man, even though they might have been locked up by a storm wherever they was at."

113

"Then," Weddles inferred, "you mean what they have stashed away up there carefully for their history's sake, for the future, is at Barren Widow's Plight. Did I catch that correctly?" It was his way of buttering the bread at the right time, when the table was set, the company at ease.

But T. Collins, suddenly and intuitively alert, shifted in place, open-mouthed, realizing he was a plain old big-mouth caught up again in bravado. "Where'd you folks say you were from?" he said. "What brought you here?" His stance had changed abruptly, a grimace announced on his countenance like punctuation. It brought with it a return to his usual business ways, not giving away anything for nothing in return, or trying damned hard to do so.

"Well, thank you, sir, for the local history," Weddles replied. "Very interesting, I must say. My son Adam is a historian of some note, loving to know what brought us to where we are."

A small grin lurked self-consciously at the corner of his lips. "And I can clarify the reason for our arrival. We are here all the way from elsewhere and I am looking for a friend who settled here a number of years ago and we need directions to his place, if you have them, if you know of him. His name is Nathan Twombly. You know the man, sir?"

Weddles believed he was gifted in some ways, one of them knowing the answers to many questions before he posed them for anybody. He felt that way now with T. Collins, the latest open book he at present was reading.

T. Collins's face was a map of information to Weddles, but all of it was mixed in a perplexity of the order of replies at his command. T. Collins didn't know how to tell this stranger, this new visitor to Great Brunswick, about a friend to each one of them, about Nate Twombly.

His mind leaped back into a host of contacts, meetings here at the livery or out on Nate's place, fishing, hunting cougar, delivering horses, fighting off brigands and Indians, going to dinner at the ranch house with Nate and his daughter, Sarah Jeanne. Nate's face, most of it, came back in quick flashes, then came the wooden cross driven by T. Collins's own hand into the ground out there on ranch property, pounded down with a sledge, the last goodbye to Nate Twombly.

Not a soul locally, it seemed, knew how Nate had been killed, the shot a long distance rifle shot in the back as he tied a rope to a dead steer and was about to drag it to a shallow place to bury it. No one saw it happen. No one reported it, until his daughter Sarah Jeanne went looking for him after he had not come in for lunch or supper.

His horse was loose on the grass and on the way home when she first saw him from a distance, her heart leaping wildly, tossed with sudden fear.

She found her father as he died, a rope in his hand, lying across the dead steer, the evening shadows falling down on him like a cape let loose from on high. The wind had taken his hat, a gray-white Stetson, almost 100 yards away. His revolver was half out of its holster, still gripped in his hand, when he fell on that side, pinning his arm through death. The bullet had ripped clean through him, striking bones, smashing them, tearing him apart. He was gone a lot quicker than he came.

T. Collins had swung the sledge atop the cross, drove it deep, and walked back to his horse, not having returned once in the four months since.

It took some time, but T. Collins related the whole episode to Weddles who listened attentively, never interrupted him once, and only asked at the finish if they knew what kind of a rifle had killed Nate Twombly.

"Well," T. Collins said, "both the sheriff and the gunsmith over at Dead River say it was a 45-70, maybe a Sharps or a Henry and owned by someone long in the tooth, and mean as hell, them thinking it's an old feud come around again. Sheriff says he'll hang him in a minute he gets guilty sworn on him."

He gave Weddles directions to Twombly's ranch and they headed out after picking up supplies. Eighteen people were in the party, and now six wagons, one rendered for spare parts, the load split up and shifted to other wagons.

A few hours later, topping a rise in the road, the Twombly ranch loomed low and squat on the far right, set against a wooded foothill that run up against a tall cliff. And the mountains stood guard behind it all. It presented a site for many lovely homes, for most anybody really interested ... and the Weddles, of course, were interested.

With one look at Sara Jeanne, a lovely creature, blonde as a Nordic beauty, statuesque, shapely even in work clothes, well-mannered, receptive to visitors, especially old friends of her father's, Weddles knew she'd be a great addition to his family ... and her ranch. Sara Jeanne and Adam would gravitate quickly, he assured himself. It would take no effort on his part.

Within hours of their arrival, sitting at two tables drawn together in the main room of the house for a dinner of welcome, she told them they could stay on the land as long as they wanted, could set up in a corner of the ranch at their choosing, all the while her eyes returning time and again to Adam as he brought his love of history into any part of the conversation it would fit.

It fit often.

Weddles was elated, that the attraction was there and that he had foreseen it all. Somewhere, at the back of his brain, in a kind of rush of pictures and strange images, he saw a huge cave filled with artifacts of Indian life, and some of them were self-illuminated by their own gold.

The call of the west was alive.

Life, again, he was sure, would be good again for the Weddles of Wellesley. He'd done his part to this point; the rest would be up to Sara Jeanne and Adam, and, as much as he hated to admit, T. Collins, the livery man, would have his part in the play.

It did not take long for Sara Jeanne to fall in love with Adam. He was interesting, he was different, and he had some distinction about his person that magnetized Sara Jeanne from the first day. And the first ride together out on the prairie, loping along on two fine horses, enjoying the rhythm of the ride, the scenery, the growing attachment and excitement in each of them, brought all of the Weddles closer to a place in the west.

Adam found her as different as she found him. Besides being lovely, she was entirely responsible for everything she did, and said, and managed the ranch the way her father had taught her. He had heard her once say to a hand, "Garvey, that's not the way we were taught, is it? You will do it the right way from now on. Right?" She had lathered it with a smile, but she was serious. He liked that in her.

Adam, too, seemed interested in her father's death, afraid at first to bring it up, speak of it openly, but Sara Jeanne felt the regard and said, "You don't have to be sensitive with me about my father's death, Adam. It was no accident. It was murder. Somehow, someway, I'll find out who did it. Then there'll be hell to play."

He loved that in her and told her so. The bond was in place all the way.

The Weddles, with Sara Jeanne's open invitation to light anywhere on the property, had set up camp in a lovely corner away from the main house.

Weddles had said to Sara Jeanne, "Among the things we want to do while we are in the area, for some months anyway, is to do some historical research that Adam is deeply interested in. We plan to do some exploring up there around Barren Widow's Plight."

The mention of Barren Widow's Plight brought up a new expression on Sara Jeanne's face and Weddles, ready to read a face at an instance, understood her fear of never having children by the man she loved, Adam Weddles, and the threat of all the Weddles leaving the area was left dancing in the air.

"Of course," Sara Jeanne said, "and if you need any help I can assign some of my men to help you, like carrying supplies or handling animals. Whatever." The sincerity of her offer was open to see.

"Oh, no, Sara Jeanne," Weddles replied instantly. "We can handle everything ourselves. We are fully equipped and staffed to take on such interesting work. Adam will be thrilled with this expedition." He patted her on the shoulder.

Weddles, his son Adam, and two rugged nephews, Paul and Clay Gentry, left on horseback and a mule loaded with supplies. They had planned for a two-week stay at Barren Widow's Plight.

As they left the Twombly ranch, Adam asked his father, "What did T. Collins say that parked your interest, Pa?"

"I was in Great Brunswick three times and spoke to him each trip and he eventually told me, on the promise of a percentage of find that all the stories say there is one cave inside of another cave that was carved out of the heart of the mountain. They say it took almost a hundred years to carve it out of rock, and he believes that every time some Indian went in there to work, he brought some gold or other piece of value with him. Said more than once, 'The place has got to be loaded with gold and artifacts we can't begin to imagine.' He swears one drunken Indian that he fed drink into, loosened up one night and told him one story that put the cave in a cave in the southern-most canyon near the high level of the Barren Widow's Plight, using their name for it which I can't collar yet."

"You believe him, Pa?"

"I have to believe him, Adam. I don't think he can lie about that, make up such a story." The sincerity in his eyes was believable and made the story carry. "Legend or lore or fancy hoping, whatever it is, we're going to check it out, and as far as we can go."

Adam thought it over for a while, and replied. "I've heard about steps and tunnels being carved over whole generations for places of worship, but never a cave inside of a cave. The Pueblo Indians and the Anasazi and other tribes did some amazing work, and did it for centuries in some places. If all of it is true, something will grow out of it."

"We will grow," Weddle said. "We will grow."

A week later they were in a large cave near the peak of Barren Widow's Plight. Sounds carried like a tunnel caught in the wind, and animals of various kinds added to the music of the cave; it was vibrato and tremolo in one sense and minutes later a basso profundo delivery came like an echo from deeper in the bowels of the mountain.

The party might have missed it, a message of sorts carved in the rock face of the cave, down near the floor of the cave, nearly out of view of dust, dirt, debris and old leavings from predators.

Adam, with a swinging torch almost passed by it, too, but a few characters reined in his passage, and he knelt to study the series of symbols. He let out an exclamation, "Aha," lowered his torch, and uttered, "Imagine, a road map."

Hastening to his son's side, Weddles said, "What is it, Adam? Can you decipher it? Is it a true sign?"

"I figure, Pa, that it's part of a direction sign, pointing the way. I'm sure we are in the right cave. And the entrance to the next cave must be near here. We'll have to go over every square inch of the place." He stood up and pointed further on. "It must be that way. This is too close to direct us to the exit. Go that way."

Adam Weddles started tapping on the walls, listening to the reply, measuring that echo. When he was sure the sounds were different from one area, he raised the torch, saw the stone set against the wall, and leaned on it.

It moved away from the wall easier that he thought it would.

And there, cut out of the wall how many centuries in the past he could not begin to imagine, was an entrance.

"This is it, Pa. This is it." The excitement bubbled out of him.

The elder Weddles, taken aback, dreams flourishing already about the find, the eventual trading with the world's ultimate powers of finance, said, "You go on in, Adam. You deserve it, but tell me what you see as soon as you can." He patted his son on the back, lit up a new torch and handed it to him.

Adam Weddles, historical student and buff of old remains, feeling the magnitude of expectation, thinking of Sara Jeanne and how she'd greet his discovery, knelt, fit himself torch first into the narrow opening and crawled into the end of one world and the beginning of a new one he was sure, seeing the harvest of all harvests.

The first thing his eyes lit on was a six-pointed star sitting directly in front of him as though set there long ago to be the lead-in piece of this most holy place. Its sheen in the flare of the torch jumped into a series of golden flashes, from the core of the star to the six rounded points. It was only as big as his hand, so he put his hand forward, grasped the star and stuck it into his shirt. The cold but wakening touch of the star seemed to make him shiver at first, and then the thought of the largest chunk of gold he had ever seen set his mind ablaze and warmed his whole frame in a burst of heat. The slight rumbles in his heart and chest, in his whole frame seemed part of that burst of heat.

Lifting the torch on high, he realized he could stand to full height, so stand he did, slowly flashed the flickering torch about him, the swift tongues of fire leaping, fading away, leaving the source of their being, and saw the treasure of treasures. There was no doubt about it ... it was the most amazing find he had ever heard about or ever read about. And nothing like this had he ever seen. The amazement touched again at the bottom of his feet, for it was running the whole length of his body, the excited shivering.

There were niches and shelves and small fissures cut into the face of the cave, hundreds of them, some shallow, some slim cuts, some vertical and some horizontal, some made with shadows so deep they appeared to be exits, cut to fit each piece contained, for in each one loomed a piece of history. The artifacts were not trinkets or trifles, were not paltry or frivolous, but were made of gold and assorted gems the types of which he had no idea, except they sat shining, shining gloriously in their settings, in the glare of the torch, in a cave in the heart of a mountain.

"We hit it, Pa!" he yelled out, hearing the echo of his words leap back at him like quick thunder, a shaking in the walls they had seemed to set off.

He yelled out again and heard the echo again before his father said, "Hold it down, Adam. Hold it down. Now come out and let me take a look."

Adam, left the torch burning as it leaned against a fissure in the wall, a gleam of gold behind it, and crawled out of the cave.

"Pa," he said as he came out of the opening, "you won't believe it until you see it. Wondrous, amazing, nothing like it ever seen. Go in and take a look. Bring a new torch with you. I don't know how long the one I left in there will last. Go now, Pa."

"I will, Adam, but go back and tell those boys out there that we want them to go back and get another two weeks supply. Tell them we have found some signs that definitely say we are on the right track. Tell them to leave what we have and be back here in three days. We will live on what we have left. Do it now, Adam, but don't be so excited. Don't give them a clue so that they'll run off at the mouth about it. Keep it in the family."

He patted Adam with his most solemn blessing.

The elder Weddles, bigger than his son across the shoulders, knelt, thrust the torch in ahead of him and squeezed his body into the opening. He had already heard his first offer to the banker who had taken the family fortune: "It's like I have said, Mr. Stocker ... this is the last offer I am going to make to buy your institution, or it will fall in ruins about your feet." It made him feel so good before he had seen a single artifact that he believed the shaking in his abdomen was part of his excitement.

Then he saw the glitter, the shine, the glory of exorbitant treasure, treasure enough for any family in the whole known world. Adam was right! It was stupendous. Glorious. Beyond dreams. He stood in the midst of glory of the Nations, back past most beginnings. Staring at the walls aglow with gold sheen and that of precious stones, he felt overcome ... but the clean break with the sorry past was at hand.

Adam, as bidden, sent the others off on the requested errand, and sat to enjoy a rest. The water was sweet on his tongue, in his throat, and he got a small snack for himself and one for his father. He was putting them in a sack to carry back to the cave, along with three other sacks folded tightly together, when his feet started shaking as they had done previously.

He stood to listen, to get away from the tremors at his feet, until he realized the whole mountain was shaking. He felt it all before he saw walls of the canyon begin to shiver, crack, give off explosive sounds, and separation from the past began in earnest.

He screamed, "Pa!" and rushed toward the initial cave entrance and the thunder came from inside as he heard much of Barren Widow's Peak feel nature's next cataclysmic struggle with its being. The roar and the thunder seemed to generate movement, shifting of atoms as large as the imagination, while the heart of one whole mountain felt the strain.

Joshua Weddles, once of Wellesley, Massachusetts, dreamer, fortune hunter, was interred forever with the greatest cache of precious items and historical artifacts of significant value that the whole continent might ever reveal.

Who knows what piece he might have held in his hand when the mountain came down on top of him, interloper at history's feet?

Sara Jeanne was glad that Adam was not too very much like his father. He didn't need all the riches that his father dreamed about, of which he had made the center of his life. Adam would be fine with just her; she had enough for both him and her right there where Barren Widow's Plight looked down them, along with Nikninisht-ta Peak, like a pair of sentinels or guardians on high.

A good life sat in front of them in spite of the magnitude of the loss.

The Hawk

The freighter stumbled into the De La Grasso Station in mid-July of 1876, more than 50 miles from Tuscon. There was blood on his arm from a flesh wound, but yelling out so everybody in the station could hear him, "I saw him! I saw him! I saw The Hawk! They was holdin' me up, three ornery cusses, and he come out of the trees like he was a fire-eater, shootin' off his guns and scarin' them critters off quicker'n any fool can imagine. Yes sir, it was The Hawk! He swooped in like he was on wings and he's wearin' a mask makes his nose hook over like he's gonna kill some critter for eatin', just like he was gonna rip it apart."

A hundred miles away, less than a full day later, a bank robbery at Wilton Ford was halted by the appearance of a man in a mask, which hooked his nose out of kilter, and who said to the lone teller a few spare words, "Keep your gun on these fellows until the sheriff gets here. Tell him The Hawk paid a visit."

Near Winslow, only a few miles out of town and only two days after the attempted bank robbery at Wilton Ford, the Overhaul Stage was stopped and three bandits were about to take the strong box off the stage, and had already wounded the shot gun rider, when they were surprised by a man in a weird mask. He seemed to appear from nowhere to stop the theft with a few well-placed shots, then tied up the thieves and slapped them over the saddles of their horses, saying to the stagecoach driver as he left the scene, "Deliver them to the sheriff in town. They're strapped on their horses and tied to the back of the coach. Tell the sheriff they're his prisoners, and you can do the charging, but make sure he knows they're a gift from The Hawk." With that said, he spurred his horse, a big and handsome paint that looked like a colored horse in a schoolmarm's coloring book.

In the first year or two of appearances of The Hawk, wearing the weird mask that hooked his nose and riding an impressive looking paint that could be seen in paintings behind the bar in many saloons, it was Tucson Sheriff Virgil Nawblock who began wondering about those appearances. At first it amounted to only mild wonder, then a sincere sense of curiosity began to work his attention to pieces, and he finally settled on a firm decision: he'd keep a little informational notebook on The Hawk. To that end, he began collecting, via telegraph, letters, stories from travelers and coachmen and freighters, and as much saloon gossip he could attend, all the adventures of The Hawk. The notebook listing showed what and where and when those sudden appearances of The Hawk's had come about with the times and distances in between as part of the listing ... and his long and arduous calculations on the possibilities that evolved.

In addition to the notebook, Sheriff Nawblock got a map of the Arizona and New Mexico Territories from the editor of the *Tucson Clarion and Herald*. It was like a puzzle to work out as he plotted each event on the spot where it happened and how long it would take him by horse to get to the site of the next appearance of The Hawk. The map, with as little traceability as possible to The Hawk, was kept in a locked draw in his office. It became his major off-duty diversion.

Doubts of varying magnitude began to foment on their own ... and a keen sense of admiration for the actions of The Hawk.

More than a few times he argued with himself about the possibility of one man making all those rescues even if half of his information was right and half the times of such happenings were even incorrectly reported by a day or two. It was after less than a year of such noting and plotting that he surmised it had to be more than one man in the strange mask and riding the paint horse.

The Hawk was not one person.

Nawblock, long retired and "on the porch" as he termed it, never made much headway in learning true identities until, with all time sitting in his lap as he sat the porch, began to plot locations of individuals he knew who could and would fit the character of The Hawk. Those who left any question in his mind were cut off from any further concern, and abruptly forgotten. He was overjoyed at arriving at a list of ten men he knew for years who could wear The Hawk's mantel.

He saw the list as men of virtue, hard work, some with great personal property, some with little property but fit for a good, clean living, all law-abiding and all with other admirable values.

Secretly, he wished he was on such a list that might be kept by one of those on his list. Those ten men, unknown to him, kept him in high esteem.

But for more than 30 years the man known as The Hawk had fought against any and all kinds of evil doers in the territory. His targets were not only thieves and murderers and rustlers and horse thieves and road agents of various kinds, but the big thieves, the land manipulators and money investors that dealt with underlings in any manner they chose to get their way, to steal properties of all kinds and dimensions, to gather the riches off someone else's work and sweat and, too many times, the loss of life in such circumstances.

Now, hastening onto 50 years of age, rancher Grover Dumont remembered where and how it all began. Each detail of that solid memory. He saw the map of the Arizona-New Mexico territory as if it was marked at the back of his mind. Saw the first appearance of the masked man the people began to call The Hawk, a new hero for the people.

The land was being savaged, not by the American Natives, but by greed, force and wild corruption that come with exploration, expansion and plain all-out adventure; and the boys of wealth in The School of the Mission San Agustín del Tucsón, unknowingly gathered their forces for a cause. They were up front with each other, an even dozen of them, in the course of many late night discussions from the start. Each of them came from decently well-to-do families that sent them to this special school, and they had measured each other from the git-go. They realized they would be harnessed to the same dollar signs that allowed them here in the first place, without a solemn promise for anyone in their lot.

It was disheartening.

At one meeting of the group, closed off from all the other students, they discussed problems, politics, law and occasional gender stuff. Much of it was illuminating; much of it saw true blame for the shape and condition of the land and the status of its people.

But it was Grover Dumont, son of a highly successful mine owner, sole heir, who made the revolutionary remarks that they'd often look back on. It was time for change.

He said, at a moment of revelation, "I believe I am not alone in this image of mine, one that has come upon me in the middle of the night, in day-dreams, in moments of extreme enlightenment. The lot of us gathered here, each one of us, can do something to help the people, the territory, and the nation as a whole. We've been a century on our own and we still have a long way to go. You all know it. You've all seen it. We're not dumb. As a group, we bring strength to a cause. This is the ultimate one. It will take a serious dedication, perhaps the loss of fortune or loss of family ties, loss of anything that you might call important to you. But when you come right down to it, when you vaguely remember who has gone before us and left little but a name or a small fortune for someone to waste, you might find the message that has come to me. And it is this group, the bunch of us that brought this idea to me. I know I didn't conceive it by myself, for I have felt what all of you I hope have felt in our meetings, some kind of belief that goes beyond us."

He paused, looked them all in the eye and said, "It's bigger than we are."

Eric Lindsey said, "Spill it, Grover. Let it go. We can handle it. Face it, if it's not for us, we won't get another chance as a group."

Dumont put strength in his voice, a noticeable demand, and a bit of illumination: "We're going to become one."

"Hell, Grover," Lindsey said, "we're one already."

"I mean one man, one rider, one figure, one hero for the people."

He let it sink in, saw some of them dumbfounded, some with a slim beginning of an understanding smile. "We will become one man who is everyplace at once, doing everything to help the people. Each one of us, when our turn comes to be the hero in this, the savior, we wear the same clothes, our own issue of course, and each one of us wears the same mask. We go as the masked rider, but never at the same time. If we plan our appearances, know the times and schedules perfectly, we can throw Hell right in the face of those who steal from the people, hurt the people, hurt the expansion of the country."

He sat back, let all of it sink in, or try to sink in. The beginning smiles began to widen, spread, began to show appreciation for the idea of one man being everywhere almost at once, a hero in a mask, on a memorable horse. Dumont already knew it had to be a paint, a horse easy to see and hard to identify from a quick sight.

"You wait here. I'll be right back." He left the room.

In a few minutes he came back, wearing a gray hat, a pearly gray shirt, black vest, and black pants. A pair of Colts was holstered on his belt – and he wore a mask across his eyes, a mask as black as a dead sky. To those who knew him better than his family might have known him, he set a striking figure, youthful but ominous, agile but proud, singular but belonging to a cause.

"What do we call him?" Lindsey asked, shouting, standing in the middle of the room, his eyes bright blue, a smile locked on his face, and his mouth ajar.

Dumont knew that his pal had an idea of his own and noticed how Lindsey set his stance, ready for what he was about to say, ready for any and all replies, questions, denouncements at the highest level. Robert Sherwood Lindsey, III, was the dearest friend he'd ever had, and he had only known him for two years.

Finally, Lindsey said, "I have a choice of two names we can give to this masked man right at this minute. We can call him The Guardsman," and Dumont saw him shrug his shoulder in a declarative but minute disdain, letting The Guardsman sit on the minds of all in the room, and then he qualified his whole approach, "or we can call him The Hawk."

The very name hung in the air, and all the romance of it sat with it.

Jumping up, exclaiming his approval, agreeing with his friend's ploy, his manner of presentation, Dumont glowed with his response. "My God, Bob, that's it! That's it! I never had the slightest idea about a name. That's it, The Hawk." Those in the room saw him mouthing the name over and over again, as if he was tasting the drama of it, the swooping beauty of it, swooping in from wherever in every place, all of them one, one from them all no matter how many times or places The Hawk would appear; the legend in the making.

He looked around the room and realized it also sat well with those who would wear this uniform of a sort, carry the name, The Hawk. He was elated. It was the best thing that ever happened at The School of the Mission San Agustin del Tucsón, which had been in place since 1775 when it was established by Father Garcés as a daughter church of San Xavier del Bac. Once the place was known as San Cosme y Damián de Tucsón. Around them sat the O'odham village of Chuk-son, some of it in remnants, some having braced the new century, moving well into it as Tucson.

Lindsey was still working the curiosity angle. "How did this happen, Grov?"

Dumont did not stop to gather his facts in a coherent order, but let his emotions carry it off. This, he fully realized, was the moment for his idea. Nothing in his life would ever be bigger, or more ready to be said.

"I was riding, just riding, looking at things, and feeling the land and what was upon it, from all angles. The lime hue of mesquite wrapped into my eyes and lingered like offering a drink of lemonade. I rode around with all the Earth calling out to be noticed, the pines, the flowers, the ridges so clearly defined in cliff faces that they came at me like pages in a book, and I knew I was being taught something. Something was right in front of me waiting to be learned, that learning never stops even if you stop looking because you hear it or smell it and you're back where you started, looking at it from an ant hill to a mountain top and the sun kissing it like a girl does her lover in morning's realization. The prairie dogs called out to me and the hawks shifted their wings overhead into a new thermal updraft and I could read their signs like a language spoken to me long ago, perhaps something my father had said. And right then, like I was looking into the face of a hawk on his prowl, it all came to me. That hawk came to me. It took me in like I was in its talons, but wrapped me in one, single and noble idea, wrapped me up forever in this idea, this being what I am, what we are, how time and history and the new century will look back on us. We are here at the root of history; let's make it happen."

He raised his empty hand and said, "To The Hawk. May *they* live forever."

The Hawk made his way across much of the territories of Arizona and New Mexico, alighting in places an ordinary man could not have reached from a previous rescue, and the rumors and the legend and the stories grew manifold until The Hawk had become a beacon of heroism, clean play, tidy and neat rescues of maidens in distress, of old men on the downside of their lives, on the feeble among the citizens of every settlement, town, moving wagon train, stagecoach or horseman alone on the grass. He came to be expected, and in truth, there were some folks who began to pray for his appearance when they were at great disadvantage, like a gun in the back or stuck in their face.

It was retired Sheriff Virgil Nawblock who was the vital witness at the end, when The Hawk was killed by road agents trying to hold up a stagecoach in which Nawblock was a passenger.

The killers, two young men in masks, stood confused, unsure of what they had done, looking down at the prone figure of the masked man whose nose seemed bent and hooked on his face.

An elderly woman passenger, unafraid of the bandits, yelled at them from the stage, "You scum of the Earth have killed the only hero we had around here. You two have killed The Hawk who has saved more lives than you can count, and whose death, you may be sure, will be avenged." She showed them her raised fist, and yelled again, "Scum of the Earth has killed The Hawk, and the fiery God will come down on them from high above."

The confused killers, forgetting what they had come after, spurred their horses and fled, and it was the retired sheriff who unmasked the dead man and saw that he was a man who was on his list of possible Hawk suspects: Grover Dumont.

He began to wonder if it really was the end of The Hawk ... as he had known *them,* perhaps *the lot of them.*

The Lost Badge

The wounded man came from nowhere, it seemed, was headed no place, had no horse, no gun and no money when he was found at the side of the trail by the Somerville Stage due hours earlier in Kellerton, Utah. And he had been mauled by someone or something, but was breathing when the driver and shotgun rider stuffed him in the coach, across the floor.

They got to Kellerton and Doc Smithers' office about an hour later. The man was bleeding still, but not heavily, and though he had regained consciousness, had not said anything useful. Doc Smithers was mystified too, not just by the man's silence, but by the abuse his body had taken.

The doc called out the window at one of the townies and said, "Go get the sheriff for me, like a good fellow, Charlie."

"Is he still alive, Doc? I heard he could have been easy dead. Gotta be a tough one to hang on like he has."

He raced off to the jail.

Sheriff Wilbur Cantry, on the job for a half dozen years, said to the doctor, "What did this to him, Doc? It sure don't look natural to me. I never seen anything like this, like he's been beat with barbed wire or shot with nails. Why ain't he dead?" He had found nothing in the man's pockets.

Doc Smithers, the doctor in Kellerton for just about as long as Cantry had been sheriff, and a poker cohort, replied, "That's as close as I can guess, Wil, and he's a rugged man in his regular shape, probably could have lasted a few more days, one anyway."

"He say anything at all? Any name? Where he's from?"

"Nothing, Wil. And I'm not sure he can. He's been pounded at his throat too. Lots of bruises on top of all those little punctures in him."

In the morning, after a fitful sleep of incoherent mumbling, some possible reactions to old pain or an ache with a bad taste, the man sat up and looked around. His hand touched his throat first where the doctor thought he might have been strangled or punched or both, and then his hand went to his left breast where he now wore a shirt of the doc's, and muttered the first words Doc Smithers could understand.

"Where's my badge?" he said, grasping a second time at his chest where his badge had been.

It meant a whole lot to Smithers, who had been imprisoned in the Great War one time without his medical bag … he felt useless amid miseries of the toughest kind. Now, sure the patient was a lawman, he was bound to get some answers. In the terrible state he was in, still clutched up in pain spasms, the man kept fishing around for his badge.

127

The doctor realized the badge must have carried a lot of weight for his patient, the way he kept fumbling for it.

"A stage driver spotted you at the side of the trail between Somerville and Kellerton, Smithers said. "This is Kellerton and you've had the hell beat out of you from what I've seen, but you'll get through all of it in time. You weren't wearing a badge when they brought you in. I'll have the stage driver look in the coach, and we can find out just where they found you and check there." He studied the man's expressions, which ran a course of significant differences, from pain to wonder to amazement in a quick hurry.

"Who are you?" Smithers said. "We have no idea of who you are. Me, the sheriff here and the folks on the stagecoach. No idea at all."

"I'm Dopper Kearns, sheriff of Lumsden, Kansas." His hand searched again for the missing badge, a most forlorn look settling on his face.

Smithers exclaimed, "Lumsden, Kansas! How'd you get over here? You're in Utah, almost in Nevada. Another thirty miles and we'd be in Nevada."

Kearns shook his head, trying to clear it of something mysterious or dark, and he looked around as if he did not believe what the doctor had told him. "Utah? I can't remember riding so far, though they had me tied up in a wagon for days."

"Who tied you up, Sheriff? Why'd they do it? Do you know who they are, where they are?"

"All I know is two of them recognized me from the war. Said I lead a charge on a Confederate position and raised hell among them when we ran over them. They said they agreed to look for me after the war no matter where they went. I just dropped into a saloon one night to get a drink, and the next thing I knew, after a fight, they had me tied up in the wagon and on the road to somewhere. I guess that somewhere was near here, though I don't know why it was this far. They beat me several times a day, but fed me when they ate, let me wash in the river a few times, but never let me near a rifle or a gun. I tried to get away a couple of nights and they beat hell out of me again."

"Did anybody ever try to rescue you, ask questions about why you were tied up?"

"Only once. An old gent heard me groaning and looked in the wagon and they told him they were a posse and had captured a dangerous killer. Said they were taking me to a town where I killed a mother and her three children. The old gent almost hit me with his rifle, he was so mad. I couldn't say a word with my mouth stuffed with a rag."

"When was that?"

"I can't remember how long ago or where it was."

"You have to talk to our sheriff, Wil Cantry. He's a good man. He'll help you. Maybe get things in some kind of order for you. He knows his way around these parts and knows most of the folks here."

"That'll help"

"How's that?"

"There are six of them. They're former Confederate Army, from the same outfit, and they recognized me by name from the battle and the sheriff's job. They might have been attached to Lomax's 15th Virginia because they were in the battle at Yellow Tavern where we captured the turnpike with a charge going at their line standing right firm at the start. I don't know if these men were cavalry or infantry but we captured two guns there. I was with Gregg when we charged in the rear and the battle was over and done. We got control of the road to Richmond and they lost a couple of their generals, Jeb Stuart being one of them. That really burned them. They ain't got over that yet and some of the other stuff that went on after the war. I guess I'd be mad at some of that too." He looked down at himself, felt for his badge again, and said, "But not this mad."

Cantry came in later on. "Doc says there was six of them and all ex-Confederate Army and you can recognize all of them if you was to see them. That right, Sheriff Kearns?"

"Call me Dopper 'cause that's my name. Yours is Wil. Right, Wil? Yes, I could spot them in evening shadows 'cause I studied them every time I could. How they walked and talked and how they wore their clothes and handled their guns and mounted their horses and took care of them before themselves mostly and how much they drank whenever they got a chance. Yuh, I can recognize them."

"Know their names?"

"Not any family names. Just their Christian names cut down or nicknames. Only one of them's a lefty and I heard his name once, but don't know if it's first or last name. Called him Maxwell a couple of times and he's like a scout, always out on the trail ahead of them. When he came back in to eat or sleep once every few days, they'd get together and speak so I couldn't hear them, and then he'd go lie down and sleep. Sometimes we moved on and left him behind, him still sleeping. But he'd come back every time and they'd talk again. Sometimes they'd tie me up in a cave and go off or leave one man with me and the rest'd go off. I don't know where, but it'd be half a day or more before they got back. And they never talked about anything when they got back. For sure, not in front of me."

"Where'd you think they went those times?"

"Up to no good, I figure, but they didn't let on to me like I was poison."

"This lefty, Maxwell. He wear a gray hat with a skinny band on it? And gray shirt, dark gray pants with a Colt on his left side, and a Winchester rifle in his scabbard and ride a pinto?"

"You been studying him, Wil?"

"Well, he was hanging around Titusville before the bank was robbed, 'cording to Harley Means over there, the sheriff. Nobody ever saw him before and never since, but that gang walked in just at the right time to run off with every bit of paper in the bank."

"Like it had been checked out by Maxwell, the scout?"

"Yup. But the sheriff down at Turner Corners, about 50 miles away, said a man dressed like that Maxwell mailed a package to Georgia a week later. The clerk never saw the gent before or since and couldn't remember any of the address except it was in Georgia and that was a whole week after it was sent."

"You thinking what I'm thinking?"

"Sure am, Dopper. They're sending money home. Robbing the haves and sending it to the have-nots, the relatives of southern boys who're getting chewed up by the Federal people. Once the package is on the train, a whole week later, they can't catch up to it, even by telegraph. Like it's gone forever."

"We can blame them for how and what they take, at the point of a gun, but can't blame them for what they do with it."

"Oh, we got to be careful there, not letting one side of it wipe out the other. They'll kill when the time comes, sure as shooting."

"How'll we track them down, Wil? They won't come back here. Best we lay out a map and put down the places we know of that've been hit by the likes of them, and plot out things. Maybe we can catch onto some scheme or plan they're using. We can use the telegraph and find out from station clerks where a package might be sent to Georgia or some other place down that way. They might not use the same delivery information more than once or twice."

"That follows, as long as they're doing what we think they're doing. We could be so far off on this, it'd look damned foolish of us. Dumb sheriffs by the pair."

"Yup, and one of 'em's without his badge. Well, I'm with you on that last part, knowing it's a gamble, but we'd be chewing on a willow stick otherwise, Wil, a whole lot of wasting our time, piddling it away like chaff in the wind."

Almost two weeks later, the sheriff of Blane Hills, north almost 60 miles, saw a stranger come into town, get a few drinks at the saloon, and saunter around town. He came back the next day and carried out the same routine, his eyes, it seemed, always on the bank and striking up conversations with bank customers in a most casual manner. He was wearing a gray hat with a thin band on it, a gray shirt, and dark gray pants with a Colt at his left hip. He was riding a pinto with a Winchester rifle in the scabbard.

He sent a telegraph message to Sheriff Wil Canty down at Kellerton, Utah.

Wil Canty and Dopper Kearns, sheriffs, headed north, one wearing a sheriff's badge and the other with a new deputy's badge, a loaner for the time being.

Dopper Kearns said he still felt undressed wearing a deputy's badge.

At Blane Hills, they came in after dark as previously planned, Kearns saying, "If Maxwell is hanging around, he'll recognize me in a flash."

"Think you'll recognize him just as fast?"

"Just make sure I don't draw on him as soon as I see him. It will tempt me."

Sitting in the hotel lobby, looking out the window, Kearns saw the bandit gang ride into town. They were visible to him in known order, each one of them clicking onto his memory banks, each off them fully familiar.

With a near single act, Kearns drew down the shade in the small window and immediately placed his hand where his badge should have been. The other sheriffs, Canty and Blane Hills Sheriff Morgan Alexander, saw the signal and alerted their men, a small force of 10, well-armed and alert, standing by for instructions or alarm.

When five members of the gang came out of the bank, Maxwell among them, money bags in hand, a teller under gunpoint as a hostage, they were forced to drop their weapons or be shot on the spot. Their horses had been commandeered and run off after one gang member, in charge of the horses, had been knocked off his saddle and disarmed by a young man carrying a plank of wood across the main street. The young man had rammed the gang member and knocked him free of his saddle with the end of the heavy plank in a sudden swing of the plank that came at the mounted man like a projectile. This was also carried out on the directions of Sheriff Wil Canty.

The first time Dopper Kearns relaxed in a long time was when Wil Canty, after a search of gang members' possessions, found Kearns's badge tucked into Maxwell's shirt pocket.

With extreme pleasure, and a smile on his face, he pinned the badge back on Dopper Kearns without saying a word.

Dopper Kearns didn't say a word either, but felt a sensation he had known before, like being on the road to Richmond after the charge at Yellow Tavern.

131

The Marker

The crude cross was driven into the ground midway between two trees still wearing remnants of rusted barbed wire. The lone man had thrown the last shovelful of dirt on top on the mound before he set up the cross that he made from two branches broken off the trees. There'd been a swing hanging from one branch for the early years, and he recalled how the remnant barbed wire whistled when the wind was strong. In a last look around, he studied the location of the marker between the two trees and lined up two other sites perpendicular to the tree line, a large rock most likely never to be moved and another rock across the grass only Mother Nature herself would ever dislodge, and which would be calamitous. He muttered a few solemn words, followed them with an epithet not repeated here, and then jammed his hat tightly in place.

He mounted his horse, a big gray stallion, checked the rifle in the scabbard, and two pistols on his belt, and rode off. Northwest he headed, far peaks catching sunlight in blue-white brilliance. Once more he framed the epithet with his lips as he spurred the gray, the August sun setting on his back a thick mantel of warmth.

He had come on this land as a new husband and was leaving it as a widower 26 years later. Margaret Mary, the best thing ever in his life, rested behind him, a stray bullet taking her life on her own porch.

The gunfight had been spurious; bandits in flight looking for horses, her exclamations from the porch that the horses were not for sale or for the taking, that her husband was due any minute and would settle the issue.

He had come in the middle of the theft, hearing her yelling at three men to leave at once. He galloped into the midst of them, killing one man, wounding another, and the third fleeing north on a tired horse.

Harland Yeats learned how to curse the moment Margaret Mary uttered her last breath, in his arms, and saying as she had said on hundreds of occasions, "Oh, Hal. Oh, Hal." His hand, under her, began to collect the flow of blood.

He'd trail that third man to the end of the world, wanting to get him before his sons did the chasing. The wounded man, not Margaret Mary's killer, was soon in jail.

On the table in Margaret Mary's kitchen, he left a note for his sons, making the message as short as he could but with purpose and intention in his words:

"Matthew, Mark, You've probably heard before you read this, but I buried your mother where she said was her favorite place outside of this room. Three men tried to steal some of our horses. One is dead. One is wounded and in jail. The one who shot your mother rode off before I

132

could get him. I am going after him. Take care of things until I get back. Dad"

He worried about how much attention they'd pay to his last sentence. And his thoughts roamed off with her always saying she had wanted Luke and John to be part of her family.

Yeats was long on the trail before his sons came back from the drive they worked on. He had seen the man who had fled, remembered his clothes, his hair when his hat fell away, that he was a clumsy lefthander. He could describe him, knew what his horse was like, could see him going for his gun and firing off that crooked shot, almost aimless, useless, until Margaret Mary collapsed on the porch.

Yeats, as time would prove, learned new curses with the continuing sights in his mind.

A full day's ride brought him to a clump of trees and brush about a half mile from a ranch house he had visited in the past with a previous owner. In the trees he spotted the killer's horse hobbled by a short rope on his forelegs, and the saddle and saddle blanket gone off the animal's back.

He found where the killer had walked off a way, found where he thought the saddle had been set on some brush, and a new set of tracks where he must have put the saddle on another horse, stolen from the nearby ranch.

Yeats approached the ranch until he realized he was facing a man with a rifle pointed at him. The rifle was as thin as the man holding it, but he had a quizzical and broad look on his face that was not entirely ferocious. He had apparently seen Yeats as harmless, At least Yeats thought so.

"Hold there," the man said, shouldering the rifle, "who are you and what do you want." There was no fear on his face.

"I am Harland Yeats from Hatfield, back a day's ride. I'm chasing the man who killed my wife when he and his friends tried to steal some of my horses. I knew Purnell who used to live here. Who are you? Have you had a horse stolen from you?"

"I bought this place from Purnell. I'm sorry about your loss. I had a horse stolen sometime during the day when I was looking for strays up in the hills. But only one horse. His friends have horses?"

"They didn't get this far."

"You get them? I'm Jeff Salisbury." He put out his hand to shake, his early assessment of Yeats confirmed.

"I got one and one in jail and still hurting I hope."

"Good man. I was going after him but my wife was too upset and worried, so I was letting her settle down before I lit out after him."

Yeats said, "I have two sons who most likely will be after me. I'd appreciate a quick meal and a promise that you'll hold them back as long as you can. Try any kind of a story you want, but I want that man to myself. Tell me what kind of a horse he stole. I'll appreciate all the help you can give me, Mr. Salisbury."

"My wife Winifred will get you a quick meal and I'll hold up your boys long as I can. I suspect that's going to take some doing on my part, considering their purpose and intentions." He was measuring Yeats again and what Yeats' sons most likely would bring to bear on their mission. "The stolen horse was a rugged paint, three white socks and one black sock and his left neck near spotted with black on white. He was getting a day's rest as I rode him all day yesterday. Your killer knows a good animal 'cause he picked my best."

Salisbury waved to a woman on the front stoop of the ranch house. She was almost as tall as her husband, and just as thin as a crane sitting a rock in a creek. "There's Winifred now. She'll have something on the table real quick. Lady's like greased lightning when she's ginning about the kitchen."

Yeats smiled as he saw a flash of Margaret Mary handling a pot and two plates and a loaf of warm bread in one dash from stove to table top. He almost found another curse framed on the instance, but shook his head.

"If I can talk her into it, I'd go along with you," Salisbury said, the chances showing nil on his face. "When she hears about your wife, she'll close down like a winter bear."

"You do me the best favor by sitting on my boys as long as you can. Give them an extra meal, a place to sleep, tell them I went right past here last night, say you don't know where."

"I'll do what I can." There was promise in his voice.

Winifred Salisbury didn't fold into a ball of sympathy, as Yeats thought she might, rather she moved into a stony and distant composure. She spun about the kitchen in her manner and had a plate set down in front of Yeats as fast as promised by her husband. She spoke once, saying, "I'm sorry for your loss. Such things worry me every day." She never said another word to Yeats, who left saying only, "Thank you for your gesture and your concern and I wish good things for you."

Winifred Salisbury was out of her mind as soon as Margaret Mary made another appearance in one of her favorite poses. Yeats heard her voice again, coming from another darkness.

Interrupted, but adamant, he rode off still on the trail, the description of Salisbury's horse locked in his mind, and the images of the killer tucked away just as clear as the moment he first saw them. The white socks of the paint floated in his mind, the spots on the neck, trying to affirm what side they were on, for he was suddenly unsure.

But the trail of the paint, with two new front shoes according to Salisbury, was easy to follow on the way off the rancher's property. It lead north as before, due north, the sun a simmering orange-redness on his left shoulder, and Yeats knew the two towns to the north, hugging the river, Litchfield and Carver. He was not sure which one he'd end up in because the regular trail would lead, in part, to each town.

And he had old friends there.

In both towns.

He'd hopefully use those friends before his sons could get there, before Salisbury wilted in front of their resolve, and perhaps joined them to the disappointment of his wife. He could hear Matthew saying, "Salisbury, you best own up to our questions with some straight talk or we'll drag you along with us to get your horse back, see our Pa is safe, and get the rat who caused all this, and we beg the forgiveness of your wife. We ain't here to hurt her or you or anybody 'cept those who delay us, like you're doing."

He could hear Matthew's words as clear as he could hear Margaret Mary say, "Oh, Hal. Oh, Hal."

The new shoes of the paint came to a decision point, Yeats figured, for they appeared to have danced around in some indecision, here and there, and finally, probably after some resolve or reason came to the rider, the trail headed off to Carver where the road broke in two parts.

One of his old hands, Jethro Kohlrausch, at last report, had become sheriff of Carver. If Yeats had a need to talk when the trail failed, Kohlrausch would be a good ear, would lend a hand.

Kohlrausch, though, had been injured in a fall, a bad fall, and was stuck to a bed in a boarding house, and had little to offer Yeats in the way of help.

So, after wishing his old hand the best of luck, Yeats headed for the livery, checked the horses, walked around town, spotted a few paints that did not fit Salisbury's description, and went off to the saloon to get rid of trail dust.

With a sense of ease, not expecting to see the pursued killer in the saloon, Yeats stopped in his tracks as he had taken only two steps into the room. There, at the bar, just spinning around to leave, was Margaret Mary's killer, who looked up, saw the look on Yeats' face, drew his weapon, and shot Yeats in the left shoulder. Yeats went down, hurting like hell, hit his head, and went unconscious.

In the turmoil, the desperado fled the saloon, saying, "That man has been trailing me for weeks and weeks, saying I killed his son. I have to get away from him."

When Yeats regained consciousness, after a fitful sleep and the pain finally subsiding after the bullet was extracted by a handy bartender because the town had no doctor, sons Matthew and Mark and Jeff Salisbury were standing over him, their faces after several moments breaking into great grins that could have been approaching significant accomplishments.

Salisbury said, with a sense of glee that he found hard to hide or disguise, "It was a great pleasure to meet your sons, Mr. Yeats. Winifred took to them right off because they were very persuasive about revenge for their mother. They convinced her to let me come with them. You ought to be proud of them."

He stepped back from the bed Yeats was settled into.

Matthew stepped up, put his hand on Yeats' hand sitting on his chest, and said, "We got him, Pa, in a ravine just up north of here, before you get to Litchfield. The paint he stole threw one of his new shoes and we walked right in on him as he was commiserating about his luck. We didn't even have to take a shot, which really hurt us, but Mr. Salisbury squashed that real quick 'cause we had that rat dead to rights and he was scared hell of us screaming at him to stand still or die on the spot. He's in jail right now and the sheriff here says we can bring him back home for a trial."

Yeats looked at Jeff Salisbury and said, "You found it hard to persuade them not to come, didn't you, just like I said?"

Salisbury looked at Yeats' sons, turned back to Yeats and said, "Yes, I did, but my Winifred didn't have any trouble with her way, did she?"

The Missing Sheriff

He was bound hand and foot and believed he was off the ground, with the falling sensation a constant threat. It was dark, he was in the air and his bonds tied him to some kind of pole with his bare feet firmly on thin limbs. He heard the trickle of water as if it was 25 or 30 feet below him, and the awed sensation of being high in the air still working through him. A hum or dull whistle of an airy sound came around his ears like the moan in a barn with at least one door open and the wind at work on all the corners. He was convinced he was not exposed to the elements, but was undercover somehow. Whoever hung him up here and bound him had to be a strong man, for he had to be unconscious when he was bound; he had no recollection of being bound up like this. Only serious deliberations kept him lucid yet thinking of odd things and circumstances that had brought him to this. He might have been tied to the pole when it was on the ground and then the pole lifted in the air. Even that would take great energy and strength. There was no smell of hay or old leather or the after smell of barn animals; no horse or mule or cow smell or dung. Those observations said he most likely was not in a barn. But there was a rancid stink that a slight breath of air kept bringing to him in odd moments, as if a dead animal was below him. He thought of snakes and rats and mice and other carrion eaters seen and unseen. Only a sense of balance kept him sane on those counts, for some of them would necessarily feed on the others before feeding on him.

He wondered if there was any balance in his thinking, or in that of his jailer or kidnapper, or between what certainly could be various kinds of life below him. Snakes could reach him, wrapping around the pole that he thought was about 6-8 inches thick, and wind their way up and around him, or spiders by the hundreds could crawl up the pole, or drop on him, and at length wrap him in a huge cocoon, making him a feast for the ages.

He didn't know how long he had been in this place, whatever or wherever it was. His gun belt was gone, his boots were gone, and his sombrero was gone. He felt naked and threatened and not long for this life. And a poor way to end this one, he thought. He didn't know who to think of at last moments; no wife, no children, no close friends, only his deputies, the two of them still strangers for the most part, young, inexperienced, but caught up with a sense of righteousness in them that he had sought in aides. Then there was Millie at The Flying Horse Saloon and the talkative and happy bartender, Paul Foxx, but they were as casual as friends could be, each knowing one thing he liked at the end of the week, and neither one of those wants being monumental or significant … a good scotch whiskey alone at a corner table or fair company for an hour in a room above.

Vantek Cawblen, sheriff of Milepost City in Montana for seven years, once of Eastern Europe, once an officer in the army of his new country, had not been in his office in three days. One of his deputies, Gavin Durstin, said he was off looking for an old friend whose cabin was burned by some maniac, but the body of Cawblen's friend was not found in the ruins.

Durstin said to one inquirer, "He was in the war with old MacPherson and might spend a month out there looking if he's not satisfied with what he finds."

The pair of friends had been in the Massachusetts 2nd Cavalry for three long years. MacPherson had been his first sergeant; found in the ranks by Cawblen and "brought along."

"Corporal MacPherson," he had said early in the war, during their first campaign battle, "you are exemplary in the care of horses and I shall reward you for that gift."

Some folks in Milepost City had not begun to worry about Cawblen. The popular word said, "He's a most able man, a staunch man, and a highly dependable man." They all agreed he had paid his dues a lot earlier, in the real rough days right after the war.

When a week had gone by, and no word of the sheriff and no sign of him anyplace around, the worrying began. It entered the saloon, the barbershop, the general store, and the livery, but in a strange way for a small town.

The owner of the livery said, "He's got the best horse he's ever rode, so don't worry there. I sold him the horse myself." The owner of the general store mentioned that "the sheriff loaded up with 60 rounds of ammunition in his belt and in his saddle bag, and that'll be enough for a small war."

Those concerns were closely aligned with personal business interests. Generally folks said, "That sheriff can take care of himself. He's done it for seven years. No reason to stop now."

Stretching continually at his bonds, Cawblen heard intelligible words, he thought, from some hollow distance, then assumed it was more moaning, as he had also done. But it surely was human. The gag was still in Cawblen's mouth and he worked his tongue to loosen it. By manipulating his chin, and stretching more, he managed to wrest free the small bind at his mouth and was able spit out the gag.

Then, in the eerie silence, in the fetid odor coming around his nose, he heard the moaning again. It surely could not be his captor, sounding as if the moans also came from a gagged mouth.

"Who's there?" Cawblen tried to shout. The voice came abruptly from him, low and half-pitched, and scratchy and, he thought, unintelligible. He said again, "Who's there? This is Sheriff Cawblen from Milepost. Who are you?"

The moaning came again, but there was a distinctive tone to it, a familiar tone, and a hopeful tone.

"Is that you, MacPherson? Is that you, Aiden?" The other voice was still coming muffled, coming through a gag.

"Once is a yes and twice is a no. Is that you, Aiden?"

One muffled moan came. "Uh."

"I've been looking for you, Aiden. Sorry I found you like this. Do you know who did this?"

Two muffled sounds came back. "Uh. Uh."

"Here's what I did, Aiden. I wiggled my chin and got the gag bind loose and then spit out the gag. Have you tried that?"

"Uh."

"Keep trying. I'll wait on you. We have to find a way out of this place."

"Uh."

"I feel like I'm suspended high in the air. If I fall I think I'll break a leg or my neck."

"Uh. Uh."

"You think I'm up high."

"Uh. Uh."

"Keep working on that gag. Mine came loose after trying for a long time."

The darkness was as heavy as it had been, with nothing visible, no reference for him at all.

"I am trying to figure out how high I am. If I could get on the surface, I'd try to loosen these ropes. Do you think I'm more than a foot off the ground? Are you?"

"Uh. Uh," then a pause and, "Uh. Uh."

"Good. I'm going to get off this limb and try to work on the ropes. Keep working on that gag, Aiden. We've got to get out of here."

With some care still working on him, Cawblen managed to get one foot off the limb or cross-arm, and then, when he held his weight in place by leaning on the pole and gripping with his bound arms, he slipped the other foot off the limb and crashed down no more than a foot. It was a sudden stop that did not hurt, but he felt splinters in his arms from the slide down the pole.

But he was upright. He fidgeted and managed to slide to a sitting position, felt for the limb, found the end that had the sharpest pieces

139

where it was broken, and began working the rope across the sharp wood. He felt strands of hemp break loose one by one.

He was hard at it when he heard a loud and victorious cry, "Ah, ha, Vanny, I spit it out. Are you okay?"

"Yes, Aiden. I'm working on the ropes. I am working through some of the hemp, strand by strand, by rubbing them on the end of the branch. Do you know who did this? Who burned down your cabin?"

"No, but I have an idea. Only an idea. I believe his voice was one I heard years ago, in the army. Do you remember that deserter you court martialed in Virginia before we got to Yellow Tavern? I can't even remember his name. I think it's him. Someone caught me on the side of the head with a good whack and I woke up here, but I heard a dozen times a voice saying, 'I owe those two, Cawblen and MacPherson, for all my troubles, and now I got one of them.' That's when he went after you. How'd you get caught?"

"I don't know. I was just waylaid, hit on the head, and ended up here. Where are we?"

"I'd guess in a cave in the Juniper Hills. Said he was going in to Milepost a few times and went out and back in about six hours. That would put us in the Juniper Hills. I hunted and fished up here, but never saw a cave as big as this one must be. You sound like you're 50 feet away."

"I remember him now, Aiden. Private Rockland. Said his wife was sick and he had to go home. But that was a lie. He was never married. We knew that. He was just a coward that wouldn't own up to it. We sent him off in irons and heard later he broke free. Never heard a word about him until now."

"I'm sure it's him, Vanny, the rotten coward, the vile sneak, the backstabber."

"Let's both keep at these ropes and get some kind of weapon in our hands. It looks like he's got some serious plans for us, the kind we won't like."

"I'm hard at it now, Vanny. Hard at it."

Cawblen felt the ropes at his wrists getting thinner, felt the hemp strands continue to break as he ran them over several sharp edges that dulled quickly, but did the job. With hard work, his breath getting labored, a few new pains building up in him arms, the last strands let go. He went at the ropes at his ankles and tore them loose.

"Aiden, I'm free. I'll be right there. Talk so I can hear you because I can't see a thing." He stumbled as he kicked a stone and heard MacPherson say, "It's my pleasure, Captain, to serve with you again, and with that rat we owe all this misery to. I'll break his neck."

In the Flying Horse Saloon in Milepost City, Deputy Durstin stood at the bar talking to Paul Foxx, the barkeep. "I'm sure he'll turn up soon, Paul. He knows we'll be concerned. He'll come in and probably go right back out if he hasn't found anything. MacPherson was one of his sergeants in the war and a hero, from what I heard. Comrades like that tend to favor each other for all their lives after going through real battles. I've heard they become instant friends all over again in a few seconds even if they haven't seen each other for years and years."

Foxx replied, "I heard that from the sheriff himself when he talked about meeting MacPherson long after the war was over, and right here in Milepost. In fact, right here in this room. I was here that night. Talk about noise and calamity and handshaking and backslapping. It was something to see."

They both turned as a stranger at the end of the bar, a man possibly torn between mountain life and town life and not having made up his mind because of the mix of clothes he was wearing, said, "Not all comrades are like that. None that I knew. Mostly they were glory hounds looking for medals, promotions, all the extras that fools look for. I know. I was there and don't ever want to see any of the faint of heart I served with. Too many of them were false to the service, to themselves, to their families, wanting glory above all things."

He drank off his whiskey and pushed the glass for a refill.

Foxx said, "I wasn't in the war, but I know nothing but heroes who came out of it and don't say a word about what they saw, where they were. You have to admire that in them. I think our sheriff was like that, now he's out there looking for an old comrade and he won't quit until he finds out what happened to him."

The stranger said, "Is that the fellow who might have died in the cabin fire over near the ridge?"

Durstin responded happily, "Oh, his body wasn't in the ashes. We know that. He might be hurt someplace or had gone off to hunt some game, but he didn't die in the fire. We think someone set fire to the cabin. Looks like revenge or an old feud come back on the surface. MacPherson did not have one enemy in this area that we know of. A good man that the sheriff really admired, a great man with horses, and that counts with all of us."

"Only it doesn't if you feel horses were just put here to take us places. They're not friends, you see, just like servants to us. My horse is just a carrier for me. I don't put any more than that on him."

"What kind of a horse do you have, stranger, and what's your handle?"

"Oh," the man said, "he's just like a mongrel dog, made up of many parts. My name is Jeremiah Rockland. I was in the army all through the war. Never met any heroes. Not real ones. I don't think they exist." He drank off a quick shot and sent the glass back to Foxx. "Do it again. I'm celebrating."

"What are you celebrating," Durstin said, "an anniversary, a wedding, the birth of a child?"

"I'm celebrating a personal victory I've been pursuing for years. But it's too personal to talk about." He drank off the next shot, put his money on the bar, and started to leave.

Durstin said, "Where do you live, Jeremiah? Are you from the area?"

"Oh, I'm from all over, but if the rights to that burned down cabin come up for sale, I'd like to buy the place. That's a nice piece of property. I saw it on the way in here. Has a great view, doesn't it? I'll be back in a few days to check on it. Did the owner have any relatives who might claim it?"

"Oh," Durstin said, "it's like I said before, we don't know if he's dead or not. Maybe just missing."

"Yah, that's what they said in the army, when they knew someone was dead … that he's just missing, and after a long time the whole thing fades away." He spun around said, "We'll see." He left the saloon without another word.

Foxx said, "That's a mean man, Gavin. Don't run afoul of him. I never saw him before. Have you? And don't hurry if you haven't. He doesn't look like good news to anybody."

Durstin said, "He's got some funny answers to questions, don't you think? I'll be checking out a few things on that gent. Sheriff would be all over him, I'm sure. Probably keep an eye on him as long as he could, which is just what I'm going to do."

Giving Jeremiah Rockland a good start, because he knew the road he'd travel on, Durstin watched from just over the crest of each hill or hummock in the road. He kept Rockland in sight, but always at a distance. When Rockland was about two hours out from Milepost City, he turned off the trail and went into a series of canyons and finally disappeared.

Durstin, now more curious than ever about the man with the strange answers and elusive actions, found three horses in a tight little natural corral at the deep end of a canyon. His heart leaped up when one of the horses was Sheriff Cawblen's bay. A second horse belonged to Aiden MacPherson.

He was into the heart of the mysteries, and had a damned good idea of who had burned down MacPherson's cabin … and where Sheriff Cawblen had been for nearly a week. The life of a deputy was going to be a good one and he was feeling it in his bones.

In the cave, a large cave with a small entrance, Jeremiah Rockland, deserter, arsonist, kidnapper, was lighting a torch to see his way to his prisoners. Now came the time to get even with all of the army through the two men who had set his conviction as a deserter in place ... and ruined his life, but only up to this moment. The torch flared in his hand and threw shadows into a flash of light, dark corners coming visible, and a stern and vile look on his face. He was ready to exact all demands upon his two sworn enemies. His lips curled in a snarl, a near exultation came from his lips and then, when he raised the torch and looked ahead of him, he saw a slim pole wedged between floor and roof of the cave and it was bare of his prisoner.

At that same moment a number of things happened: Deputy Durstin had drawn his revolver in deep expectation of using it and was entering the cave, his heart fluttering for his first gun fight; Aiden MacPherson uttered the ugliest of cries in the depth of the cave; and a thrown stone bounced against a far wall of the large cave attracting Rockland's most immediate attention, just as a second stone, in a raised arm, came hard against the side of his head.

He went down like the first rock thrown against the far wall.

Most all of the expectations fell away in subsequent reality: Deputy Durstin did not get to fire his revolver in a gunfight; Aiden MacPherson didn't get to strangle Jeremiah Rockland; Jeremiah Rockland did not get to exact his revenge on old comrades or buy the selected property he had his eye on; but former Captain of the Union Army, in the Massachusetts 2nd Cavalry, Vantek Cawblen, was able to exact the military penalty against a deserter and send him off to do his sentence at the federal penitentiary.

That very evening, in the Flying Horse Saloon, the favorite customer of Paul Foxx settled into a corner table with a bottle of scotch and overhead, in a corner room, Millie Courtney heard that Sheriff Vantek Cawblen had been rescued and Deputy Gavin Durstin had a hand in the rescue.

She was as happy as the sheriff.

The Old Man from Pueblo Ande

They were near Pueblo Ande, at the old walls, and talking to the old man who could have been 70 or 90 and no difference to them. And he could have been as old as the mountains or the winds that played around up there. And that no difference either. He might have been as old as the walls. Maybe he had put the last stone in place. It was all gone now, or almost. Like him, the old Mex.

And Thorsen, riding up front of him like he was the only trail blazer in the world, was acting funny, thought the kid; had been acting that way for a week or more, since they had pulled off the last robbery, stuffed themselves with carry-off money, all currency.

Thorsen said, in a casual way, but hard, like a final wish being made with disappointment already loaded up in it: "Don't get upset with him. It won't count. He only speaks Mex, that old man, so you can shoot him if you want. If you do, watch your trail though. They all say he talks to the mountain gods. You and I know they're up there, they talk so much to us who can listen good." He let out a laugh, a long laugh that had echoes and said, "If we could only speak Mex, we'd know better."

Thorsen laughed all the way out of Pueblo Ande, on the trail to Escalendo on the river, the young woman Cielo in her new place on the edge of Escalendo, a nice little cabin an old man had died and left to her, and Thorsen showing eager all over the place. It was his regular style after a job was done, the proceeds gone their ways, the kid's share showing a bump on his saddle bag, Thorsen's caught up in his shirt as though it might get away from him otherwise.

The kid didn't care what Thorsen felt like, what he knew, what the girl Cielo might say to him in the night, what he had said that one time about his sister and Thorsen not knowing he was right behind the door in the cantina. He kept hearing the words and all that time he kept seeing the eyes of the old Mex staring at his pistols all the time, like he might have been juicing up a curse.

The kid was thinking up a dust storm: "I should have done it. Should have shot him right there. Who the hell will miss an old Mex like that? It wouldn't bother Thorsen at all."

But all down the trail from Pueblo Ande, the kid couldn't shake the old man's eyes from the back of his head, like they were in there, staring him out of his mind, seeing what he was thinking, what he might do if he saw him again, what Cielo really said to Thorsen in the night. If she meant it.

Three times Thorsen spoke back over his shoulder to the kid and the kid didn't hear him or couldn't hear him, locked up the way he was.

Thorsen was smarter than the kid, that's why he was the boss, and now the boss knew what was working at the kid: it was nothing but the old man, just like he had figured.

If someone else got rid of the kid, he wouldn't have to do it. His conscience would be clean. He could tell his sister Melva how it went. She'd understand. Real beauties always understand what you tell them.

The kid was a killer from the first time out, shooting the stage driver when he was just trying to set the brake so the horses wouldn't run away with folks aboard.

"I thought he was going for a shotgun," the kid said, but there was no real apology in it; just plain fact for a shooter. Thorsen had seen them before. Mickey Crystal showed it early, and Crazy Albert from Alberta, and Thorsen's first pard, Slip Mackro.

It would all go so quick it could take someone's breath away. They'd throw off guilt like an old shoe on the trail. "Shucks," they'd say, or "Tough," or "Served him right," or a plain old off-handed "Ouch." That's how they looked at death from their hands, saw it drifting off as if there never were any consequences.

But there were consequences; serious ones.

Slip had gone missing in a wild hotel fire that had been set; Crazy Albert fell off a cliff when his horse got stung by a whip. Mickey, as good as a shooter can get, also became a liability, and a victim; Thorsen knowing he couldn't carry their weight for longer than a few jobs. Two at the most. Three if they were lucky and had any money left over.

But the kid was the only one with a great looking sister who sizzled under Thorsen's skin. He'd lasted for four jobs now. But the old man from Pueblo Ande had done his job. It would be easy. He thought on it more; how it might look best to Melva when he told her, in the kitchen before they went to bed ... never in the bed. She could move in any room better than any woman he ever knew, and that included Cielo.

Maybe, he thought, on the bridge over Little River, at the gorge, where the downriver waterfall at the end of the gorge and the half mile of rapids would swamp a man to death on the rocks ... steal his hat, his guns, maybe his boots, and leave him so far downstream it might be a month before he landed some place, all bubbly and pimply and marked for Hell.

"Listen, Melva," he would say, "there was an accident down the river, near the gorge below Escalendo." He'd hold his breath, let go a moan from down in his gut, take her lightly by the arm, and say, as light as his touch, "It's Rico. His horse fell off the bridge when it broke under us. I was a little ahead of him. I almost went. I looked real fast. But I didn't even see his horse in the water. They must have been deep down in the water. I raced downstream, but nothing showed up. I waited for hours and hours, just hoping."

He'd shake his head, hold her lightly, let her cry against him, show her into the bedroom, let her lie down, cover her, say, "I'll be outside. I'll wait until you're sleeping good. I'll see you tomorrow, if you want some company." He'd walk away, stop, and say, "And I'll go down river again. See what I can do."

That ought to do it.

Now all the old man had to do was go to work on the kid.

Every few hundred yards he'd take a skinny look at the kid, look at his eyes, and check his expression, measuring the old man's gift. The gift would show. It'd be in the kid sure as snakebite has its way, slow, sure, or sometimes it might hit like a .45-.70, not leaving anything tied up.

Behind Thorsen, his saddle bag bumpy, wanting to put his head down and sleep, the kid had finally moved his worries away from the old man at Pueblo Ande, left him sitting against the old wall, the sun dancing on his hands, part of his face, as the afternoon sun started its decline, as shadows moved like a lame horse, slipping onto verticals, falling down to gravel and grass, head off to evening.

From another scene, one he could not find background in, hazy, misty, damp as pre-dawn, Slip had winked at him, and Albert and Mickey, each of them like they were saying statements he had not heard before … and he wasn't sure he was hearing it now. But he began listening.

The lisp in Slip's voice came alive, but without words, and Albert had a way of stuttering that made you catch your breath sometimes, and Mickey could talk like a steam engine pounding down the tracks, none of it audible, understandable. The words didn't come from any of them … just a feeling he tried to corral, tried to rope, and saw the noose slip off each time it seemed to fall correctly in place.

But what was unsaid came anyway, less than a whisper, but finally an understood statement … CAREFUL, KID.

The old man was looking not at his guns, but at his eyes. It was not his voice that spoke to him. His eyes said he should listen to whatever was said, from any source but one.

CAREFUL, KID.

He saw Thorsen slow down, fall in line with him at regular intervals, so regular he could almost time them. The geography came at him as he reflected on all he saw, heard, imagined, felt. The gorge was there off to the left and the roar of the water could be heard as it washed and slammed against the rocks and walls of the strict enclosure of the river. Often spray was seen in places flying up over an edge along the gorge, the roars coming thick as drum beats in one of the old villages near Tetu-twante or Val-merte in the canyons up north … one drum beating was loud in a canyon, 100 drums made it another world.

Coming out on top of an abrupt rise in the trail, he saw the bridge running over the gorge a few hundred yards ahead, and there was a minor sway in it as though the ground at each end trembled. The bridge was older than he was, he was told one time. Did it now tremble as he did, thinking of Slip and Albert and Mickey … and Thorsen? CAREFUL, KID.

He heard Cielo laugh in the night, and Melva singing in another room, and Thorsen talking only the way he could. Once Slip had said, "For us, there's never a wrong time. It always has to be right. If you ever think it's the wrong time, you got to change your boots in a hurry or it'll be all over for you."

He looked it over, the whole view of the bridge, saw the trail coming up all the way to Escalendo, the shadows that would soon cross the bridge much as slow as they would.

Now, there was no doubt in his mind. This would be the place. The only place. He had to move fast. Hailing Thorsen, he said, "I gotta go in the woods. I'll be right out. My gut is busting."

His horse, nudged, trotted off the trail into the wooded area, as Thorsen waved that he'd wait for him.

Quickly as he had moved all day, he took his money from the saddlebag and hid it under some leaves, dropping a small log on it, and then filled his saddlebag with sticks and leaves so it looked like the money was still there.

He rode out rubbing his hands with leaves and throwing the leaves away to the wind. Some of them flew into the gorge. The kid, in a swift look, made up his mind that the leaves looked like currency caught in the wind and then floated down into the gorge and the river. It was the sign of signs.

The old man was smiling at him.

Thorsen smiled too, a new thought in his mind, though he didn't say anything at all. He rode slowly onward, moving his head as though he was singing, things all in their rhythm.

Ahead the bridge was two-oxen wide, looked passable but possibly treacherous, at least faulty. It was wooden and often repaired as seen from the color of weather-beaten wood versus newer pieces of wood. The stanchions, two at each end of the bridge, looked solid enough, their feet caught down in crevices in the rock walls the thousands of years of flowing water had carved apart, split in a cataclysmic rumble and shaking.

As Thorsen neared the bridge, he looked back again at the kid a short way behind him and smiled and waved him on with a hearty voice. "Thing still looks good enough to get us across, Rico. Good enough to get us across."

Thorsen rode onto the bridge, and eased his horse, which seemed somewhat unsure on his legs, but under control.

He smiled again.

And the kid thinking right then it was the first time Thorsen had ever called him by his born name.

As the kid came up to the entrance to the bridge, his horse treading gently, Thorsen was at least 20 feet ahead of him. His horse slowed again and it appeared he was waiting for the kid to come abreast of him.

"Now," the old man said, mysteriously, from wherever, perhaps still sitting at the edge of the old wall, but it was Albert's face the kid saw. Then the kid grasped his whip by the handle as it sat on the pommel and said loudly, "Hey, Ted," calling him by his first name for this one time only, "this one's for Albert."

The lash went in a swift arc, snapped at the rump of Ted Thorsen's horse and the horse stumbled when one leg broke through a plank. Thorsen and his horse flew off the bridge into the swift current below.

It took the kid a whole day to ride upriver to cross over at a fording, thinking of Melva and Cielo and Thorsen and Mickey and Slip and Albert, as well as the old man, all the way home.

He said to his sister, "Listen, Melva, there was an accident down the river, near the gorge below Escalendo."

He held his breath, let go a moan from down in his chest, held her lightly by the arm, and said, as light as his touch, "It's Ted. He didn't make it."

The Silent Horseman

Javer Moncton, who owned a decent-sized ranch with a decent-sized herd of cattle in Nevada foothills near the town of Jasperville, woke with a start, and recalled the sound that roused him, one that plunked at his cabin door. The first thought was an Indian arrow, but there were no follow-up cries, no ungodly threats, just silence. Besides, the Indians had been quiet in the area for half dozen years.

He found a note printed on a remnant from a sack tied to a small arrow stuck in his door. In rough letters it said, "The cattle rustled yesterday from your herd are at the end of Coyote Canyon. Bring enough men to get them and bring them back." A large "X" in a circle sat at the bottom of the message. Coyote Canyon was a dozen miles up the river.

When Moncton tracked horse marks from the spot where the arrow was apparently shot, the trail quickly faded by the river and was lost.

Moncton gathered his few hands and a few neighbors' hands and they rode into Coyote Canyon and retrieved the cattle stolen from him and at least two dozen head rustled from the neighbor's herd, which was a surprise to the neighbor. No rustlers were around the stolen cattle that were penned in place by brush and rope at the deep end of the canyon.

The sheriff of Jasperville, Will Almsby, was surprised at the outcome of the note when Moncton told him the story, but admitted it was not the first time that some thievery or other crime had been uncovered by an unknown person who never made an appearance, so far as he knew, but had nevertheless provided explicit instructions on how and where to find stolen goods. "He's like a righteous angel or a gent too good to be true," the sheriff commented, nodding his head in added approval.

"This fella, the one who leaves notes around, he leave you any notes, Sheriff?" It was asked by Rag Tolman, a cowpoke locked up a few times by Almsby for being drunk and waving his gun around the Rocky Tor Saloon. The question sounded like sour grapes coming into the mix, as if Tolman was asking the sheriff if some unknown person was doing the sheriff's job.

Almsby, a quiet man with a dozen years of service to a couple of communities in Nevada, did not show contempt for the pointed question from Tolman. On the job he'd often seen, or heard, doubt coming from some men who, in his mind, would never make it even as a part-time deputy, never mind being saddled with a sheriff's responsibilities. Often he had judged men not in the throes and difficulties of danger, where survival instincts would kick in, but in those moments when contemplation and self-doubt marked the character of a man.

"None that I ever read first, Rag, though I've now seen two notes brought in to me. This one to Moncton and one a week ago. Looks like we have a quiet ranger or invisible lawman on our side and I'm not disregarding any of it. Everything helps, you have to admit. Like having a new man on the job. 'Course, if you want my job, Rag, I'll step aside for you. You can have the badge right now."

Almsby's hand went up to his chest as if to unpin the badge. His way of getting to the root of a man's doubt was straight on … with just a little bend in it, he might qualify if asked.

Tolman shrugged off the challenge with a face still looking sour, but did not reach for the badge. The sheriff obviously was getting some help, and that meant the town and the folks benefitted by the extra help, so there was no use in making off what it wasn't.

It was only a week later that a ranch hand from the KA-KA spread raced into town and dismounted hurriedly at the sheriff's office. "Someone grabbed Kurt Agular's little girl, Will, little Kedie. God, she's only eleven years old. Took her right off her pony on the back end of the KA-KA's north pasture. We looked all over and can't find her, and her pony had a hunk of rope on him where we found him pulled up and looped to a fence pole. Hell, Sheriff, Kurt's out there going crazy with six or seven men still looking and they can't find a thing. Told me to tell you. But you know what something like that can do to a man. Kurt's bound to shoot at the first thing looks out of the ordinary to him. And I suppose his boys'd do the same thing. Kedie's the little pet of all of them."

Almsby grabbed every able-bodied man on the street and emptied the saloon, swore them in as deputies, and the whole posse rode out of town, headed for the Agular ranch. Rag Tolman was one of the riders, a half a body more in a posse is better than no more of a body in a search.

The sun was setting behind the Rockies, a cool breeze had come into play tempering the heat of day, and the force of men had ridden and rumbled to a head of steam and anger and violent promises of what would happen to any man found with the child.

Almsby, in his time on the job, had seen some strange and unwarranted actions from misguided people caught up in mob anger, mob mentality. He knew he'd have to hold them in place.

The posse was rushing down the riverside, bent on anger and annihilation of a perceived coward and child molester, when one of them spotted the girl sitting on the bank of the river. She was muddy and incoherent and cried and shook the whole time the sheriff tried to ask her questions. Her dress was ripped in a few places and red marks circled her wrists. At length she pointed downstream and said, still in a near hysterical voice, "There. There. Down there." Then she began to shake again.

Almsby said to his regular deputy, "Go down there and take a look, Thorny, I'd guess near that bunch of trees. From these tracks, I think she came up here from down there. Probably crawled half the way."

In no time at all the deputy called back loudly from the middle of the cluster of trees and said, "Better get down here, Sheriff. Somebody's here but he ain't goin' no place now."

The sheriff found "the someone that ain't going no place now." He was a complete stranger, in regular cowpoke clothes that were in absolute tatters. He wore no regular boots but rugged pelt-made moccasins appearing to have had constant use, and he was hanging by his neck to a stout limb on a tree in the middle of tree shade. A note had been thrust under one suspender loop and said, in large letters on a piece of tanned hide, "This will happen with no trial to any man who risks a child's life." A large black "X" closed the message.

"Look for tracks," Almsby ordered as he held Kedie Agular in his arms and waited for her father who had been summoned.

An hour later Agular was reunited with his daughter who clung to him still sobbing, and all traces of the unknown person now described by various men as "the unknown hangman," "a righteous angel," "a gent too good to be true," "a quiet ranger or invisible lawman," "the quiet rider," or, finally, "the silent horseman." That man so described had been swallowed up by the river and its current, which was born in the mountains and headed southeast on a dead run, mostly silent except at certain points, much like the silent rider, the silent avenger of wrongs done to the innocent or the helpless or the unwary.

Will Almsby had no idea who the mysterious and silent rider was. There were some men he knew who might be capable of these deeds, but most of them could not keep quiet about such doings. Not with the notoriety that soon gathered around the image of the unknown person avenging the victims of all kinds of crimes.

In the Rocky Tor Saloon at night there were arguments galore about the hanging of Kedie Agular's tormentor, some saying that his hanging without a trial was a crime in itself to the full reverse of the argument where some men loudly affirmed that he got what he deserved.

Almsby never entered into such discussions, either keeping quiet in a corner of the saloon, where folks most likely would not bother him except the truly outspoken and inconsiderate ones, or he'd walk out of the Rocky Tor and leave his drink untouched on the table --- a sign to those who could read it.

The area generally was quiet for a few months, fall and its cooler weather coming down from the mountains in the north, with the slow evolution coming across the foothills, and the wide grass and the rivers joining in the spell of daily changes. The sheriff was content with the quiet turn of events, not looking for or wanting a posse chase or a shoot-out on the main street or any kind of deception pulled across the eyes of the community and its folks.

Quiet for him was always better for him. It was better than hard chases and gunshots and show-downs where mostly immature men tried to be other than what they really were ... just growing boys reaching for manhood and woefully equipped to do so. The frailty was too common where life of the times demanded much of a person.

Almsby could be happy in a variety of pastimes, like watching for hours for what he doted on. He liked the slanting sun as it crawled into secret places only to let go its grip earlier than it usually did. He liked to hear a song come from the saloon when a traveler with a penchant for music and its delivery spent a few nights within hearing distance of his office or his small cabin just off the main street, his horses letting him know they were still close by, comforts reigning. In the mornings he was just as happy when he woke to birds putting their voices to the start of a new day, and the soft, durable pleasure of the time was suitable to him.

But, as the Earth changes in its seasons, so changes came in the temperament and attitudes of folks. The thought of winter sat harshly in a goodly number of them and he saw the differences ... which told him that other elements would change: man would change the neighborhood as well as the neighbors ... the environment would change the people and the people would change the environment.

In one night, near cataclysmic for the quiet sheriff, there was a shoot-out that shifted from the Rocky Tor Saloon to the street that resulted in a needless death, then revenge came from a bushwhacking of the survivor early on the following morning, before the sun rose, and two days later the bank was robbed by two hard-eyed men who shot a teller in the arm as he tried to draw a weapon from under the counter. His blood spattered on some of the currency, which the robbers left scattered on the floor.

The town of Jasperville was once more torn asunder by anger and hatred and frustration and murder of its citizens. The hue and cry was loud and often went directly at the sheriff, who was too often seen sitting and enjoying life, but there were no clues about the bushwhacking or the robbery and shooting at the bank. The three days of calamity was a force that kept surfacing in discussions of every gathering, the saloon, the

152

store, at the cemetery when the dead were buried, in any passing of neighbors on their rounds.

It worked on Almsby with a vengeance, but three more days passed and nothing surfaced about any guilty parties ... including silence from "the avenging angel," "the silent rider."

A rider, in the early morning five days after the town was turned on its head, slammed his fist on the sheriff's cottage door, yelling, "Hey, Sheriff. He's done it again. Them bank robbers is tied up in a wagon that rolled into town a bit ago and if someone didn't stop it the danged thing would have run clear through town. The whole shooting match is hitched to a rail down at the livery and they's waiting on you."

When Almsby threw the door open, the rider mounted up again and said, "I'll tell 'em down there you're comin'." And he rode off in the same hurry he had arrived.

The sheriff knew the day was no longer his, figuring it would belong to "the silent rider."

At the livery, the wagon was a strange one to Almsby; he had not seen it before, at least not noticed it. But the message painted on its side was clear as an advertisement. "Here are two hombres who robbed the bank and all the money is in the satchel, every dollar is here but five I took for fee for my horse waiting on these scoundrels." Followed by "X."

Almsby attached a veiled sense of humor to his first question, smiling slyly but not carried off by laughter. "So tell me, boys, how one man got you wrapped up so tenderly and delivered here in style?"

The livery man and a few folks gathered for the interrogation tittered at the twist of the sheriff's words.

"It weren't fair, Sheriff," one of them said. "He was just sittin' on us, waitin' all the time we was robbin' the bank, sittin' right there in the cabin of our'n and chowin' down on our grub, and his horse, a big gray one, relaxin' with our mare, all 'em waitin' for us to come back with the money and that's just plain cheatin' stuff."

"Know him?" Almsby said. "Know him at all? Anything about him say who he is?"

The second robber, just as irritated as his pard, said, "This I know, Sheriff. He's nothin' but a plain all-out, all-aces coward who wears a mask so you can't get back at him later on. A plain all-out, all-aces coward. That's just what he is." He looked at the folks gathered around the wagon, his arms tied to one side of the freighter's wagon and legs still roped to the tail gate but hanging over the back end, like he was ready to jump off ... but couldn't.

"He call his horse by name?" The sheriff had tempered his humor a bit.

"Yah, that's a good one, Sheriff, like he was gonna tell us his own name, huh? Called the horse "Horse" every time he spoke to him. Just 'Horse' and nothin' else. I guess he ain't as stupid as you think, is he?"

"Nope," Almsby said, as he fingered the money bag. He told his deputy to handcuff the pair before he untied them, and then get them into a cell at the jail. He took the money bag and rode off, saying to his deputy, "I'll be at the bank, returning the money."

As he rode off, he looked at the mountains touching the early sky with their magnificence, and dwelled on the bold meeting the beautiful and then wondered where that thought had come from. Joy swept him as he realized it was some spark in him that kept getting ignited by certain things … which included his outlook on life in spite of some sheriff duties and a hopeful look for the good people of the area, most all who only wanted a chance at independent living … and having unknown friends in the ranks of those people.

At the bank he spent a good hour in the office of the bank president, outlining an idea he had and making certain demands on the banker concerning the returned money and all the new money that had come into the bank in the last week or so. Then he swore the banker to utmost secrecy.

He made two stops after that, choosing the two after deep consideration. One was at the barbershop knowing he could trust the barber without any doubt, and then at the general store, which was run by a similarly trustful person. He had eliminated the saloon because he could not trust any element there to keep quiet.

With nothing more than hope on his side, and a bit of faith, he set his plan into operation and planned his part in it. Each day he ambled slowly around town, fortunate that things had quieted down … the bank robbery solved, the bushwhacker had come forth on his own … and his ambling, slow walk brought him to the barbershop and the general store several times a day.

On the third day, the barber nodded as he sat down just to read the paper, and the barber placed a five dollar bill in his hand and a small note that contained the name of a rancher. Almsby knew the man whose name was printed on the note, nodded in agreement, and stuck the note in his pocket. The barber swapped the five dollar bill for one Almsby offered as he left the shop.

Almsby had not told the barber anything about what he was up to, and told no one else. Not even the banker knew. The five dollar bill from the barber went into a drawer in his office desk.

But now Almsby knew who the Silent Rider was, and deliberated for days about it. The man was married, had two children, and was a solid citizen on all orders.

On one ride for a mile or so out of town the next morning, the air chilly but the sky bright, pretending to the livery man that he wanted to get his horse some exercise, he thought it all over, and weighed all the crime solutions that had involved the man he'd come to know as the Silent Rider, including the hanging of Hedie Agular's kidnapper, and finally agreed he would do nothing.

Again he dwelled on the mountains meeting the sky, "Glory unto glory" he thought, and fully comforted himself with the things his eyes fell on, scanned, or saw more in them than what was visible.

It was settled and done in his mind; he was, after all, the law and order in Jasperville, and that included the protection all the local homes and ranches for 50 miles around, and their occupants and workers; a heady summary of a lawman.

He'd let the Silent Rider do what he could as long as he could; it was like having a silent deputy on duty, from wherever he'd see or hear of a crime against the people and start solving it on his own.

He knew the possible luxury of his decision.

The Trooper and the Dog Star

Pvt. Alexander Mulvihill, still bleeding from a serious wound, sat with his back against a big rock, the Texas night sinking like a lost swimmer, a breath of prairie air mixed with a promise of cool shadows. He kept thinking of home and the smell of a roast from his mother's great iron stove, her voice lilting and lifting angelic in the kitchen all the way back there in Pennsylvania, and the hills around home lit up in the leaves like flares the whole length of the Allegheny Valley.

He waited through the long night for the sun to come up.

It didn't.

A raiding party of renegade Cherokees, behind the chief on the big white horse, found him before his comrades did. The lead horseman was Tsewogi Awenitsa, the Cherokee Avenger, still doing what he said he'd do against the white man as long as he lived ... and then after. "I will be true to the Nations in the face of all powers," he'd said at many powwows, and the echoes of his words were steady on the Plains from Texas up to the Canadas. Some of the Indians agreed that Tsewogi Awenitsa had to be 80 years old in that year of 1872.

Two days later, Co. F, Fourth U.S. Cavalry, his outfit, found Pvt. Alexander Mulvihill, who hadn't moved a muscle since Tsewogi Awenitsa had put him down, buried most of him under rocks, the avenging Cherokee sending his own talk to the soldiers from Fort Wilson; Mulvihill's body, most of it, was covered with rocks. In the beginning only his head was visible ... and his left foot, the foot that he mounted his horse with, those end parts all torn, gnawed, chewed beyond recognition.

Those parts of him had been fed upon by predators.

The troop doctor said he had been dead for at least two days, maybe three, the way he was picked apart, the scavengers coming upon him from different directions and in different forms. But only the purposely exposed parts of him gnawed, pulverized and eaten, head and foot. His uniform and the contents of his pockets made the identification positive. The doctor was particularly alert to the left foot having been left exposed; he'd seen it before, and it was supposed to be a subtle message from the Indians, especially the Cherokees in the long and unfortunate war with them, with Tsewogi Awenitsa always in the forefront.

This newest act was his deciding mark. "It's supposed to be subtle," the doc had said to Captain Lattimer, troop leader, "but we see it better than that."

Private Mulvihill's Smith & Wesson .44 revolver, issued by Co. F, Fourth U.S. Cavalry, lie in scattered pieces on the ground beside his grave, his Spencer carbine long gone with those who had interred him, Tsewogi Awenitsa and his renegades.

It was 1872, near Wells, Texas.

Most of the Cherokees had been expelled from Texas in 1840, but out there, in 1872, the Great Avenger moved with his warriors like ghosts in the woods or plains, *Gihosti Ini Wudis*, or the devils from the grass, *Dewili Womi Giwas*, as the Cherokee nation called them in turn.

The International-Great Northern Railway had built a rail line in 1872, which became the Missouri-Pacific line, and the Kansas & Gulf Short Line had run a line north to south, to several new towns. Wells was a new town and the cavalry was stationed nearby at a temporary fort.

The closest friend of Mulvihill's in Co. F, Brendan Croughmartin, tried to relax with the troop commander who had called him in and asked him to tell him how he had escaped and tell him all about Mulvihill, all of it on a personal basis. Croughmartin thought at the time it was an act of self-appeasement on the captain's part.

"Private," Lattimer said, "tell me all you know about Private Mulvihill before you tell me how you got away from those redskins. It's important to me, as the commanding officer, in order to process the information further." He made a sudden point of conciliation: "You must know it's miraculous that you escaped from that horde of savages." Abruptly he held his hand up. "Time enough for that. Tell me about Alexander, all you know." There was no twinkle in his eyes in a deeply-bronzed face, a rugged face, the face of a man with five years of service beyond the Mississippi River, and all of that time out on the Plains. He could remember the day he crossed the Great River and it always made him wish for one more sight of the Hudson. Just one more evening with Claire Reynolds. "Dreams have such bounty," he could have said to himself.

Croughmartin responded, aware of some minor inattentions of his commander, "He hailed from the Allegheny Valley in Pennsylvania, sir. One night on bivouac he told me his mother had run away from home as a teen-ager, from down there in Roanoke, Virginia, and met his father, Silas, who was a good and sage man. The father died, though, and his mother remarried a widower with kids. Mulvihill left home because of that. I think he was about 12 or 13 at the time."

Croughmartin, exhibiting still some of the embarrassment crawling upon him as he talked about a dead comrade, offered up a series of hesitations in his delivery.

"Once he told me that when his father died, there were no sounds left, just a void. Their old barn had become a mausoleum, like he meant the actual full grave, the real grave. The father had been caught by a

157

storm and taken down a rushing river in spring with his horse and wagon. They were heading home from selling some farm products. They never got there. His mother eventually married the widower with kids ... and with money ... planning that she could care for her own son, Alex, and have her new husband's children about her to care for, to cook for, to tend to, and she could please a man again. She could be as happy with herself as she could be, but felt sad that her son had to leave, to make his own way, for that's what Alex did."

There came a pause of delivery as though he was measuring the impact of what he would say, could say, meant to say, and finally had to say.

Lattimer sensed a core of knowledge was about to be explained and that it might indeed cause a deal of discomfort to Croughmartin.

"Worry not, Private," the captain said, "this is really about Alexander at this point. But it is no longer personal, with him gone. It's all right to let him be known again. It's really all right."

Croughmartin continued on, the air apparently clear of responsibilities. "That's when he really told me, sir, about his father who had told him, many, many times, 'Make sure to cut your own star, Alexander.' That's the exact way he said it, 'Make sure to cut your own star.' Then he tried to make it clearer and said, 'See it, haul it down, and hold it for yourself.' I'd guess I first knew his father then. He was just like my grandfather from Roscommon in the old country. That's just the way the old timers say things that count with them, that really matter in all the words they might have uttered in their whole lives."

Lattimer was tuned in, he seriously knew, to a privacy he would otherwise never attain.

"Why did Private Mulvihill join the army?" Lattimer said, aware that Croughmartin was still uneasy answering questions about a comrade of the ranks, a dead comrade.

"It was the uniform, sir. He said he loved the uniform, like it meant something, had some meaning to it."

"That's was noble of him, I'd say," the troop leader said, with a taste of drama. "He must have known the perils in his path. Life will be uneasy out here for a long time to come. These renegades will keep at it until we leave or they're dead ... and we're not leaving."

"Now, and this is highly important, for the whole troop, for Alexander's memory, for you above all the troopers, and for the whole United States Army after it has just gone through a most horrible campaign within its own ranks, if I may say that about the Great War, and finds itself in another war with the renegades and Tsewogi Awenitsa and his cutthroats."

158

There was a summation pending, Lattimer sensed, as he studied Croughmartin.

"He knew the stars, Alex did," Croughmartin further explained, "saw them coming in their turns, and saw this one coming, this special one. We were tied up inside a tipi, bound real tight to a pole, but we could move our butts a bit to rest a bone or a muscle, and we could wait for the sun to come up. We could see it through an open flap when a pelt of some kind was pulled aside."

"The Indians on guard never said much to each other, always two of them, but the funny thing about it was, they always stared at Alex, like there was something special about him. It was eerie if you ask me, like they knew if one of us was going to escape it'd be Alex for sure. But it wasn't that at all, it was something else."

"Why do you say that, Private?"

"You might not believe me, sir, but Alex was different, different from all of us, all the other troopers, and I swear those Indians knew it as well as I did. It was like it sat on him or came lifted out of him and danced in the air, but unseen, like a piece of a ghost before it's time to be seen, to scare people."

He remembered something else; "One time one of them rushed out and came back with a couple of others, older braves, and they all kept staring at Alex who never once said anything to them, and he knew a bit of Cherokee too, sir. But didn't say anything to them. Even those older ones."

"Don't stop there, Private," Lattimer said, his voice carrying a nervous anxiety, as though Croughmartin would suddenly forget what he had known, had seen, had brought up out of his soul. What next? "It was the star, sir. The one star that Alex knew was coming right in through that opening in the tipi, like it was meant to happen. That star came over the peaks in the southeast and it sat right there in Alex's eyes and I was staring at him and the reflection came right into my eyes and those braves were sure something was going to happen. Those two on guard started jabbering to each other, getting agitated, making all kinds of gestures up to the sky, what they could see out there on the horizon through that open flap. And one of them went out again and others came back, but not the big chief.

They were talking and I caught a few words and don't know much, but Alex had pointed out the star to me before and called it the Dog Star or Sirius, bright as all hell, if I can say it, sir. Then I heard them say and I'll say it the way I tried to remember it. It was like *Gitli a-i-sv no-qu-si* and I sure guess that's Cherokee for Dog Star or Walking Dog Star or Dog Star Walking or something so close to that that they were concerned both about Alex and the big chief because some of them kept pointing to Alex and then to the outside and I knew it had to be the chief because they were not pointing at the star."

Croughmartin took in a gulp of air.

"It sat right in Alex's eyes and I stared at him and the reflection came in my eyes and the Indians started talking among themselves and I knew there was some kind of apprehension there, not real fear, but a concern for something beyond them. In Alex's eyes, and in mine, too."

"Captain," the trooper said after a long pause, as though he was reconstructing images or events, 'It's just like Alex, I'll swear it forever. Like he just reached up and grabbed that mutt by the tail and hauled him right down there twixt us and those Cherokees, like his father said – and they damned well knew it. A couple of them went near white in the face for a few seconds and bolted out of there, almost tearing down a pole from its roots, and then the big boy, the one that rides the white horse like he's the king almighty himself, he came in for a look on his own."

Croughmartin rubbed his wrists again, as he had on several occasions, and then Lattimer knew he was still feeling the cut of the ropes on his wrists.

"And you know what, Captain? I wasn't afraid any more. Even when the chief came in and his face painted up like he was going to a masquerade party, looking like the devil might look at the Horrible's Parade back in Massachusetts. Not for one damned minute was I afraid 'cause Alex, that good old boy, had the sign on them and they all knew it ... and they knew I knew it. That's one hell of a feeling when they have you all tied up like you'll never be anyplace again, like you won't even be able to mount your horse or run like hell if you even had the chance."

Lattimer was silent for long seconds at a time, his eyes drifting off now and then, looking for answers in clouds, bushes, shadows, hoping for resolutions and images as bright as his mind could stand.

At length he found a firmness setting on his chin. "This we will do, Brendan," Lattimer said, in the most secretive way an officer had ever spoken to Private Croughmartin and the very first and last officer of rank to address him as Brendan. "We will make an agreement. I will make you Alexander's star. I will send you off to the academy at West Point with a Medal of Honor citation. And you can become Alexander's star, become an astronomer. Go beyond yourself. We should be able to explain to the whole country, and the entire army, how Tsewogi Awenitsa felt about this, what he knew, what he feared if anything."

He waited for it to sink in with the private, and then said, still as secretive as ever. "Remember this, Brendan. It is for the extreme good of the service, and for the 4th Cavalry. And somehow it will touch Alexander Mulvihill wherever his soul abides."

He looked overhead, perhaps seeing Alexander Mulvihill's face in a far reach.

"Oh, I know, sir," said Croughmartin. "I saw all that in the chief's eyes a bit later, though he could not let his braves know. That's why he let me go, making off like it was another message from him, one of those subtle messages he's so good at."

He nodded and said, "He's awfully smart, sir, but Alex had his number. I'm sure of that. I saw it in his eyes more than once, that he knew Alex had a connection with whatever was overhead, who ran it all up there, who kept the stars in place yet kept them moving at the same time. And who brought the sun up every morning and brought the moon around in a cart every so many days, who changed the moon's dress each time it was to be done, who colored it each time. Oh, sir, I know ... and he knew that I knew. And Alex, bless him, sir, saw everything, like his father said. He never had a minute's fear."

Lattimer had a citation prepared for Croughmartin, processed it properly and to fulfillment, and transferred him to the Military Academy at West Point, "for the greater good of the service."

The citation read:

Private Brendan Croughmartin
Rank: Private
Organization: Company F, 4th U. S. Cavalry
Place and date: Near Wells, Texas, 29 September 1872
Entered service at: Gloucester, Massachusetts
Birth: Ireland
Medal of Honor Citation: After insuring that a dead comrade, brutalized by Indians, was properly buried, he escaped from long-time hostile Cherokee renegades led by Tsewogi Awenitsa, "the Great Avenger of the Cherokee Nation." He escaped from the hostiles and reported all details to his superior officers in a brave and circuitous and illustrious flight from captivity.

Croughmartin became, after his separation from the service, a noted astronomer and late in his exemplary life collected funds to build on a broad hilltop in Pennsylvania's Allegheny Valley, the Mulvihill Observatory of Stars and Other Celestial Bodies.

A boy, visiting the observatory one night and using one of its telescopes, turned suddenly to his mother and exclaimed, "Mum, I saw a man's face up there right near a star!"

The Trouble with Sheriffs

First the trail came, a rough ride to the river towns of Beaumont and Breadloaf, then the stagecoach line opened and that was followed in a dozen years by the railroad. People in both towns knew many in the other, from relatives to old riding pards on the trail to acquaintances in the beef business. And from the first the sheriffs of both towns held up their records as the best law-controlled town on the river.

Often, as propelled and fomented by jealousy or ambition, justice took a backseat to personal gain. It seemed a certainty that each new sheriff would get the job because he'd owe allegiance, and experience, to his predecessor. It was bound, one day, to end up in the wrong hands. That thinking was often the general consensus as the two towns spread and grew in their own ways.

Jazco Collins, newest sheriff in Beaumont, once chief deputy to his pal and cousin Lorne Comiskey, now retired to a ranch in south Texas and not to be seen again, sighed as he rode back into town after a visit downriver to Breadloaf. Jazco, just short of six feet tall, wore his blond hair in curls that fell over his ears, and came at people with a firm jaw that gave him a sense of solidity.

The trip between towns usually took under a full day, with plenty of sights and sightings along the way and precious time for thinking of valuable things, like his sweetheart Alma, his last arrest, and the most recent poster placed on the wall of his office.

The purpose of his trip was supposedly a secret between him and the Breadloaf sheriff, Walt Carmichael. In each town, on successive days, a Wednesday and a Thursday for four straight weeks, a major crime had been committed. The Wednesday days were alternated by the criminals, times were random, and sightings were non-existent: not one witness had stepped forward on five murders, two barns burned in the night; one person kidnapped from his bed, a five-year old boy, son of a rancher with a large spread. The father wanted to wage war on somebody but had no idea who had taken his son, or why. He had haunted the sheriff's office every day since the kidnapping, asking questions, making suggestions, getting more lost in his misery.

So, the conversation between the two sheriffs had been odd, each man generally knowing only the "what" but unsure of the "who/why/where."

Jazco Collins sensed Carmichael's uneasiness. "Something's on your mind, Walt. What's going on with you?"

"I got the strangest feeling, Jazco, that someone is setting us up. Pulling us in from each town, or stacking things up against the both of us. It feels like it's all planned, even the targets. I don't think any of this

162

is random, not the work of some idiot out for revenge. I don't think it's anything like that. Have you had any of those feelings? I mean, really asked yourself about them?"

"You mean like each of us saying our town's been the cleanest, and all of a sudden it ain't that anymore? Yuh, I've been on that side of the wire for a week or so. But I don't have any idea of who would gain by all this stuff. Nobody I know is out to get me, 'cept maybe a few guys I put in jail for a good spell."

"Or their kin," added Carmichael, "some young cousin or older gent ought to know better, but it takes all kinds. It says we ain't going to get much sleep on this matter. Keep me fixed about what's going on in your town. I'll do the same."

They had parted company, each to their own troubles, which to any outsider were affecting both men, both offices and both towns in a concerted effort.

When the kidnapped boy was found wandering out on a wide section of grass near the river, only a few miles from Beaumont, Collins realized another statement was being made, more so to him than the boy's father. It almost said, "I can do what I want to do and there isn't much you as a sheriff can do to stop me."

Collins, after the euphoric reception by the boy's parents at having their son back in their arms, went off by himself into the hills above the wide grass. He spent two days looking for something ... and found it ... the remains of a small fire high in the hills with an exceptional view of the area where the boy was found. It set him to thinking about the kidnapper's intentions ... that the boy was being watched and protected from the high point. Then he found a rifle shell beside a nearby rock. He could picture the kidnapper taking aim at something, perhaps an animal that was intent on hurting the boy.

The big challenge came when Collins's sweetheart, Alma Dixon, a cousin of Carmichael's who lived on a small ranch halfway between each town, was whisked off her carriage one afternoon and hustled off into the hills. A note, tucked under the cushion, said, "So much for those who can't take care of their own." And the horse had developed a bad leg from being run into a rocky area.

The two sheriffs, each with a separate posse, had scoured the hills for more than a week and not a sign was found that would give them a lead. The teams of men came back exhausted, and fully dispirited. The evenings were long and bothersome in the saloons. Talk passed there of ghosts at work or unseen men who had secret passages and hideaways up in the hills and amid the towering peaks.

For three weeks there was quiet, silence at night, little of crime. Sleep came back in a slow approach to many of the townsfolk, except for the two sheriffs, really under the gun of some unknown foe.

In the midst of silence, Collins, at a terrible loss without his sweetheart, rode out of town to seek out an elderly Indian high in the hills.

The old Indian, a mix in himself of Comanche and Kiowa, never seen in the company of another brave, elderly or not, eked out a solitary existence in a corner of the mountains. Other red men stayed afield of him, talk of danger and evil spirits circulating in their comments about One Dog True.

A few years earlier, at the end of a hapless search for a bank robber and killer, the search extending deep into the mountains, Sheriff Collins had spent the night at One Dog True's fire, both men speaking of justice, loss, what God spoke fairest on the mountain.

This trip Collins did not mention the kidnapping of his fiancé, but One Dog True said, "I have heard that a strange woman, very young and with hair of the raven, is kept under guard by a band of renegades of all mixes in the Valley of the Washato."

Collins leaped at the information, seeing dark tresses his fiancé kept in long, luxurious waves, seeing the smile that still haunted him.

One Dog True held up his hand. "An army cannot get in there, but one man or two good men, can make an entrance, escape with the girl. In the far end of the valley, under a huge overhang, a narrow crevice allows a person to leave the valley and come out after a long walk at the end where the river runs below an opening. The river must be crossed at that point, for there is no crossing for many miles below, and no way to go up the mountain."

Collins, in full excitement, leaped to make his way north. One Dog True said, "I would go if I were younger, but take your brother badge man. You will be a force, the two of you, but no more. That would be foolish. Move swiftly, silently, with guile if need be."

The next day, packed for their undertaking, routes planned and understood, the two lawmen took off at midnight in a circuitous route to their destination. One Dog True had advised, "Beware of those close to you. Bear no good wishes for your journey but mine."

With a few minor distractions along the way, losing the trail for a time, scattered by a bear and her cub on a narrow trail, smelling smoke from a fire, the two lawmen made their way into the hide-out valley in the reverse route outlined by One Dog True. The trip was on foot through the heart of the mountain, through tight places, low overheads, on a slim ledge that poked above unseen but heard water.

They had more than a few precarious escapes, near falls, and heart-stopping moments when rock falls threatened not only their lives but their route in and out of the secret valley. It was Carmichael, only a cousin as he would say time and again on the trip, who made the best decisions, took the least chances, made the most of each moment; he realized he adored his cousin but Collins loved her beyond bearing at the moment, and that was as keen as a knife edge.

"Jazco," he'd say time and again, "take a deep breath every time you feel you heart pumping. If this trip takes us ten days instead of one day, it'll be worth it. The old Indian was right when he said, 'Take deep breaths and make no noise when you do. It will do you well.'"

So it was, two days later, after a scare from spiders, unknown creatures making night noises in a tunnel section, daylight a full 48 hours behind them, that they saw a glitter of light ahead of them. It sat out front of a small entrance like a glowing diamond with all the glitter.

"Don't rush out, Jazco," Carmichael warned. "The sunlight will blind you. We'd be cooked if some lookout saw us and we were half blinded by the sunlight. Let's go slow, pace it, be ready for anything. The old boy said we'd only get one chance. Just one chance. We have to make it good." He paused, put his hand on Collins's shoulder, and said, "I want to be an uncle. It's my only chance too."

From their retreat in the side of the mountain, they had a full view of the valley, a tight and narrow valley, a small waterfall at one side that seemed to disappear into the ground again, and a cabin that looked as if it was wrapped around three or four rooms. One room had shades or curtains on two windows at the back side of the cabin. There was no rear porch, but there was a large one out front, with a scattering of wooden chairs and benches tight to the wall. One large door, of two sections, sat in the center of the structure. At an early part of evening, smoke and attendant food aromas spilled from a stone chimney in the center of the front roof with a steep pitch.

Collins pointed to the four horses tied at the hitch rail directly to the side of the cabin, on the side closest to their lookout site. "Might be four or more of them in there, Walt. That big gray looks familiar to me but I can't place it. Wish I could see the saddle he wore getting here." He pointed to a small shelter near the far side and said, "Might be more company in there if there's any more horses. Maybe we can figure that out when they feed the animals."

He sat back, and said, "I wish we could rush in there, but you and One Dog True are right in all this. We have to plan our one chance. I think it's gotta start with their horses, then get Alma out of there and up in here. We can hold off an army if we have to from in here."

At that moment both men heard the rattler in a corner of the tunnel. Carmichael, his hand near a rock, clutched it and fired it into the corner and then threw three more stones. There was no more rattling. He slipped closer, kicked at the prone rattle snake and brought the butt of his rifle down on its head. He hit it three times, crushing it. He could already see the sweeping loop of the snake winding through the air at the horses. The picture pleased him and he explained the plan to Collins.

They sat back and set their plans, excluding the one guard who sat way out in front of the cabin and changed places with a replacement every two hours. They guessed the room with the shades was Alma's, that she must have hung the curtains. There were no bars on the window, for there appeared no way out of the valley this rear way.

They waited until full darkness came, armed themselves to with only their side arms and the dead rattler and set out on the next leg of the rescue mission.

In the dead of night, in complete darkness, in mountainous silence, the tapping on the window seemed perilously loud. Collins, at the window, waited, counted to ten and tapped again. He did it three times and then the curtain parted, Alma peered through the opening. Collins put his hand against the window, and the youthful scar borne there was full evidence of his identity. She peered closer, saw his eyes, lifted the window and slipped out without a sound.

She did not kiss him. He did not kiss her, but took her hand and led her away from the cabin. He got her almost to their tunnel when an owl screeched, a horse snickered, and Carmichael flung the dead rattlesnake onto the top of two horses in the leaning barn at the far side. The three of them said later it was like the screech of banshees if there were any banshees around, and the horses broke loose in a thunderous calamity and rushed, all of them, down the known trail.

Several bandits rushed out of the cabin and chased the horses on foot, screaming at the far guard to slow them down, shoot in front of them, somehow bring them to a stop. Half a dozen shots rang out even as the threesome reached their escape tunnel.

None of the shots came their way, and they were into the tunnel and on their way to freedom before any accounting was made ... except Alma kissed Jazco and Jazco kissed her back for a long while and Carmichael thought he might get to be an uncle sooner than later.

All other accounting was done in town as Alma, on the day of her marriage, pointed out the culprits one by one, each one naming another in a move to get control of the two towns, all headed by one teller at the bank who knew more than any of them how the two towns were doing.

Torby Glibstone's Enterprise

Torbert "Torby" Glibstone was about the smartest young man ever to come west in a wagon, helping his grandparents to move to a piece of land they had inherited from their son when he was killed in a gunfight in Dawson, Wyoming. Torby was fifteen at the time the wagon set off from Independence, Missouri, part of a large wagon train. His grandparents were both just turned 61, on the same day, which got them married in the first place like a celebration was in order, and they were game for the move west. Torby had lived with them for seven years and they made sure some of Torby's reading books were in the wagon, "But not all of them, son, 'cause we couldn't carry half of them in one wagon," Toby's grandfather said, knowing his grandson was an avaricious reader at all hours of day and night.

Almost a year later, after leaving Independence, they were settled on the small ranch a few miles up-river from Dawson, Wyoming, comfortable in their new holdings, some left-over cattle remaining from a broken herd, and some good elements left in the property. The mild preservation of the property was due to two individuals in Dawson, the sheriff and the banker, who made sure the land, in essence, was kept intact, though some thefts from or damage to the property had occurred. It was not far from Good Grace's Pond that was fed by a spring from a mountain fall that didn't stop until winter froze it up tight, as well as Good Grace's Pond, some nights that winter looking like a mirror in the moonlight.

Both men, Ben Silverwood the banker and Jess Sturgiss the sheriff, were taken with young Torby who they found willing, determined, loyal to a fault to his grandparents, and the most imaginative and lively talker they had met in a long while. There were no other young men like him in all of Dawson. Nearby ranches that reached all the way up the river to the mountains sat like sentinels of the territory, huge, rugged guardians who stood silent until thunder came over their tops swift as rockets, or falling stars, heading east or west in the night, ran across the sky like runaways. For hours on his arrival, when his day's work was done and enough light still shone on the rugged peaks, he went back into his reading and found old mountains in a new place; craggy tors from Scotland, Bavarian mountains lyrically found in an old German translation, pieces of the Pyrenees and Alps and the Andes brought to him by thin paper in leather bound books he'd treasure every day of his life.

Wyoming gave him his own ranges to discover. Around him he knew The Teton and Rocky Mountain and Gros Ventre Ranges. His interests were well known in a short time.

"He's as bright as a new spoon," the banker once said to the sheriff, "and he's the breeziest and quickest and most entertaining talker we've had around here since a mare gave birth to a dogie. One day I'll bet he's the mayor of the town or the head of the council."

"And maybe the bank president," the sheriff offered in his pitch at humor. They both laughed.

But for all the talking he did, Torby Glibstone did a lot of watching and listening, and one thing came ringing true to him once he had his first beer at the Four Horse Saloon in the heart of Dawson. It was the day he finished a trail drive for a neighbor who needed help and offered him a beer as part token of thanks at the finish of the drive.

The neighbor was Cal Thumblick, an old timer in the region who had lost his only son in a landslide.

Thumblick said, "I'm damned sorry your first beer is so warm, Torby. I don't much like it so warm, but warm beer is better than no beer from where I stand." He tapped his mug on Torby's mug and added, "Here's to better days and better beer."

Torby Glibstone, that very moment, was off and running with an idea that he had not given birth to, but which had come out of his reading a letter from one old friend of his father's to another friend. It mentioned a cave where ice had been stored from winter months until late in the summer of the year.

He found the letter to be revelatory.

Dawson was built against a solid foothill of the mountain, with the river only a few hundred yards from the center of town, and little was known about the buzzing that went on in Torby's mind about the condition of his first beer, which he liked but knew it would be better if it was cooler … especially on a hot day or the end of an arduous task, like a month-long trail drive … or longer. "Cowpokes," he thought, "might taste that cool beer for the duration of a drive."

He asked the banker about a small piece of property that was pretty close to a large rock wall at the north edge of town. "Mr. Silverwood," he said one day as they sat in front of the bank on a bench, "that little piece of land over by the cliff at the edge of town has sparked a fair amount of interest in me. I posed a few questions to some local folks and they say it's the property of the bank. Is there any chance that I can gain possession of the site to step off in my business career without having to produce much of a down payment on the site? If I find a business opportunity to set off there, might such a down payment on purchase of the property come from business profits, thereby not requiring me to make any cash deposit on it from this end?"

"Son," Silverwood said, not knowing what the lad had in mind but sure he'd make a go of any venture, "You come down to the office in the morning and I'll have proper papers drawn up with a minimum down payment on your part. I can't let it wander off without something, that's the banker's way, but it won't be a whole lot and you can even work it off in a week or so if need be."

He slapped Torby on the back and said, "Good talking to you, Son. See you in the morning." He could not wait to share the news with the sheriff.

After the papers were signed, Torby, a land owner by agreement, went to work every time he was free from ranch duties, and he'd work dawn to dark on every Sunday digging a huge hole in the ground. It took him months of labor, in which he managed to put a little money onto his mortgage, all which was deemed appropriate by Silverwood. The banker was eager to learn what Torby was working on but never asked him, thinking all the time it was the foundation of a building he had brought out of his reading, a special place of some sort or other, but beyond his guessing.

The hole eventually was about 19 feet deep and 5 feet on each of its 4 sides. Onlookers were amazed to see, when he was finished, tossing some of the rocks he had uncovered into the base of the hole, lining them up like a square floor; bigger rocks were packed with smaller rocks, the whole bottom of the hole eventually covered with stones and rocks. On this foundation he erected a wooden platform made of squared logs or cut beams set apart from each other by a few inches.

Folks stood wondering at the site, asking questions and opinions of each other.

After that effort, Torby started building 4 walls, each one of loose but wedged stones so that they fit tightly together. In another few months the walls were complete, and the last few feet of the rock walls were set with a kind of mixture to hold the stones fast in place.

To everybody's surprise, including the banker and the sheriff who visited the site each day, Torby started to dig a trench around the walled hole, out about 3 feet. He built a new foundation in that trench, on which he built a platform and started to build new walls on the new foundation.

Silverwood said to the sheriff one day as they were enjoying a few drinks at the saloon, "I think winter is about to catch up to Torby and his project. He won't be able to work much in the cold weather. Well, it's a great start on something, we can agree to that. Boy works like a dog working an old bone right down to dinner."

But Torby kept at it, building double-sided walls about 8 feet high on the exterior foundation, then put a roof over the top and filled the in-between section of all each wall with sawdust and hay mix, including the separated partitions of a double roof.

Sheriff Sturgiss said to his banker pal on another night in the saloon, "I think I have an idea of what Torby's up to."

"Oh, c'mon, Jess, law's your business, not buildings and property. That's my business. What the devil can you make of this, on the chase most days after someone escapes your jail or tries to rob my place or the store, or the damned livery for that matter. I'll leave the law to you and you let me keep my mind on that Torby. Makes me shivery, he works so hard."

Well, the winter came down hard, pounding at local folks, and shutting ranches into long days trying to keep cattle fed, and just getting by as they looked forward to spring when the harsh grip on Earth would be loosened and slip away toward summer.

But one day, winter well onto its coldest spell, Torby Glibstone started the second leg of his business: cutting ice from Good Grace's Pond in big chunks that he levered onto wagons some days and onto a large sled other days, and hauled it to his new enterprise, dropping the ice into the hole through a trap door no one had seen him cut, crushing it down into his own icehouse in Dawson, the first of its kind in Wyoming.

Word ran around the territory as fast as a rabbit on the move.

"Well," the sheriff said to Silverwood, "it's like I figured that time you didn't want to hear from me." He had the needle in place, poking with it.

"Ah, Jess," Silverwood replied, "I'm sorry about that. What do you think he's up to now?"

"If you're asking me polite like, Ben, I'll make a wager that the next thing that boy does is build the second saloon in Dawson, and it's going to be right next to his own icehouse, practically on the spot, and he'll have his loan paid off quicker'n you can smell rabbit stew out on the grass. Boy's got the handle on business and nobody knows how far he can go with it. He might even own the bank someday."

The needle was home as Silverwood shivered. It was the second time Torby Glibstone had set it off.

That winter the icehouse was crushed full of ice from Good Grace's Pond, and Torby started work on his own saloon, where he was sure to enjoy a cool beer on a hot summer day, all because he had read a letter in a book about an earlier icehouse in Philadelphia, Pennsylvania.

The saloon, Bookman's Cool Paradise, was built and in place by the following April and cool beer was the main attraction, Torby's grandfather the bartender and his grandmother making and selling the most delicious sandwiches this side of either Chicago or San Francisco, according to all reports. The Cowpoke's Special, a thick sandwich with ham and several cheeses the main ingredients, was the big seller, most cowpokes tired of trail beef and beans and loving the change. The avaricious reader had made his start in a unique way and folks all over wondered what he'd do next. It was a steady point of discussion, and all guesses were mostly treated with a sense of possibility.

It was Sheriff Jess Sturgiss who said to his banker pal one day, "If I was you, Ben, I'd try to find out what book that boy's been reading lately."

Silverwood hadn't thought of that at all, but the more he did think about it, he figured he'd better get as smart as Torby Glibstone, and in a hurry.

Two Guns West

Prior strangers, leaving Boston on the eve of May 1st, 1867, heading west on a train, neither married, both in their early 20s and veterans of the Great War of the States where they met in the ranks of Company B, 2nd Battalion of the 4th Massachusetts Cavalry Regiment, Merlin Lockland and Pouvard BeLaire knew their friendship truly began aboard the steamer Western Metropolis. The steamer had left Boston, their whole regiment on board, bound for Hilton Head, South Carolina three years earlier in March of 1864, with a gritty piece of the war in the offing.

Lockland and BeLaire were from small towns south of Boston, loved horses and wanted to "get their way west one day," to see the country grow, to see the Pacific, and eventually to see adventure coming at them other than, after they had seen it during the campaigns, massed infantry and cavalry on a headlong move. The latter they met in strange, once-seen locations as they earned their veteran status in such places as Gainesville, Gum Swamp, Front Creek, Boyd's Neck, Beech Creek, Honey Hill and Smith Mills.

"No big names there," Lockland said to his pal once, "but all damned memorable." They had counted their blessings on a number of occasions.

"Someday," BeLaire said as they boarded a train out of Boston, bound for any place where they might jump off for something that looked promising, "I'll write a song about those places we've been to, and swiftly thereby said adieu." Lockland had learned a lot earlier, even in some ticklish battlefield situations, that his friend's predilection for rhyme was always alive, "Sitting on his forked tongue, so to speak," he'd quickly qualify.

Lockland, to balance things between these pals, had his own special talent; in most usual circumstances, and with people of ordinary dialect, he could read lips as long as he had a decent view of them, not too far, not too dark, and rarely when delivered in screaming rages whereby all messages became distorted. With this talent, learned in school, perfected in hallways and then in command posts, he often knew what sergeants and lieutenants had in store for them. It had proved both valuable in an instance and treading on the dangerous in other developments.

Both men laughed religiously whenever lips or tongues or such associated figures of speech were employed by one of them or heard from a bystander. Their friendship came fast and sure, each of them aware of what the other brought to that quick alliance, including humor of any sort.

Lockland looked the part of a very young professor who had sped through classical ranks of education. He was the taller of the two, with a continual studious look on his face and about his person, though he would often prove to be the lark of the pair, full of fun and frolic as if his studies needed to be set aside for a short while. His long frame alluded to quickness and an athletic prowess he could have exhibited on most occasions. BeLaire thought him "pretty as boys go," but didn't hold that against him at all; the fairest blue eyes that lit up on occasions, a perfect nose that balanced out the blue flame of the eyes below a wide brow, sandy-colored hair often loose on that brow, and a skin texture and color the sun never seemed to hurt.

BeLaire, shorter by two inches, with broader shoulders and thicker arms, wrist to shoulder, was a dog for work, the broad shoulders surmounting most of his appearance except for his laughter, a constant sidekick that he brought to his work, and that sometimes infuriated others around him, generally those given to bitching and bellyaching and finding themselves matched by a laughing cohort. With one quick assessment, Lockland found him boisterous, friendly, humorous, and fervently devoted to a determined goal.

It was at an evening stop in a saloon for a drink, a few days out of Chicago, that the first encounter for them as a civilian team arose. Lockland, having watched a group of four cowpokes at the far end of the bar, said to BeLaire, his voice low, cautionary, "Pouv, we're not getting out of here without some kind of trouble. Those fellows at the end of the bar are ready to start something about 'them eastern dudes looking out of place and ought to be put where they belong.'" He paused in his warning to amend his alert; "The tall fellow in the gray vest said he bets we're damned Yankee Blues, and his name is Big Brit."

"Sakes alive, a way to survive," BeLaire said, and quickly followed with, "Here's me and you, like we're dressed in blue." His eyes rolled at his friend as though he expected a critique on his pitch. He laughed loud and long and Lockland knew exactly what his pal was up to, for he might have called him The Infuriator more times than he could remember. It's how BeLaire's hand was dealt, and how he used it.

It usually worked the way it was planned.

It was Big Brit who jumped in with his raise, saying loudly down the bar, his eyes straight on BeLaire, "You got something funny to laugh about, mister? Why not tell us about it?" The tone of his voice quickly showing his origin.

BeLaire, suddenly wobbly on his legs the way a drunk might assemble himself, his left hand holding onto the rim of the bar, said, "You bet, Big Brit, and this is it: laughing's great except at Hell's gate."

173

Big Brit reacted. "What the hell are you talking about, mister, and how do you know my name? Have you been poking around my business, my concerns?" He stepped casually away from the bar, a well-known move by a challenger, separating himself from his pals, standing tall, hands loose at his sides the way he might wish to be remembered. And ready to toss out the next barb, or the next challenge.

BeLaire came right back at him. "That's it, Big Brit. That's all of it. You have something to prove, make your move."

"You calling me out with some brand of silly talk?" and he turned to his pals and Lockland saw him whisper, "Watch me drag this Blue dogie down."

In his own whisper, Lockland advised BeLaire of Big Brit's message.

Big Brit yelled out loud and clear to everybody in the saloon, "He called me out," and his hand slipped haphazardly toward his holster.

The entire room, all its occupants, went into a stunned silence. Outside a horse rode past the door, hoofs at rhythm; a wagon followed, then a child rolling a hoop threw a quick shadow into the room. Death and punishment seemed in the offing. A mother's voice, anxious, demanding, called a child from somewhere out of sight.

The stunning continued when Big Brit raised his pistol to see BeLaire's pistol, only 20 feet away, pointed right at his heart. He made no further move. His pals made no move. Lockland watched for lips to reveal some intent, some piece of a concentrated reaction, and saw none.

"Hold it there," a voice from a corner of the saloon said. "I'm the U.S. Marshal hereabouts, and all this stops here."

He looked at Big Brit and said, "Go back with your pals, Clifton, and be quiet. Next time ask me politely if you feel like calling someone out. I'm always ready for you."

He turned to BeLaire and Lockland and said, "I know you gents are passing through. Which way you headed?"

Lockland stepped right in and said, "We're heading back east, getting away from all the do's and don'ts you folks have rigged up. We're heading back to peace and quiet where a man can have a quiet drink and not worry about a known big mouth tossing out a chance for personal heroics."

Big Brit yelled, "Pay him heed, Sheriff? He's mocking me."

The sheriff came right back at the loudmouth. "Sure I can see it and I can also see if you tried him on a hundred times, you'd be a hundred times dead. Consider yourself lucky one more time, Clifford." The two pals understood the sheriff's taunting use of Big Brit's given name.

The sheriff turned back to our adventurous pair and said, "Well, get on your way right now. These gents will stay here until I leave. I guarantee you that much," and he leaned in close and whispered, "Don't close your eyes or ears for a few days. That's my best piece of advice. The Brit's a dangerous phony."

The pair started out and BeLaire, over his shoulder, said his goodbye; "Adios, amigos."

There was no answer. None that BeLaire heard or Lockland saw.

They rode east out of town, turned north immediately when they were out of town and swung west again.

Riding into the setting sun, BeLaire said, "That was keen. We're looking clean." But Lockland kept looking back over his shoulder, the sheriff's words coming along with them.

In one moment of revelation, Lockland said, "Pouv, do you understand what we're doing? What's ahead of us? Do you really know what I'm thinking about all this that's around us, looking us in the face, or creeping up behind us? Do you have it locked up the way I have? Do you really know where we're going?"

BeLaire, comfortable in the saddle, caught in the music of the gait, swung easily in the saddle as he twisted sideways to look at his pal, said in his best western diction, "Merlin, I've known it from the shipboard cell: we un's are headin' straight for Hell."

They laughed again, their gusto being laughter's companions, pleased with each other, the stars showing early statements no lip reader or rhymer could miss. They tried to sleep under those stars after a small fire set a pot of coffee for them, the horses cared for and tied off, the wide skies coming full of greater demands, the stars appearing by a seeming thousand-fold, and finally putting sleep in order.

A few hours later they were awakened by gunfire from a nearby canyon, the sounds of shots arriving like brittle pieces of rock whizzing into their hearing.

"What do you think that is, Pouv?"

"Might as well be the start of Hell," and they were up and saddled and racing toward the continuous rounds of rifle shots, those sounds so familiar to each of them.

In the dying flames of a late fire they saw a wagon under attack, rifle fire coming from higher on the canyon wall, return fire now and then coming from darkness under the wagon. The shooting was spasmodic both ways, as if each party knew they were shooting blind and wasting ammunition.

Lockland said, "We'll be taking sides here, Pouv, and I'm all for giving the folks in the wagon all the help we can."

"Let's fire away," BeLaire said, and when the couplet was not finished, Lockland knew fate was afoot.

The two pals let loose with repeating salvos at the upper reaches of the canyon wall. The return fire from that target was hesitant, and then it all stopped.

The sound of hoof beats on the run came dimly from an upper level of the canyon, then that too disappeared completely.

A woman called out from the wagon. "Hello out there. Thanks for the help. I need some help down over here right away. My husband has been seriously wounded."

Even in despair, under great duress, not knowing who her saviors were, her voice came to them as sweet, melodic, Lockland thinking it was operatic, BeLaire as if a poetess was reading only to him.

And it was the romantic BeLaire who made the first announcement for the rest of their lives. "That's it. That's her. I'm in love." For the second time in as many opportunities, there was no couplet from BeLaire.

Lockland said, "You beating me to the prize, Pouv?" His voice too had become new.

They laughed together, but it came weaker than usual.

Fate had moved in on the pair.

The woman, in the flash of dawn, shone her beauty right from the first glance despite her predicament. She was kneeling beside the lone wagon, leaning against one wheel and a wounded man was in her arms, his leaking blood evident.

"He's badly hurt," she said. "My husband, Earl Dumas. He has two bullets in him and he's losing a lot of blood. I stuffed much of my petticoat in there, but it's not enough. Do either of you have any medical experience?" Her voice was still full of a quality timbre, though dawn was shredding some of her appearance.

Lockland was about to step forward, but BeLaire said, "Yes, Ma'am. Let me help. You let me look to him and let my pal do what he can to help you." He lifted Dumas from her grasp and Lockland held her hand and walked away to the fire. He placed a blanket tenderly around her shoulders. He saw, reflected in her eyes, some of the flames and some of the starry sky not yet letting go its handsome grip.

There was no doubt in his mind that she was an unnatural beauty of a woman. And Pouv had spoken his mind.

She said to Lockland, "I'm so glad you two came along. I hope your friend can help my husband, but he's been hurt terribly bad. I don't know how much he can do for him."

She had not yet shed a tear, holding herself together.

176

"Do you know who those bushwhackers were, Ma'am? Any idea at all?"

"My name is Tricia Dumas. I used to be Tricia Walker, from Maine. We've only been married for less than a year and he had a big dream about a ranch out west and lots of cattle and lots of kids and the whole new dream that's working on people back east." She paused and said, "Who are you folks and where did you come from?" She looked back at BeLaire still working on her husband. Once or twice she saw his shoulders slump, but kept it to herself.

"Oh," Lockland said, "we're Merlin Lockland and that's Pouvard BeLaire trying to help your husband. We're both from little towns near Boston, and just out of the same cavalry outfit in the army after the Big War, and trying our hand at that western dream you just spoke about. We're in it for the long haul, whatever it brings, adventure, excitement, riches or a life of labor. We'll take what we can earn."

This time he saw BeLaire's shoulders slump and knew the reason immediately. Each of them had read that sign before in their campaigns, death marking the living as well as the dead. BeLaire stood up, turned around slowly and shook his head. He walked to the back of the wagon, found a shovel and said, "Ma'am, he's gone on you, Ma'am, and we have to bury him now. You take care of the lady, Merlin, while I get things ready."

Tricia Dumas looked at Lockland and said, Bury him way out here? Where are we? I don't even know where this place is." Her shell was in danger of collapsing, Lockland noted.

"It's best to get them in the ground, Ma'am. We'll mark it real properly, and make it deep so the carrion eaters won't get at him. It's best, believe me." Softly he draped a comforting arm over her shoulder. "We're in Nebraska, fairly close to both Colorado and Wyoming. I'd say a half day's ride would get us to either one of them. There are some towns on the way, too, from what I've heard."

His tone changed, even as he heard BeLaire working away with the shovel, a rock sounding out once in a while. "You didn't say if you knew who those bushwhackers were, Ma'am."

"Oh, I have a pretty good idea. We stopped only a few miles back at a small camp and Earl swapped some things for food. Some men were two damned interested in us for what I could tell. Three of them, and the dirtiest lot they were, cussing and swearing and making noise like they owned the place and could have anything they wanted, anything in sight. Earl didn't see it, but I did. A woman knows such things."

"You think they were after you, Ma'am?"

"Yes, I do. Earl had us sleeping over there," and she pointed to where a blanket still lie crumpled on the ground. "The second time he

177

got up to put some wood on the fire, two shots rang out. I think those are the ones that hit him, and he was standing right in the light of the fire. He went down right away and I dragged him near the wagon and started shooting back. Then you came." She placed a hand on Lockland's wrist. It was like a lilac bloom had graced him. And there floated an essence in the air that was new to him.

They buried Earl Dumas in a deep hole, put some rocks in the hole to thwart the carrion diggers, covered it all over and marked it with a cross. Each one said their impromptu words over the grave of Earl Dumas. The words of his widow were not audible to either man, and Lockland saw nothing from her immobile lips.

Lockland told BeLaire her whole story, and Tricia Dumas kept nodding at each point of information, acknowledging its veracity.

It was Pouvard BeLaire who said, his chin firm as a rifle butt, his voice hard as the barrel of the rifle barrel, "And the first order of business is to go back to that camp and finish this up. They'll only be setting on others who pass through. This is part of our destiny." He looked at Lockland and added, "Among other revelations this day that is a prime order of business. The west has to be safe for grand ladies."

Tricia Dumas blushed for but a second, and rushed to agree with him. "Let's do it now. I can point them out for you, all three of them."

BeLaire slapped his pal on the back, nodding in quick agreement. When she lets us know who these bushwhackers are, and you can find out from their own lips that they're really the ones, we'll wrap it up in a hurry." In a hesitant side note, he said, "And make them scurry," but it was, as of late, a rather indecisive note.

The hand-painted sign above the door of the clumsy-looking cabin on the edge of a fordable stream said in clumsy black paint, "Burke's Sidewinders Stoar." A few barely readable corrections had been added by odd hands, none of which were incorporated onto the sign. At the water's edge a raft sat idly on the edge of the banking, its stream-wide rope hanging down into the soft flow of the ripples, the raft a mess of ropes, planks and logs in a twisted but floatable condition. The whole arrangement said it could be swept away in the first cloud burst rushing out of the mountains; such events were historical in the confines of the mountain stream; Teton waters had already swept away a few towns in the foothills, along the streams unloading high waters rushing out of the mountains, taking the easiest route.

The two men and Tricia Dumas sat their horses in a copse of young trees a bit upstream from Burke's Sidewinder Stoar, their mounts quiet and feeding on clutches of grass. Lockland noticed again, for the tenth time, that his pal Pouv was not able to take his eyes off Tricia Dumas.

178

It was settled.

One man came downstream on his horse, entered the store, and left shortly thereafter. Then a pair of riders, on big grays and both wearing old Confederate military pants, came down along the stream. Tricia Dumas stiffened up in the saddle. Her horse made notice of her change. The two cavalrymen saw it and took additional note.

"That two of them, Ma'am?" Lockland said. "Do you recognize them?"

"They're the ones, I'd swear on it," she said. Her hand was on her heart. And Lockland saw a grimace crossing her face that was as deadly as a knife or a bullet. "The third man did not have the same outfit. He had a funny hat on his head, like an opera hat, tall, black, like Mr. Lincoln wore to Washington."

Lockland and BeLaire reined up in front of Burke's Sidewinders Stoar and tied their horses to the tie rail, Lockland stretching like he just got out of bed as he dismounted his horse, flinging his arms in the air and loudly saying, "I am tired of running all day and all night and now I need some rest." He was loud and boisterous, his voice carrying the words all around him, like a bell sounding its knell. "Liquor," he proclaimed to the heavens, "You got any liquor in there?"

Inside, at the simple and crude plank bar that Ordinary and Legal Judge Jud Burke had set up to dispense drinks and local law, they demanded whiskey and "the best you got and no rotgut. We got some gold wrapped up out there and we plan to drink our way for a week of Sundays, if no preachers mind us saying so." He let out a Dixie yell he had heard a thousand times, and he delivered the oft-sensed fervor in that most generally came with the cry.

BeLaire dropped a small sack of coin on the bar top and said, "When that's done gone and drunk up, let us know where we're at in accountability. We ain't any too particular about small change, if you've a mind of skimpin' off the top or neither the bottom." Their laughter was loud, boisterous and entirely too damned amusing for the fellows that Tricia Durham had identified without doubt as "most possible bushwhackers in the canyon."

She had fervently declared again, "They watched us like hawks and we saw them cross our trail, behind us, several times. I know they saw Adam set up an empty tin and we went on a decent way and he took his rifle and with one shot sent that tin flying into the air. It was his warning to anybody who might be looking on and contemplating an evil of any kind. That empty tin bounced around behind us more than 100 yards away, he was that good a shot."

Lockland said in a whisper the devil couldn't hear even if he had a mind to, "You keep making noise of any sort, Pouv, and I'll keep my eye on them. They have to tell us straight out if they're the ones, and if I catch it from them, we'll keep our promise to the lady and her husband we buried out there."

In his own too-busy and slowed-down rhythm of language, BeLaire, into main-stream action again, loudly said, "Dog gone you, Merl, that's about the funniest thing you ever said. You keep that up and my britches will be outgoin' on their own. Yore damned right about gettin' back at our strike, damned if you ain't. I swear on a stack of 'em books, it's the most pleasurable work I ever done in my whole life, diggin' that pretty stuff near right off the top of the ground. Yessiree!" He slapped the bar top again, the plank rattling all the way down its length to where the suspected fellows stood muttering among themselves.

Leaning over the crude bar, his elbows supporting his chin and his hands over his face, Lockland peered through slightly parted fingers and saw one of the suspected bushwhackers whisper, "Think them's the ones shootin' at us out there in the canyon?"

A second seedy looking character, his sidearm sitting knobby in a belt holster and a strap barely visible under an open-collared shirt, telling Lockland he was wearing a hidden chest holster, said with a quiet voice but loud lips that Lockland read with ease, "Nah, that noisy one said they got a strike somewhere. We gotta track them to it, only don't get caught like that woman's gent caught onto us last night. Shore missed her. Hope we run across he ag'in."

He got his wish quicker than imaginable, for a horse pulled up in front of Burke's Sidewinders Stoar, the door opened, Tricia Dumas walked into the room, pointed at the suspects gathered at one end of the bar, and said to Lockland and BeLaire, "That's them, Sheriff. Those bushwhackers killed my husband last night. Shot him while he was unarmed and putting wood on our campfire."

Lockland and BeLaire, with suddenly new titles conferred upon them by a lovely lady, and new widow, were as surprised as the bad guys, as well as self-proclaimed Judge of the Territory, Jud Burke.

There was, of course, a scramble at both ends of the bar. The suspects had forgotten in a hurry the two men who talked freely about the big strike at their mine, who now had four guns drawn and pointed at them. They scrambled again, going for their guns, the shots ensued, and the three bushwhackers who probably had more in mind than robbery on the Dumas wagon, went down in a heap, smoke pouring from their useless weapons.

Tricia Dumas, still in the doorway, her shoulders slumped in release, revenge caught up in place, turned and walked out the door.

They found her crying as she leaned over the tie rack, all the emotions, however many there had been, draining away from her, her horse nuzzling her shoulder, the sun sitting on the white of her neck.

She eventually married Pouvard BeLaire, on the ranch the two men tore right out of the heart of the earth. They built two cabins, one in which a daughter Amie was born to the BeLaires of the lower Tetons. A few years later, rustlers working to gain a portion of their herd, Pouvard BeLaire was killed in a running battle with the last of the rustlers, the other gang members killed by him and Lockland, and it was Lockland, many hours later tracking through the lower Tetons, who killed the man who killed his pal and best friend.

His own love for the woman they had rescued from who-knows-what in a dark canyon came his way when Tricia Walker Dumas BeLaire married him, Merlin Lockland. Tricia gave birth to two boys, Pouvard Lockland and Earl Lockland, the two boys fiercely loving their older sister Amie. Their parents had more than 60 years of a happy and truly blessed marriage at the foot of the Tetons, at the end of a long journey that had begun outbound from Boston aboard the steamer Western Metropolis as it left Boston for Hilton Head, South Carolina, a gritty piece of the Civil War sitting in the offing, in early March, 1864.

Everything about the Locklands moved right on past the first quarter of the following century.

Two-Gun Rock, Singer

Even now, 150 years later, within the family historians, and we have a few of them, old Uncle Joshan Rock is more than a legend, and though none of us have a recording from that time, the stories still pass down through the new members of the family as soon as they are keen on listening, paying attention, hearing the music in the words if not in a song.

Some of the stories go like this one, and every once in a while a pair of young eyes find an incandescence telling another chapter is taking root:

Joshan Rock left Cobh (Cork) in the old country aboard a ship bound for America on March 5, 1862; he was sixteen years of age, last son left to Anna Rock on her death bed, dragging the promise from Joshan to leave on the next boat and "get out of this cursed place that's taken two sons and takes my own life in the next day or two." She was dead before the ship left port, and Joshan Rock was alone in the new world coming at him.

In the shortest order possible, he was in the states, in New York and in the Union Army before he knew what a salute was. He lied about his age to gain entry.

He had been a stable boy for a British land owner, and a pub singer of note on his rare nights free from duties at the stable tending horses, He was a decent horseman and a better singer. He ended up in the cavalry, was promoted to a corporal and discharged from service as a sergeant at the end of the war, coming onto his 20th birthday.

With two comrades also discharged the same day with him, he headed west, and ended up a month or so later, in Independence, Missouri signing on with a wagon train as scout. On the first night out, around the campfire, he sang his first western song. It was this display that said he owned all the unmarried girls on the train with his songs, his blue eyes, his fair looks, and a sense of confidence in all things that he brought to hand. That confidence soon was attached to his ability with the two guns he wore on his belt; one he bought from an old drover knocked down for good and one he had lifted from a dead Confederate soldier in the last battle fought, a Remington Model 1858 .44 revolver. By 1868 he wore on his belt two .46 Rimfire revolvers, the new Remington on the market.

He was a good rider, a good singer, and soon became a good shooter with the new weapons. Ready for all the wide west was he.

But he was lonely, somewhat rootless, having a lone known cousin in Chicago, and bore the heart of the dreamer that he often sang about. It was the lone cousin in Chicago to whom he sent the occasional but long letters that have brought much of his life forward into the family history.

The cousin was Mary Elizabeth O'Sheehaughn Cassidy, married in 1866 to Peter Joseph Cassidy, from Elphin, Castlerea, Roscommon, whom she met on the ship carrying her to America. Peter Cassidy was a fiddler and a full life was promised her ... but in five years no children blessed that marriage. On a cold December day in 1873, her husband in a sick bed for the second week and Mary Elizabeth working as a waitress, two things happened that changed her life: by noon of that day her husband was dead, and a letter came to her from Joshan Rock, announcing that he was the lone cowboy in the family and was working his way all around the western states and territories.

After Peter Cassidy was buried, and Mary Elizabeth was back to work, she read at ease the letter again, treasuring it as the first entry in a family book she promised to maintain. She subsequently found a bound book of blank pages in a used items store and decided she would begin a family record of sorts, hoping that life would change for her with a new interest.

Joshan Rock's letter in 1873, when she was only 24 years old, in a good and bold hand, said:

Dear Cousin Mary Elizabeth,

I obtained your address from a friend from Roscommon, William Doherty, a musician I met on the trail who had played with your husband Peter on several occasions. William wants to be remembered to Peter, and you, of course, as he was on his way to San Francisco when we gathered as musicians for a rather nice weekend in a small Nevada town with music holding sway for several of us from the old country.

You are, dear cousin, the only person I know from the family who is here in America, though many more must have come since I left there in 1862, landed in New York and was in a rapid hurry placed into the army of the Union and fought in many battles along with many Irishmen who had made the same journey, though I never met any relatives of ours.

I was let out of the army immediately after hostilities were over and headed west. I have been a wagon scout, a drover, a wrangler, a musician, a saloon singer, a shooter when necessary to protect my life, or those of the fair side of life. I've been on cattle drives, freighter's wagons, posse hunts, and a sworn deputy for half a year in a town that was burned to the ground in New Mexico. For a half year I mined for gold and barely received back my investment of $100. I left that occupation and that dream when I signed on with a freighter's company, only to give that up as it paid less than other tasks I had undertaken. I have not yet married though I seek the ultimate in a relationship within a family. I hope that things of this order have come to you in our new land of promise.

I have no address where you can reach me, because I move continuously looking for the perfection in matters, if it is available, which may be beyond the next hill, over the next mountain, or in the passage that follows this one I am on now.

William Doherty was ecstatic in his praise of Roscommon and I have retained much of what he said to me in our few weeks together. It was a sad time at our departure, probably not to see each other again, and I have promised to keep to mind the good things he said of his home, which you can relate to your husband, whom I am sure will remember and enjoy some incidents or memories that William's words that we played with music and come to me with each note, and thus shake free: (Please take note that all which follows belongs to William until the double star intrudes on these thoughts.)

A Dream from a Roscommon Emigrant in America

There is a land though far away that's very dear to me, an island in the ocean most picturesque to see.

As each day goes by I heave a sigh for those lovely native scenes: Ah! Isle of Saints and Martyrs,

I see you in my dreams. I'm at the gate of Clooniquin, I hear the pearling stream now wend its way to Ross and then to far Culleen. I hear the thrush and blackbird in the holly and laurel tree; my soul says I must loiter in this fair locality.

I cross the bridge and up the walk and toward that lovely grove; with ecstasy my heart does bound as onward I do rove. From the countless pines a shadow runs to meet me on the hill where the pheasant and Rabbit doth wander there at will. Ah, solitude, thy charms are dear, to me how sweet they seem as I set me down and look around on Nature's lovely scene. The hills of Ross are beautiful, and so the lovely glen and meadows fair that stretch between those hills and dear Elphin.

From Castlerea to Carrick I see the places all, from Roscommon down to Lulsk and to the Plains of Boyle. As I travel o'er that scope, with Nature's gifts so strewn, I stop halfway where I was raised now aided by the moon. I look around bewildered on all that I behold; the tree of ash, the hawthorn bush, now burnished in their gold.

The cottage I was born in and raised by parents kind, I enter with impatience but there I could not find the one above all others whose love was dear to me. She has gone to her heaven for all eternity. Father, brothers, sisters, I join in fond embrace as tears of joy and sorrow roll swiftly down each face. I see the gold old nabors, each remembered a pleasant day, and shake each hand with affection as I did when going away. In harmony we all did join and traversed those weary years since that eventful morning when I left them steeped in tears.

Now fond adieu to all my friends around the dear old isle. Though adopted by Columbia I am Erin's faithful child; for the Stars and Stripes with the flag of Green will line in unity. Adieu again, old Ireland, farewell my dear country. **

I promise that I will provide more communication from this far western land, as often as I can, and while I can, until the day I might present myself to you and Peter and have a pint or two to celebrate the family in whatever shape it is, known or unknown, though I hope that you hear from other members from Cork, Youghal, Wexford, and Limerick.

Yours with all graces and best wishes upon you and your family, your fond cousin, Joshan Rock, last living son of Anna Rock, once a Rooney before marriage to John Martin Rock, gone too with the blight upon him in the year 1854.

In quick order, amidst her sorrow at losing her husband, not having any children of her own to console, and unable to advise Joshan Rock of her husband's death, Mary Elizabeth began her history of the family, in a bound book of once blank pages that she had paid only $.30 for. (At discovery, in 1952, in a box in an attic in Oak Park, Illinois, a short way from Chicago, the book had only 26 blank pages of 300 total pages.)

The widow did not get another letter for almost a whole year, in 1874, when she was 26, this one from Montana, and was received two months from the date it was written:

Dearest Cousin Mary Elizabeth,

I sincerely hope this finds you and your husband Peter and any blessed issue in good health and fair circumstances. I am in Montana and working on a ranch for a wealthy man who raises beef and sends his product your way in Chicago and to all the great cities east of the great river that I have crossed several times in my treks across the prairies of the country, though I have not yet gotten close to you in Illinois. Be advised that if I ever get with a couple of hundred miles of Chicago, I shall pay my respects at the Cassidy household.

I thought I might have found a soul mate and future wife on a stagecoach between Denver and Tucson on one trip, but learned in time that she was misrepresenting herself to me and me to her parents and *siblings, which alarmed me a great deal and caused me to thwart any attempt on my part or her part to engage in all plans for the future.*

I have met two comrades from the ranks in my travels, both of them from the old country, in Waterford and Cork itself, and one more from Peter's Roscommon, from Elphin. His name is Dermot Clougherty and his father was a publican in the village at which Peter may have enjoyed a pint or two, and more if we might have joined him back then.

As for my relaxation from all sorts of labors I find myself in, I continue to sing new songs learned here and the favorite songs from the old country. I sing to those who will listen to them or me in whatever venue I can come forth with these musical contributions, campfire, fireside, summer porch, saloon or social gathering in any barn available for such gaiety. The real crucible in this endeavor is to sing for group of drovers in from the end of a long drive and see them standing, mouths agape with drinks still in their hands and granting perhaps 5 or 10 seconds of silence before they begin their roaring of approval. That acceptance is the real test out this way; the west has its own manners in lots of ways.

I can also say at the same time that my proficiency with side arms, a necessary activity on these rounds I must make, has increased dramatically and some posse members, at which we avail ourselves when most serious crimes have been committed, call me Two-Gun Rock, the singing shooter, or have chosen such equivalent language. In fact, I have proved myself to be most capable in the face of dastardly men who threaten the peace of the land. I have enabled the incarceration of noted killers, kidnappers, bank and train robbers, which you might likely read about in the simple magazines that some literary men, writers, journalists and other sorts have managed to gather in their chronicles, accounts, missives, billets, commentaries or editorials that befall their pens.

If you chance to read about the Masked Lawman of the Teton Embankments, it is one that has grown from rather a simple and easy-to-subdue encounter with a child kidnapper I found by accident while he was dismounted off his horse with a crying female child that alarmed me. The young girl, son of a well-to-do rancher, explained the entire event of kidnap to me and we were able to produce the culprit at the same time that one of these journalists or penny-dime writers had come on the scene at her father's ranch. The grateful daughter, with a grand imagination at her grasp, was able to enthrall the journalist with the most fantastic story he could imagine in his own right (write), which he sent off to his magazine post haste. Needless to say, though I am in print, it is not the real Joshan Rock there chronicled.

Devoted to writing to my dear cousin Mary Elizabeth whenever I can, I remain your casual correspondent, Joshan Rock.

She read the letter a dozen or more times, imagined well the girl trying to make a greater hero out of Joshan, and found herself trying to portray him bigger than life herself. In fact, with a secret of her own, and her husband being dead longer than a year, she began to have dreams about the singing gunman. He invaded her nightly thoughts, and soon invaded those of her lively hours, and found herself enamored of him. She eventually agreed that she worked hard and dreamed hard and felt no shame in any portion of her thoughts.

Nor would Joshan Rock, if he knew her secrets.

He was about 29 years old and unmarried, according to the letter, and that fact fluttered around in her heart. She was 26 and afraid of never having a child of her own; some things stood in the way of her motherhood. She might dispel them if she was a different kind of woman. The thought did not linger.

She had taken on the care of an elderly woman of means, both of them finding dear companionship in the other, and Mary Elizabeth shortly moved in with the woman in her most decent home on the North Side of Chicago. Her very first duty was to ensure that mail to her old address was delivered to her new abode.

That precaution assured the delivery of a letter in the following year, in early spring, 1875. She remembered the first thought that came to her when she saw the envelope with the fair and bold handwriting that shook her name right off the envelope in her excitement. She hastened to her own room to read the letter. There was no disappointment in its contents:

Most dearest cousin, Mary Elizabeth Cassidy,

I write from a small town in Kansas to which I had been directed by my employer to arrange purchase and delivery of a special breed of horses, Percheron, most stately equines of enormous strength and character, which I have accomplished and have arranged their shipment by railroad back to Montana by way for most part of a new railroad, the Northern Pacific Line. I have found that many of our countrymen have worked on the construction of the railroad, most of them also being comrades on either side during the Great War Between the States, and most appreciative of some lively nights here after rigorous days of labor. Their requests for songs at various celebrations far exceeded my memory, but all were heightened by demonstrative fellows seeking a night with the song and the pint. I was most happy to do my share ... of each element.

And it is, my dear cousin, my most happy opportunity to tell you that my employer, knowing of our relationship, has provided me with time and funds to engage a visit with you and Peter and I will be there within two weeks after my completion of assurances on the delivery of the Percherons at the delivery point. It is April 17, 1875 as I write this and I am sure that I will be able to engage in a visit by the first week of May.

You have no perception of the joy that crowds me now envisioning my visit with you and yours, to sing some of the old songs, to celebrate a union a long time in coming.

Be of patient hopes that we find mutual likes about us, my dear cousin. I look forward with eager anticipation. Your most fond cousin,
Joshan Rock.

He had no idea of her anticipation.

She hurried to her old address and made sure that the new owner would provide one Joshan Rock with her new address, and even supplied a hand-drawn map to ensure his arrival at her new home.

Her patient was almost as happy as Mary Elizabeth was, knowing the fondness her caretaker had for a loyal cousin who wrote interesting letters to her, keeping family ties well knotted. She had none of her own, which was good reason behind her asking Mary Elizabeth to stay in her home.

She did not know Mary Elizabeth's secret, or her captivation by Joshan Rock.

In the few weeks of expectancy, she filled page after page of the book with her dreams, fantasies and hopes of things that might come to her, along with a series of sketches of what she thought Joshan Rock looked like, including the type of hat he wore, and the weapons he carried while he enforced the law, and watched out for the unfortunate. In particular she admired his stand for women, upon which she entered many significant observations garnered from her dreams and his letters.

She did have fears come upon her; that Joshan would not get to her old home, or the new owner would be away or suddenly dead, or Joshan would be killed by robbers, or he would not even get to Chicago because his employer changed his mind on the liberties granted. When the reverse happened, when good hope and fortune countered her fears, she imagined him walking to the front door and catching her in her best dress, her hair adorned full and properly, her smile anxious but full as a blossom.

The book, in the end, told the story:

May 8, 1875

Oh, he has come at last to this door, providence bringing him here, and the lady of the house invited him in and told him he could stay as long as he wished as a guest in her home and that I could have all the time I needed to catch up to family history. He is more handsome than I thought and none of my little sketches show him in proper manner. I must tell you how it happened, myself in a full working dress, in the front garden, my patient Maureen Cudahy sitting her porch chair under a shady arbor of vines with bright sunshine in bars and rays plummeting down through a morass of leaves and vines in their early crawl of the year, the shadows all moving on her in flits the way a shallow wind found leaves to twist and cast their element of shade upon her face, which I must say said she saw him first, a smile lighting up the small shadows that found her as she found him.

I saw the glimmer of expectancy, then one of reality, as she looked, at first toward me, then on past me. It was a telegraphic smile and I was initially afraid to turn, knowing that my working dress was far from my best introduction. But he was so handsome when I spun about, his face lit with a smile as he sat his horse, a huge black animal that surely must have owned the wide prairie that he told me about. Joshan's hat was as white as a lily the garden had promised already, a wide hat that sat down atop his shattering smile, a mustache decorating his upper lip, his shirt a pale green as if he was announcing the old land itself, his weapons out of sight, perhaps packed away in a saddle bag or under his shirt for quick protection if needed, his stature that of a god on that magnificent animal, and me on my proper knees on the cultivated earth I had just turned to stay ahead of promising weeds.

Oh, Lord, he dismounted that horse in a majestic swing of his leg, looked me in the face across the front yard, dropped the reins that he commanded in his hands, and rushed to me, sweeping me up in his arms, saying, all in one breath, to me, "Oh, Mary Elizabeth, my joy swells at sight of you," and to Maureen Cudahy, "My pardon, dear madam, as I find my lone relative in this wide land, a new heart within me, and one now in my arms."

Maureen Cudahy blushed in a sweet happiness, and I, I swooned in his arms, and the first words out of my mouth, were, "Oh, Joshan, I have misrepresented things to you. I am not a cousin. I was taken in and raised by your family, the O'Sheehaughns. I am not your cousin, I am not a blood relative. That has been my secret."

And my heart leaped wildly, again and again, and Maureen, dear soul, clapped her hands in joy because she knew what she was looking at, two souls in love, for Joshan said, as he hugged me and kissed me on the forehead, "I have dreamed of nothing but you for a few years, never

189

once faulting at making you a cousin, for damned the difference or indifference in the matter.

Then, sensing my reception of him, and my employers, this cowboy gunman and singer kissed me as my dreams had brought to bear.

We were in love, after all stories had been told, all explanations put forth, two people cast out from home by the troubles that ran from person to person, home to home, village to village, throughout a whole country, and brought together by chance and the intervention of the good Lord. Even my hand feeling the revolver under his shirt as he hugged me brought no more fear rising in me. For surely it must have aided him to come to me. And that evening, to the joy of Maureen Cudahy and her neighbors, he sang on her wide porch songs from the old country and from the prairies of our new country in a voice that descended on us as if from on high, and I imagined all the campfires on the wide grasses and all the saloons that he had dashed into momentary silences, all those gone on behind us and a full life in front of us.

I have seen that book, that thick volume from an elegant pen, the one from Mary Elizabeth (O'Sheehaughn Cassidy) Rock, the one found in an attic in Oak Park, Illinois and brought inquisitively to one of my sons, now of that fair locality, by a friend. That friend's grandparents found it in their attic in 1952 and it came to that friend when he inherited their home. He noted the names O'Siodhachain and O'Sheehaughn on the inside of the front cover and read the full story of the fair lady and the singing gunman who were married, had seven children, and saw them and their descendants spread across The Land of New Hope; in Maine, Massachusetts, New Hampshire, Rhode Island, North Carolina, Illinois, Wyoming, Mississippi, Louisiana, California, and beyond, some still on the move outward from dear Elphin.

About the Author

Thomas F. Sheehan served in the 31st Infantry, Korea, 1951-52, and graduated Boston College, 1956. Books include *Epic Cures; Brief Cases, Short Spans; The Saugus Book; This Rare Earth & Other Flights; Ah, Devon Unbowed; Reflections from Vinegar Hill.* eBooks include *Korean Echoes (nominated for a Distinguished Military Award), The Westering,* (nominated for National Book Award)*;* from *Danse Macabre* are *Murder at the Forum, Death of a Lottery Foe, Death by Punishment, An Accountable Death and Vigilantes East. A Collection of Friends, From the Quickening, In the Garden of Long Shadows, The Nations, Where Skies Grow Wide, Cross Trails, The Cowboys,* and *Beside the Broken Trail* were published by Pocol Press, and *Six Guns, Inc.,* by *Nazar Look,* in Romania. Sheehan has multiple works at these sites: *Rosebud, Linnet's Wings, Serving House Journal, Copperfield Review, KYSO Flash, La Joie Magazine, Soundings East, Literary Orphans, Indiana Voices Journal, Frontier Tales, Western Online Magazine, Provo Canyon Review, Nazar Look, Eastlit, Rope & Wire Magazine, Ocean Magazine, The Literary Yard, Green Silk Journal, Fiction on the Web, The Path, Faith-Hope and Fiction, The Cenacle, etc.* Sheehan's tales have produced 30 Pushcart nominations, and five Best of the Net nominations (and one winner) and short story awards from *Nazar Look* for 2012-2015. *Swan River Daisy* was recently released by KY Stories and *Back Home in Saugus,* 200 pages, 90,000 words, and a chapbook, *Small Victories for the Soul,* are on proposal. (His Amazon Author's Page, Tom Sheehan -- is on the Amazon site.)

www.ingramcontent.com/pod-product-compliance
Lightning Source LLC
Chambersburg PA
CBHW070016260626
47159CB00005B/1824